Praise for *Island of a Thousand Mirrors*

"The paradisiacal landscapes of Sri Lanka are as astonishing as the barbarity of its revolution, and Munaweera evokes the power of both in a lyrical debut novel worthy of shelving alongside her countryman Michael Ondaatje or her fellow writer of the multigenerational immigrant experience Jhumpa Lahiri."

—*Publishers Weekly*

"[A] verdantly atmospheric first novel . . . expressive [and] deeply felt." —*Kirkus Reviews*

"Munaweera's first novel is a breathtaking work of lyrical prose and vivid, transporting imagery. Part historical fiction, part family saga, it is most of all an ode to the Sri Lanka of the past and a hopeful wish for the country's future."

—*Booklist* (starred review)

"A lush family saga . . . *Island of a Thousand Mirrors* reads quickly, though it's unsparing. With the same, rich strokes she uses to evoke exquisiteness in preparation of coconut sambola, Munaweera . . . describes rape, massacre, and all matters of wartime evisceration in pulsing, sensory detail. In one breath, it's as much a swift inhale of trauma as it is a romantic epic, embracing both pain and nostalgia from earlier times. In the style of García Márquez or Allende, the story traces love lines from nineteenth-century generations—then surfaces in the recent

past, when the narrator goes back to Sri Lanka only to encounter new tragedy."
—*Mother Jones*

"This beautiful, heartbreaking debut novel is completely arresting, both as the story of two young women whose lives take different paths that circle back to each other, and as a history of Sri Lanka's civil war . . . one of the best war novels I've read, and the best book that's come my way in 2014. May it be widely read—in Sri Lanka, the United States, everywhere."
—Minneapolis *Star Tribune*

"Munaweera's writing is everywhere remarkable: a concentrated lyricism that is supple, and at the same time, muscular."
—*Hyphen*

"Though *Island of a Thousand Mirrors* staggers with its explosions of violence—the burnings, the rapes, the suicide bombings—what stays with the reader long after is the lovingly meticulous rendering of coming to consciousness, and learning to love, in the midst of a warm and multifarious family: the hidden blue rooms where lovers find one another. We take away from these pages the scents and colors of a faraway Sri Lanka become strikingly close and familiar. A hauntingly beautiful book."
—Mark Danner, author of *Stripping Bare the Body: Politics Violence War*

"A searing tale of the Sri Lankan civil war, told through the intertwined narratives of two women, one Tamil and one Sinhalese.

Nayomi Munaweera breathes life into the beauty and terror of that era through her delicate, bittersweet prose. An unforgettable novel."   —Yangsze Choo, author of *The Ghost Bride,*
international bestseller in Southeast Asia
and Oprah.com's Book of the Week

"Nayomi Munaweera pulls you into this book's big-hearted embrace with fierce, poetic language and striking imagery. The three women at the core of the ambitious, globe-spanning story show us, heartbreakingly, that we are linked by more than nation, more than race—more, even, than blood. A dark, beautiful, transporting debut."   —V. V. Ganeshananthan,
author of *Love Marriage*

"*Island of a Thousand Mirrors,* and not one left unshattered . . . This searing novel brings the story of Sri Lanka full circle to present day . . . Here is the beautifully told story of two families . . . A good novel leaves one forever changed, and wiser. *Island of a Thousand Mirrors* is one of those novels."
—Michelle Latiolais, author of *Even Now,*
A Proper Knowledge, and *Widow*

"In *Island of a Thousand Mirrors,* Nayomi Munaweera writes with ferocity, fire, and poetry of the incomprehensible madness of civil war and its effects upon those caught within it, whether in the villages and cities of Sri Lanka or half a world away. A masterful, incendiary debut."
—Janet Fitch, author of *White Oleander*

"Reading *Island of a Thousand Mirrors* is a throwback to the wonderment one felt with Arundhati Roy's *The God of Small Things* back in 1997. Nayomi Munaweera's debut novel is lyrical, awash with the topographic charms of Sri Lanka, and of meals of rice, fish, and coconut sambol. But it is harrowing in equal parts, with the graphic violence of the island nation's post-1983 history detailed in naked words." —*Vogue India*

"*Island of a Thousand Mirrors* is a slim volume that packs in multiple layers . . . with its flawless prose." —*Harper's Bazaar India*

"Brimming with vivid imagery: Lyrical and languid in its beauty, brutal and merciless in its violence. You are left with visions of a beautiful, tranquil island shredded with unspeakable terror and loss." —*Forbes India*

"Lyrical, heartfelt, and awash with imagery."
—Shehan Karunatilaka, author of
The Legend of Pradeep Mathew

"Minimalist yet skillful. In beautiful and lucid prose, the author is able to present the various worlds that are shattered by the civil war between the Sinhalese and the Tamils."
—TheBookOutline.com

island of a
thousand mirrors

NAYOMI MUNAWEERA

St. Martin's Griffin
New York

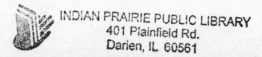

ISLAND OF A THOUSAND MIRRORS. Copyright © 2012 by Nayomi Munaweera. All rights reserved. Printed in the United States of America. For information, address St. Martin's Press, 175 Fifth Avenue, New York, N.Y. 10010.

www.stmartins.com

Map and family trees by Rhys Davies

Excerpt from *What Lies Between Us* copyright © 2016 by Nayomi Munaweera

The Library of Congress has cataloged the hardcover edition as follows:

Munaweera, Nayomi.
    Island of a thousand mirrors / Nayomi Munaweera.
        p. cm.
    ISBN 978-1-250-04393-1 (hardcover)
    ISBN 978-1-4668-4227-4 (e-book)
    1. Female friendship—Fiction.   2. Family life—Sri Lanka—Fiction.
3. Tamil (Indic people)—Sri Lanka.   4. Sinhalese (Sri Lankan people)—
Fiction.   5. Ethnic conflict—Sri Lanka—Fiction.   I. Title.
PR9440.9.M865I75 2014
823'.92—dc23

                                                                    2014016826

ISBN 978-1-250-05187-5 (trade paperback)

Our books may be purchased in bulk for promotional, educational, or business use. Please contact your local bookseller or the Macmillan Corporate and Premium Sales Department at (800) 221-7945, extension 5442, or by e-mail at MacmillanSpecialMarkets@macmillan.com.

First published in Sri Lanka in 2012 by Perera Hussein Publishing House

First St. Martin's Griffin Edition: January 2016

10 9 8 7 6 5 4 3 2 1

To my parents,
Upamali and Neil, who made it all possible

And to my sister, Namal, who fought for this book,
earliest and best beloved reader

The struggle of man against power is the struggle of memory against forgetting.

—MILAN KUNDERA,
The Book of Laughter and Forgetting

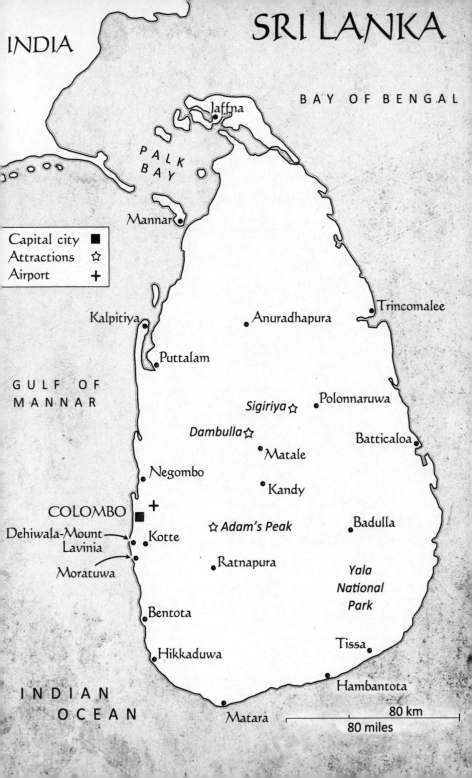

Colombo and Hikkaduwa

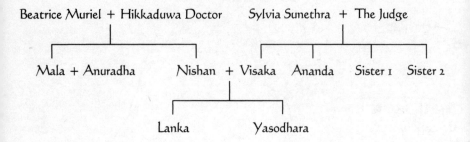

Beatrice Muriel + Hikkaduwa Doctor · Sylvia Sunethra + The Judge

Mala + Anuradha · Nishan + Visaka · Ananda · Sister 1 · Sister 2

Lanka · Yasodhara

In the North

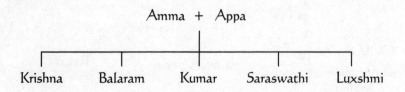

Amma + Appa

Krishna · Balaram · Kumar · Saraswathi · Luxshmi

PROLOGUE

I lie in the cave of his body, fluid seeping from between my legs. Shadows spin slowly across the sky-blue walls of this humid, airless room and my limbs are heavy, weighted with exhaustion and frantic, war-like lovemaking. Sweat beads on our skin, it runs in thin rivulets between us so that we are stuck together, glued one to the other, conjoined twins. He sleeps with an arm thrown across his face to block out the silver threads of dawn, the sugary-sweet film sound tracks rising from the neighbor's radio, the roaring of that fierce and relentless ocean. His lips move. From the drowned depths of his sleep, it is my sister's name, the single syllable of it that emerges over and over. A whispered keening of the sound I bestowed upon her lifetimes ago. I stay perfectly still, perfectly quiet, my hands folded on his fluttering heart. From here, this close to him, I can still hear her breathing on the other side of him.

part one

one

It is 1948 and the last British ships slip away from the island of Ceylon, laboring and groaning under the weight of purloined treasure. On board one such vessel, the captain's log includes the tusks and legs of elephant herds; rubies, emeralds, topaz; fragrant mountains of cinnamon, cardamom, mustard seeds; forests of ebony, teak, and sandalwood; screeching peacocks; caged and pacing leopards; ten-foot-long monitor lizards whipping their razor tails; barrels of fermented coconut toddy; the jewel-encrusted thrones of Kandyan kings; the weapons of Chola warriors; priceless texts in Pali and Sanskrit, Sinhala and Tamil.

At the foam-drenched stern, a blue-eyed, walnut-burnt sahib searches for the vanishing island and says to his pale young wife, "A shame, really. Such a nice little place."

And she, only recently having left Manchester for the colony and now returning in triumph, a husband successfully hunted and captured, says, "But so hot! And the mosquitoes! It will be such a comfort to be home again."

The Englishman contemplates the meaning of this word, "home," remembers decades of waving palms, soft sarongs against his thighs, the quick fingers and lithe embraces of burnt brown bodies. He has not seen the dome of St. Paul's for ten years. On his last visit to the frigid metropolis, he had felt an odd creature, neither fish nor fowl, smirked at by elegant ladies, his skin chaffed, fingers stiff and unable to determine between fish and salad fork. A sort of anger rises in his throat.

He tells himself that he will no longer dream of palm trees and sunshine. His wife takes refuge under his arm, her breast knowingly close to his fingertips. She utters a quick, coquettish laugh. She knows she has sufficient charms to distract him from his island memories. He turns his head resolutely away from the fast-disappearing island and toward the other, colder one ahead of him. His eyes are bone dry.

Behind the retreating Englishman, on the new nation's flag is poised a stylized lion, all curving flank and ornate muscle, a long, cruel sword gripped in its front paw. It is the ancient symbol of the Sinhala, who believe that they are descended from the lovemaking between an exiled Indian princess and a large jungle cat. A green stripe represents that small and much-tossed Muslim population. An orange stripe represents the larger, Tamil minority.

But in the decades that are coming, race riots and discrimination will render the orange stripe inadequate. It will be replaced by a new flag. On its face, a snarling tiger, all bared fang and bristling whisker. If the idea of militancy is not conveyed strongly enough, dagger-clawed paws burst forth while crossed rifles rear over the cat's head.

A rifle-toting tiger. A sword-gripping lion. This is a war that will be waged between related beasts.

My name is Yasodhara Rajasinghe and this is the story of my family. It is also one possible narrative of my island. But we are always interlopers into history, dropped into a story that has been going on far before we are born, and so I must start much earlier than my birth and I must start with the boy who will become my father.

As the last British ships slip over the horizon, my seven-year-old father-to-be, Nishan, cavorts on beaches he does not know are pristine. He dives into an ocean unpolluted by the gasoline-powered tourist boats of the future.

In the months before the thunderous monsoon, the ocean tugs at his toes, wraps sinuous limbs about his own, and pulls him into its embrace, out until it is deep enough to dive, headfirst, feet overhead, inverted and submerged. Eyes open against stinging salt, he sees coral like a crowded, crumbling city, busy with variously marked, spotted, dotted, striped, lit, pompous, and playful sea creatures. Now and then, he encounters the curious, swiveling eye of a small red octopus emerging from secret passageways. Approached recklessly, the octopus blanches a pure white, and with an inky ejaculation torpedoes away. So he learns to approach slowly, in rhythm with the gently rolling water, until the creature coming to know this stick-limbed biped is lulled enough to allow his quiet presence.

Farther out beyond the reef, where the coral gives way to the true deep, at a certain time of day a tribe of flat silver fish gather in their thousands. To be there is to be surrounded by living shards of light. At a secret signal, all is chaos, a thousand mirrors shattering about him. Then the school speeds to sea and the boy is left in sedate water, a tug and pull of the body as comfortable as sitting in his father's outspread sarong being sung to sleep.

When he emerges dripping from the sea, it is to find this father, the village Ayurvedic doctor, perched on an upturned catamaran, deep in conversation with the fisherfolk who squat on their heels before him.

The fishermen wear sarongs splotched with octopus ink. Their hands are leathered by handling rope, mending nets, wrestling sharks by their tails onto the beach. They are ruthless with the flesh of the creatures they catch, upturning gentle sea turtles in the sand to carve off chunks of the living flesh. The turtles bleed slowly, drip salt tears from the corners of their ancient eyes. In this way the meat stays fresh for days, the fishermen explain. For similar reasons the fishermen grasp just caught octopuses and turn them inside out, exposing delicate internals that flash through cycles of color. Decades later, in America, when my father sees Christmas lights for the first time, he will astound us with the observation that they look just like dying octopuses.

The sun drops fast, blazing momentarily crimson on the horizon. Father and son wander home. At the front door, his mother, Beatrice Muriel, waits, a lantern in her hand. In her other hand, she grips the shoulder of Nishan's twin sister, Mala, who by dint of her girlhood is not allowed on beach wanderings. Beatrice Muriel ignores her husband. She is angry that they have spent the day with the fisherfolk, listening to fisher songs, picking up fisher habits, coming home covered in beach sand. It is too dark to bathe, she scolds. Cold well water after the sun has set will result in sneezing and a runny nose. "Running here and there, like a savage. One day I will find you up a coconut tree with the toddy tappers. That's the day I will skin you alive. Wait and see if I don't."

As she scolds, she pulls the bones out of fried fish with deft fingers, mixes it with red rice and coconut sambal into balls, which she pops into the mouths of her children: a bird feeding its chicks. Her monologue ceases only when the plate is empty.

Afterward, he goes to sleep on the straw mat next to Mala, sea sand frosting his limbs and gritty in his hair and eyelashes, the dark shapes of his parents on either side of them, their breathing soothing him into sleep.

His mother, Beatrice Muriel, comes from a prominent southern family peopled with Vincents, Victorias, Annie-Henriettas, Elizabeths, and Herberts in tribute to the former ruling race. Now, after marriage to the Hikkaduwa Ayurvedic doctor, she is the village schoolteacher. In the small classroom, open to the sea breezes, she teaches the children to read, leads them as they chant loudly an English menagerie: "Q IS FOR QUAIL! R IS FOR ROBIN! S IS FOR ESQUIRREL!" In the sultry afternoons, she teaches them to work numbers so that they will not be cheated when the Colombo buyers come for fish.

Seven years before, Beatrice Muriel, at the age of sixteen, married for a year, finds herself bloodless and nauseous. Her new husband examines her tongue, pulls back her eyelids, nods his head, but propriety will not allow him to name her ailment. Three months later, as custom demands, he sends her home to her mother by swaying bullock cart.

In the ancestral house, she is fed and pampered, stroked and coddled. When the pains begin, she labors surrounded by the various women of her family. Her mother parts her thighs, whispers endearments and encouragements into her sweating ears.

There are the usual hours of sweat-drenched, pushing, ripping pain before a tiny creature slips forth. A boy! The gods have been benevolent! But wait, Beatrice Muriel on her childhood bed is still sweating, still straining and pushing. With a final effort, a great gush of red, another child slips headfirst from salt water into the wide, airy world. The women submerge the child in the waiting basin of water, hoping to reveal some lighter, more appropriately golden skin tone. The water turns hue, but the baby does not, and Beatrice Muriel, taking in the pair, one eggplant hued and the other milk-tea fair, cries, "If only it had been the boy who was so dark! This black-black girl! We will never get her married." To which her mother joins, "A darkie granddaughter. Such a shade we have never had in our family. Must be from the father's side!" There, revealed for all to see, on the skin of this girl, the stain of low-caste origins. Beatrice Muriel, torn and exhausted from birthing, hangs her head in shame.

Because by this time what had not been known before the nuptials has since been revealed. Namely, that sometime in the years before seeking out matrimony, the Doctor had paid a visit to the local registrar's office, where he had worked a sort of alchemy. A handsome bribe to replace his family name, Aposinghe, with its fishy associations and marketplace odors, for the princely sounding Rajasinghe. In this way the Doctor, like so many low-caste persons, had escaped the limitations of fate to win both medical training and wife.

The back room of the house is the Doctor's dispensary. On the walls, dusty emerald bottles display their variously oily or transparent contents. On the verandah, patients gather each morning. They are fishermen and farmers who often pay in kind. A large thora fish for the health of a child, a pound of paddy rice for an ointment to ease a grandmother's arthritic knees. The Doctor is dedicated to this motley group of patients, but lacks further ambition and is most satisfied walking the beach with his children.

Often Beatrice Muriel finds him in conversation with fishermen, toddy tappers, servants, sometimes even the Tamil coolie who comes to empty the latrine buckets each dawn. When she sees him talking to this blackened djinn who smells of shit and carries the stiff-bristled broom with which he performs his inauspicious duties, it takes all her willpower to walk past them, her stiffly held head eloquent in its disapproval.

She has been brought up with definite ideas about the value of each thing and person, its significance and appropriate place on a strict hierarchy. She is unable to tolerate this laxity, her husband's inability or indeed conscious decision not to treat each person according to ancient laws. Her anger takes aim for her husband's head through her children's ears.

"In my father's day, those people kept out of sight. If one of them had come into the village spreading misfortune and bad smells everywhere, he would have been beaten with his shitty broom. This is your father's fault. Talking to these people. Treating them like every other person. If it were up to him, you know what you all would be doing?" Big-eyed children attempt to imagine. "You would be gathering up shit with that one. Would you like that? Going door to door in the morning emptying out the buckets of kakka with your hands and a small broom?" Children shaking their heads emphatically. No, they would definitely not like that.

To counter her husband's carelessness, Beatrice Muriel buys thora fish. She boils it slowly and then pours the water on the thirsty earth of the front yard. She sets the dish in front of her family with great festivity. "Now they will know what kind of people we are." Outside, the pungent odor rises. Passersby inhale with distended nostrils and know that the family has feasted on the most expensive sea fish.

Those less fortunate eat dried fish while the truly destitute fight with the spiny shells of crabs or lobsters. Decades later, my father will find it incomprehensible that Americans crave what in his childhood was considered repugnant fare. He will look at seafood menus with wonder and shake his head at the truly inexplicable nature of human beings.

One midnight, the singing of bullfrogs is shattered by human pandemonium. Shouting men burst into the house. They grasp a young fisherman by the arms and legs like a heavy sack of rice, heave him onto the Doctor's table where he writhes and sobs. The family, torn from sleep, witnesses the great, medieval lance skewering the boy's kneecap. The beak of a swordfish, the fishermen say. They had hooked the fish, were reeling it in, when it turned and pierced through the wood and knee as cleanly as if it had aimed exactly for this place. They had to saw through the thing's beak to free him while it smashed itself against the catamaran over and over again. One amputation is rewarded by another. The Doctor must saw through flesh and break through bone by the light of a spluttering kerosene lamp. Outside the window, the entire village gathers, an agitated anthill.

Afterward, the fisherman is kept in the dispensary, battling infection, drifting between throbbing pain and dreams of the sea. His name is Seeni Banda and it is Nishan's job to feed him and accompany him to the outhouse. In later years, Seeni Banda will acquire his lifelong companion, the three-legged dog, Kalu Balla, who unlike so many of her four-legged colleagues survives the quiet morning train, losing only a leg to the Doctor's merciful knife.

For Beatrice Muriel, marriage has not been the pleasant idyll she had been brought up to expect. In an astonishingly short time, the pleasant softness of her body melts away, corroded by relentless sun, salt air, and marital dissatisfaction. Overnight she becomes gaunt, her nostrils pinched, her gaze sharp as knives. She develops the schoolteacher's uncanny ability to detect and subdue childish mischief. Nishan must watch his friends being sent to squat at the back of the schoolroom, arms crossed to grasp opposite ears. As they walk home together, these boys say, *"Aiyo, she has two eyes in the back of her head."* And only filial devotion keeps him from replying, *"Machang,* you should see her at home."

Because marital disappointment has bred maternal ambition, Beatrice Muriel dreams of the day her son will enter university and reverse the legacy of a father who is content in daydreams and beach wanderings. Daily, she squats over the open flame, her sari pulled up between her knees, and cooks. Into the fish curry she stirs coconut milk and heady perseverance. Into the sambal, she mixes red onion, green chili, and expectation. Under her breath she mutters invocations to protect her son from *as-vaha,* the poisonous darts of envy thrown by the gaze of those with less illustrious sons.

The days of ocean diving, octopus communing, sand-covered sleep become rare. He spends all his time over books that she has gathered. Head bent over the small pool of light that falls from the lantern, he struggles to memorize English poems and mathematical equations, trace winding Sinhala hieroglyphs. His mother sits by him, her fingers quick with needle and thread. She will not go to sleep until he has finished.

And now leaving Nishan struggling over his books in the seaside village, we journey northward into the smoky realms of Colombo. Just sixty miles away but a world apart. This is the humid and pulsating capital city where the crowd spills over the pavements and onto the belching buses that swerve around bullock carts, and every language and every god of the island is in attendance over the multitudes. Here, where Galle Road reigns supreme connecting the city to the island and giving way to the quiet residential streets, here on one of those quiet and leafy lanes in the private ward of an exclusive nursing home, Nishan's wife-to-be and subsequently my mother-to-be, Visaka Jayarathna, is busy getting herself born.

Having accomplished this feat with no more than the usual traumas, she grows up in a large white house in Wellawatte, one of the more distinguished neighborhoods of Colombo. Separated from the ocean only by the railroad tracks, and a short but dignified distance away from the Wellawatte vegetable market, the house is ruled by Visaka's father, the Judge, who, Oxford-returned, insists upon a painful formalism learned in undergraduate days when he was made to feel the unbearable shame of brownness. In tribute to those frigid days, ankles are crossed, accents carefully monitored, pinkie fingers trained to point away from teacups. The family eats puddings and soups, beefsteaks and muttonchops, boiled potatoes, orange- and crimson-tinted sandwiches. They take tea at five, with sugar and milk, choose pastries off a multilayered silver tray. In December, there is Christmas cake, fruitcake, cheesecake. The dressmaker comes monthly. Visaka is chauffeured to school in her father's car and picked up at the gate after. On Tuesdays, she has elocution lessons and on Fridays she practices Bach and Beethoven for two hours on the baby grand piano.

Yet the heart of the house is an interior courtyard, built in the days of the Portuguese, who liked to keep their women sequestered in these interior gardens, full of spilling foliage, birdcall, and monkey chatter. Annoyed by this exuberance and lack of order, the Judge sends the gardener to rip and uproot. But days after these attacks, the mutilated branches send forth vines to once again wind into the embrace of the wrought iron balcony. Birds return once again to build nests in the outstretched arms of the trees. The queen of this domain, an enormous trailing jasmine, impervious to pruning, spreads a fragrant carpet of white. When the sea breeze whispers, a snowy flurry of flowers sweeps into the house so that Visaka's earliest and most tender memory is the combined scent of jasmine and sea salt.

It is into this pulsing, green space that she escapes after the boiled beef and vegetables. It is here she plays her childhood games, befriended at a distance by the birds, the geckos and squirrels. She says of her variously prim and jungled childhood, "It was like growing up in a garden of Eden in the middle of coldhearted England."

A photograph from this time witnesses the whole family suited and saried on the front lawn, Colombo heat perceptible only in the snaking tendrils that cling to the women's cheeks and necks. Our mother is flanked by her two much older sisters, each beautiful in an entirely different way. One, round-faced and dark like a plump fig, succulent. The other tall, slim, and elegant, calling to mind something lunar.

Our mother, a sapling next to these hothouse beauties, poses on the edge of an ebony chair. A serious, spectacled schoolgirl in long braids and a stiff, ironed uniform, she is caught in a blur as if about to run off. Her formidable mother, Sylvia Sunethra, wears a sari in the old Victorian way, all ruffled sleeves, starch, and ramrod straight posture, her hand on the girl's shoulder holding her down. Behind them all, her handsome brother, Ananda, debonair in a three-piece suit. In the chair sits the Judge, who despite his profound baldness looks too young to be the father of these grown children.

The photograph gives no forewarning. Yet it captures the end of my mother's childhood, because if we enter with the certainty of history into the secret, red passageways leading to my grandfather's heart, we see lurking within his tissue-thin arteries an amoeba-shaped blood clot that will lead him to sit up in bed six months later, clutching at his chest. He will not die of this first stroke, but some years later under the assault of successive ones and in the midst of his house-building obsession.

It is around the time of this photograph that our mother remembers the coming of Alice. Male relatives from the Judge's ancestral village squat on the verandah waiting for the Judge. With them, a woman, face obscured behind her sari pallu. Our mother remembers the outline of a large, fair-skinned face, round as the full moon, long, she-deer eyelashes. And over the left shoulder, stretching the cheap cloth of the sari blouse, an enormous, quivering hump. "This is Alice Nona," the men say and meticulously retrace the capillaries of familial blood that make her "our people."

She is unmarried for obvious reasons. She has been living with her aged parents, taking care of them. But in the last year there has been trouble. The men are vague. They will not specify. The Judge thunders, "What is this nonsense? You have brought a fallen hunchback woman to my house?"

The men shift on their haunches. One says, "She can cook and also clean . . . only take her as a servant."

The woman is silent, her eyes pulled earthward. But there must have been some mute appeal implicit in the twisting of her large-knuckled hands because now, Sylvia Sunethra, twelve years younger than her husband, but already becoming the iron-handed matriarch of her later years, says, "I will take her."

The Judge is aghast. But there is something in his wife's eye that threatens unknown violence if he does not comply. So as the men breathe sighs of relief, he says only, "Alright. She can stay and join the staff. But one problem and I will send her packing."

The men leave, and Alice is installed somewhere between family member and servant. She sleeps on a mat outside Sylvia Sunethra's bedroom. For three months, her face is a study in impassivity, she moves as if in a sleepwalk, and not even the crashing of a dish just behind her causes the slightest of reactions. Finally Sylvia Sunethra, annoyed beyond endurance, says, "Oh, enough with this long face all the time. Tell them to bring the child."

The very next week, a wizened woman arrives at the gate. From within her sari folds comes a hungry, kittenish mewing and now Alice goes about her day laughing and with a baby clinging to her breast. At night, mother and infant fall asleep, rolled together outside Sylvia Sunethra's door, and even the

Judge, afraid of the venom of his wife's tongue, dares not question the origins of this baby that Sylvia Sunethra has decided to shelter along with its wayward mother. It is in this way that we who are not yet born acquire Alice, that beloved Quasimodo of our childhoods, and also her son, Dilshan.

two

In the southern fishing village, under his mother's eagle eye, Nishan develops the aura of nascent success, evident in his newly acquired eyeglasses and paid for by the loss of cricket games, bicycle rides, and beach wanderings.

During the school holidays, hooligan cousins are sent to spend their days under his mother's command. They run through the garden like wild hares; spin marbles with the concentration of gambling addicts; hold their noses to dive into the deep, chill well; but when they walk through the house they are quiet, respectful of their cousin's head bent over outspread books. Beatrice Muriel warns, "The rest of the house you can demolish any way that you like, but stay away from Aiya and his studies."

Yet even as she is proud of her son, a pointed thorn pierces the tenderest areas of Beatrice Muriel's heart. Neither her prayers nor the village women's many potions have made the slightest difference. Mala, the boy's twin and shadow, remains as stubbornly dark as at birth.

A slip of a girl, she is quiet in company, silent in her mother's presence. Next to her, Beatrice Muriel grows in bulk, the solid folds of her sari firmly anchoring each of them, the wispy female child, the dreamy doctor, the scholarly boy, to earth.

Witness, however, a daily transformation. At noon, Beatrice Muriel returns from the schoolroom for lunch and overcome by the heavy afternoon air, withdraws into her bedroom for exactly two hours. In these hours, a different Mala awakens. Assured of Beatrice Muriel's immobility by the snores erupting from the bedroom, she is in the street lightning fast, playing cricket with the boys, making sure that her voice does not join their cries. Someone screams, "Look out! There behind you! The ball!" and Nishan knows that Mala is bowling. He goes to the window, sees her poised like the Nataraja, arm over knee, a ferocious whirlwind of limbs, and the ball goes whizzing past heads.

In these magic hours, Mala climbs high onto forked branches and throws down fruit to the other children too afraid to follow her ascent. She cavorts on the beach. Stands on her hands, her dress inverted, a billowing tent, white shorts and black legs exposed.

When Beatrice Muriel awakes, there are twin furrowed brows, twin pencils working in tandem, four legs swinging under the table where Kalu Balla scratches fleas in his sleep. When the villagers come to complain, "That daughter of yours has been in our avocado tree. Stealing all the ripest." Beatrice Muriel points to Mala, innocent and scholarly at the table, bellows, "What nonsense! Look at my girl, doing her work. You mad fellows think you can come and insult us. Better you get out of my house before I call Seeni Banda." And the poor man, knowing Seeni Banda and his ancient rifle, scurries off the porch, cursing the uppity nature of high-caste neighbors and their spoiled children.

As they walk to school, Nishan's friends will say, "*Aday machang.* That sister of yours can bowl like a goddamn champion. We should have her on the school team, even Ariyasinghe doesn't have an arm like hers." And he will feel the stings of pride and resentment at this sister who exists for exactly two hours of each day.

At dusk, Beatrice Muriel and Mala gather soiled clothes, ash to brush teeth, a sliver of soap, and walk toward the river. At water's edge, a flock of women gather, loud as birds. They wear sarongs tied above their breasts. Their shoulders gleam like polished wood in the dying sun. They pull fingers through buns and braids, freeing streams of hair that unfurl along their spines. Water slides over ankles, calves, knees. The river is warm from the day's heat. The women wade to their waists, pour buckets of water over their heads, soap dark limbs white and frothy.

On the riverbank, Beatrice Muriel squats with Mala clasped between her knees. She pulls a comb through the girl's hair, fighting the knotted curls, laments, "Look at this hair. Won't straighten no matter how much oil I put on it."

The women scrutinize Mala's scrawny figure. They offer advice. "Rub a coconut husk on her."

"River sand is better."

"Bathe her in buffalo milk."

"Grind turmeric and spread it all over her. My sister's girl was black like that. Every day she put turmeric and now the girl is smooth and white as buffalo curd."

"Nonsense. I've seen that girl, she's still dark like a demon's backside! My advice, take her to the devil dancers. Maybe they can improve her color."

Beatrice Muriel grits her teeth. She has tried these various suggestions to no avail. Between her knees, Mala practices bowling imaginary cricket balls. Feels the swing of her shoulder, the perfect arc of the ball, the astonished faces of the women before they are split wide by the smashing ball. She smiles into the quick-falling darkness.

Seeni Banda, the one-legged fisherman, spends his mornings at the tea shop sucking steaming, sugary milk tea from the saucer. At the Doctor's house, he gives the children lessons in tea shop politics: "Of the two races on this island, we Sinhala are Aryans and the Tamils are Dravidians. This island is ours, given to us from the Buddha's own hand long, long before they came. And now they have come and we are forced to share this place. But really it belongs to us."

Mala says, "But Seeni Banda, our teacher says the Tamils have been here just as long as we have. She says that no one really knows who came first."

He flaps a loose-fingered hand at her, continues in the mode of the local pundits. "Tamil buggers, always crying that they are a minority, so small and helpless, but look! Just over our heads, hovering like a huge foot waiting to trample us, south India, full of Tamils. For the Sinhala, there is only this small island. If we let them, they will force us bit by bit into the sea. Swimming for our lives."

The children listen, their eyes big. They had not realized that the Tamil children they go to school with harbored such insidious and watery intentions.

In the dry season of the year 1958, Nishan is a gawky teenager, black spectacles slipping down the sweat of his nose, the weight of large textbooks curving his spine. The tea shop rumors have turned into the smoky scent of sulfur drifting down from Colombo. Whispers flutter like insects drawn to the lamplight: "They are killing Tamils in Colombo." From the opaque darkness, an answer: "This is a Buddhist country. Such things cannot happen here."

He is rendered immune to these rumblings by the drama of his own adolescence. Each night, a Beatrice Muriel–faced vulture gnaws at his liver, his failed examination papers clutched in her curved talons. He wakes sodden in a chilling sweat. His exams are upcoming and wrapped up in a fog of equations, memorized test papers, and complicated mathematical proofs. He is not consciously aware of the fear on people's faces, the way in which his parents or Seeni Banda greet strangers with a new suspicion, his mother's hoarding of red rice under the kitchen floorboards.

At dawn, he and Mala walk along the silver ocean toward the railway station. It is quiet, until the terminal. Then schoolboys and girls, giddy in this brief interlude between the authority of parents and that of teachers, chatter like mynas. There is a girl in this crowd that he likes. She is a few inches taller than him, so the other schoolboys tease him mercilessly. But there is invitation in the girl's eyes, a certain glance he is sure she reserves for him that allows him to endure the ribbing and gives him thrills of pleasure when she looks his way.

In the darkened carriage, boys talk of cricket scores and slide their eyes surreptitiously toward chattering girls. The forward motion of the train rocks them into delicious, early morning languor.

All this is smashed open with an ear-shattering shriek of metal, the train thrown against some hard, resisting object. Boys and girls are flung like bits of paper from an enormous and uncaring hand, bright blood blooming on white uniforms, and bare-chested, saronged, machete-armed men enter the carriage, stalk heavy-footed down the aisle. Schoolkids cower, arms over heads. The men breathe words flaming of coconut toddy, "Tamil devils. Get up! Stand up! Stand up!"

"Look at this one." A man grasps Radhini, object of Nishan's ardor, by the upper arm, above the elbow. She is jerked upward like a fish plucked out of water by a cormorant's skewering beak. A machete tip traces her upper arm where uniform gives way to smooth flesh. Cold metal on skin. A tear trembles on her lash, catching light in that dark interior.

"Tamil? No?"

Shamefaced schoolboys turn their faces. The odor of panicked sweat settles like a cloud. My father cannot avert his eyes, Mala claws his arm. "Do something," her fingers beg, but though his heart drums staccato, his feet remain leaden.

"Tamil? But no *pottu*? Trying to get our boys to think you're a Sinhala girl?"

"Maybe we should make a *pottu* for you, no? In the middle of the forehead. Nice big one. Red, I think."

Swift as a striking cobra, a streak of red across the girl's curved forehead. The sudden and unmistakable smell of urine. The front of her white uniform yellowed, spreading. From the back of the carriage, a loud voice. It is a teacher of the fourth standard, a tiny fury in a pink sari and thick glasses. "Leave them alone! They're just schoolkids." She pushes past hefty shoulders, wraps her arms around the girl. "This girl has done nothing. Let her be."

"She's Tamil. That's enough. They take our land, our jobs. If we let them they will take the whole country." Miss Abeyrathna, sari rustling like angel wings, says, "Look at her. She's a Sinhala girl. Only a little dark. You goondas can't even tell the difference."

A rustling in the mob. A collective pushing forward, and from the back a single, toddy-slurred voice: "If she's Sinhala, prove it."

Miss Abeyrathna pushes Radhini's shoulder. "Girl. Recite something . . . the Ithipiso Gatha, say it."

In a shivering, breaking voice Radhini recites the Buddhist verses preaching unattachment, impermanence, the inevitability of death.

For the rest of his life, the cadence of this particular verse will cause my father's bile to rise. It will conjure grasping fingers of guilt that wrap about his throat and make him remember Radhini in that dark compartment, the Tamil-inflected undercurrents of her accent hidden by her years in Buddhist schools, the front of her uniform sodden yellow with fear and shame.

She was saved, he will tell us, by the courage of that teacher. The mob, deterred by her bravery, left then. But there is something that lingers in his eye when he tells this story that makes us know the weight of it upon his heart.

There is, of course, another child in this tale, a Tamil child growing up in the north where grasping fingers of land reach into the frothing ocean. While Radhini recites terrified verses, he is four years old. At the age of four, the course of any life lies uncharted; there are perhaps no fangs in this mouth, no incipient claws in evidence. He is perhaps too young to remember these days of lootings, when houses were surrounded and set aflame with children crying inside them. He is perhaps too young to have this memory, but he claims to remember these things. Most specifically, he remembers an old Tamil woman beset by Sinhala youths, who beat her with sticks and then, laughing as if at a fair or some other amusement, set her alight so that she squawks and screams, her sari flapping like the wings of a great flaming bird. Perhaps he is too young to remember, but these are the images that filter into his dreams. In the decades to come, when he has become the Leader with blood-drenched claws and ripping fangs, a tiger-striped army ready to die at his command, these are the images he will offer when asked why.

three

In Colombo, weakened by his first stroke, his ramrod straight walk broken by an insistent limp, the mutton soup dripping disobediently out of the corner of his mouth and onto his starched white shirt front, the Judge dreams of demolishing his meandering mansion. In its place, he wishes to install a simple modern two-story house.

An army of sarong-clad men is moved in to trample the carefully laid flowerbeds, spitting betel like blood on the floors and abandoning tools everywhere. In daylight, the ground shakes incessantly and the family must shout to make themselves heard. At night, they are kept awake by the laughter of the men who squat in a circle smoking *beedis* like buzzing red fireflies and drinking arrack before falling asleep in the room erected for this purpose.

While a fine cement dust falls on their heads, rendering all white haired and aged, the Judge spends most of his time railing against these sons of the soil. "These bastards will be the death of me! If I look away even for a minute they have put in the staircase facing the wrong way. Country going to these uneducated dogs."

He bangs about the property, crashing his cane against walls and doorways. The men humor his violent moods, but when he turns his back, they snigger and imitate his uneven walk. The country is theirs now. The reign of brown-skinned sahibs dreaming of Oxfordshire and sweating in three-piece suits is ancient history.

As her husband battles contractors and shrieks at laborers, Sylvia Sunethra negotiates marriages for her children, spreading photographs and astrological charts of Colombo's most eligible sons and daughters on the dining table. A single dream emerges: to build a house and fill it chock-full of dutiful children, illustrious sons and daughters-in-law, an army of projected grandchildren stretching into the distant future.

Trying to ignore the chaos around her, Visaka does her schoolwork out of dusty textbooks. She works with ears blocked against the drilling and sawing by puffs of cotton wool. Despite these distractions, she is a good student, bringing home distinctions and prizes, managing by intense effort to leave the house immaculately uniformed. Secretly, she wishes to follow in the steps of her brother, Ananda, and become that most respected and rare of persons, a doctor.

But in her room, hidden behind the tall mirror, taped to the wall, are posters of clean-shaven, fair-skinned boys, Elvis with his cocked hips and Pat Boone. At surreptitious moments, she listens to tapes cajoled from her older sisters, dances across the room to "Love me tender, love me true." Presses her lips against the slick paper on the wall, imagines what it would be like to fall in love. To be swept away and destroyed, merged with another so that your souls are one, one heart beating in two bodies.

At family parties, tottering in their first heels and the unfamiliar weight of saris, she and her cousins look furtively at the shy boys gathered on the other side of the room. Which of them will it be? Who will sweep her away on a wave of love, into her real life? Who will love her tender, love her true? Her heart beats erratically with these questions, a throbbing in her head.

Unable to wield a pen between increasingly stiff fingers, Sylvia Sunethra enlists the hand of her youngest daughter so that from the age of ten, Visaka is familiar with the intricacies of the Colombo marriage market.

The eldest child and only son of the clan, Ananda, is encamped in England, studying for his medical degree. He is the jewel in Sylvia Sunethra's crown. For months, she searches fervently for a bride suitable to his eminent doctorship, scrabbling among Colombo's most elite daughters like a gem miner searching the riverbank for hidden sapphires. She finds one girl too plump, another too gaunt, and a third's eggplant curry an insult.

But all of this picking and choosing, weighing and consulting, is undone by the closing lines of a letter penned by an Englanddwelling female relative. "Why didn't you tell us that your son was seeing such a pretty Burgher girl? You must be more forth-coming, my dear, after all it won't do for outsiders to hear about these things before the family does."

Sylvia Sunethra rages, then pens a hurried letter to her son: "What nonsense is this? Aunty Malini says you are going here, there, and everywhere with some unknown, unplanned girl."

When the reply comes weeks later, her son writes that, yes, he has chosen for himself, worse, he is in love, and even that his love is a Burgher, her bloodlines infused with who-knows-what dis-tillations of Dutch sailor and Portuguese soldier.

Sylvia Sunethra fumes and cajoles, writes ponderous letters alternately pleading and menacing. But her son will not give up his beloved. She is after all, he says, Sri Lankan. What does it mat-ter if some of her ancestors were of the fair-skinned variety? He does not believe in the primitive custom of arranged marriage, he says. And if Sylvia Sunethra cuts off his allowance, he will wash dishes and sweep floors, immigrate to the United States. Nothing will induce him to return to that backward island if he cannot bring his love with him.

Sylvia Sunethra wrings her hands and whispers to her daugh-ter so that her husband doesn't hear, "We sent him to England to become a doctor. And now he is taking a Burgher wife and mov-ing to that bang-bang, shoot-shoot country. What am I to do?" She holds her head and says, "This will kill your father, I just know it. It will kill him dead."

They keep the secret from him, but in the end this effort

proves unnecessary. In the midst of these chaotic months, the unfolding of further catastrophe. The Judge, lying in bed next to his wife, contorts like a marketplace marionette, utters a sound like a water pipe bursting, and gasps his last. The family has no time to mourn because immediately after the funeral, it is revealed that in order to fund his house-building obsession, he has emptied all the accounts, sold all the lands.

Sylvia Sunethra, who as a bride of fifteen left her mother's bed for her husband's, whose sole monetary experience has concerned the payment of servants, must find ways to spin the empty echoing coffers into gold. Overnight servants are dismissed. Piano lessons, tuition, Tuesday elocution classes rendered a dim memory. Ebony furniture and previously coveted dowry jewelry are sold on the black market.

Only Alice remains. "Where is there for us to go?" she asks, the gaunt, large-eyed child peering from behind the folds of her sari. And Sylvia Sunethra, moved by this example of need so much greater than her own, allows them to stay and share in the family's misfortune. In return, Alice is granted reign over the kitchen, where she learns trickeries by which to stretch dhal and rice into all their mouths.

During these days, Sylvia Sunethra grows even more steely eyed and fierce. Women say, "My! How she has changed. So strong and all. If it was me, I would just die." What they do not see: the nights in which Visaka lies in her mother's bed, arms wrapped around the back of the rigid, unmoving woman who does not cry and does not sleep. Together they listen to the waves rising in the darkness.

When the rooster calls before light, Visaka wakes to see her mother, wraith-like in her white sleeping sari, rise to sitting, wind the long, thin hair into a bun. The mother-ghost rises and walks barefoot across the silent house, making her way through the dark with a blind person's certitude. She slips past Alice asleep on the floor, through the front door, past the slumbering dogs on the verandah. She walks across the street and the railway tracks, not looking, as she has warned her daughter countless times, for the rushing morning train. She walks down to the sand and sea.

Behind her, the young girl follows, afraid of the mother in her ghostliness, afraid of what will happen if she does not follow, sits on her slim, adolescent haunches in the sand and watches her mother climb high onto rocks, face oceanward. She knows that now the tears are falling, mixing with the salt spray, the sobbing lost behind the water's roar. She waits, teeth chattering in the morning chill, arms wrapped about knees until far on the horizon there is a single hair of pink and suddenly the skies are alight, the ocean sparkling emerald and her mother is climbing back. They walk home together and no mention is ever made of these sobbing dawns to which the sea and Visaka are the only witnesses.

It is in these days that my mother learns survival is the walking of a tightrope stretched between hunger and satiety, that relatives will mock and look away, that fathers die, that the sensation of being held and given succor is an illusion. These are the lessons she will carry with her into adulthood and whisper into the ears of her children.

. . .

A year after the Judge's death, the house is finished but the family's accounts are empty. Only one thing of value remains. Sylvia Sunethra has started to notice the love-struck boys who cycle up and down the lane, hoping for a glimpse of her youngest daughter. She has noted the scouring eyes of male cousins, the dresses that need to be let out at the bust and hips, cinched at the waist. She has made measurements and calculations.

One morning, she calls Visaka into her room, pulls her stiffened fingers through the girl's bath-wet hair, massages coconut oil into it, and lets the mass fall from one of her forearms to the other. Fingers pulling gently, easing knots, Sylvia Sunethra says, "You're a big girl now. We have to start talking about what will happen to you. This studying business was fine when your father was alive. But now what good can it do? We must start looking for a boy who can take care of you."

Visaka cries, "But Amma, what about university?"

To which Sylvia Sunethra purrs, "No, my darling, there is nothing to be gained from bending over books all the time, except a hunch as big as Alice's. We must start looking for a nice boy. Amma won't be here to take care of you forever, you know."

Visaka sees her best-laid plans, nurtured over dusty textbooks, over nights of sleepless study, softly gasp and die. There is a corresponding constriction in her throat as if suddenly the air itself is in short supply, it too regulated by maternal will.

• • •

Soon afterward, searching for other ways to stave off her mounting debts, Sylvia Sunethra places an advertisement offering the upstairs of the house for immediate rent. When an extensive family of Tamils collected under the name of Shivalingam telephone, she is wary. "Named after Lord Shiva's privates. These Tamils. So shameless. Who can tell what all kind of nonsense they could get up to. Anyone but them."

But when the Shivalingam patriarch shows up early the next morning with a fan of rupees, spread beautifully blue-green like a peacock's tail, an offer of three months' rent, she suspends her suspicions.

Soon thereafter, ancient furniture, cooking pots, bags of flour, statues of Ganesh and Shiva, Tamil and English books are borne upstairs and the Shivalingams settle in.

Overnight, the upstairs becomes foreign territory, ruled by different gods and divergent histories, populated by thick-braided, Kanjivaram-saried women; earnest bespectacled young men; a gang of kids; one walnut-skinned grandmother; and the unsmiling patriarch.

This is the beginning of what we will come to call the Upstairs-Downstairs, Linga-Singha wars. When Sylvia Sunethra calls Buddhist monks to the house, their monotone chant is interrupted by the voice of a Tamil film heroine winding seductively down the stairs. When her flowers die, she is convinced that Shivalingam boys hold pissing contests off the balcony. When she finds splashes of red among the yellow, she is sure the ancient grandmother shoots betel as expertly as her grandsons shoot urine. Counting her rent money she mutters, "Bloody Tamil buggers. Hanging their washing from the balconies. Dirty water dripping on our heads. Enough to give a nonstop headache."

From upstairs, too, come complaints. Once a week, the Shivalingam patriarch comes to grumble that his grandchildren cannot study because Sylvia Sunethra's daughter is again playing her Western songs too loudly or that the smoke from Alice's kitchen is rising into his windows.

The two heads of state engage in battle.

"Please, lady, understand that this all-the-time singing of Elvis the Pelvis, as he is known, is not suitable music for the ears of my various unmarried daughters and small grandchildren. In our house, it is permitted for the females only to listen to classical music and sometimes the music from Tamil films. Perhaps, it is advisable that you, likewise, restrain your good daughter in her musical tastes."

To which Sylvia Sunethra responds, "Yes, Mr. Shivalingam, having only just come to Colombo from the outstation places, you are not yet familiar with modern music. But in my part of the house, we embrace change and progress."

"Yes, but perhaps you will be kind enough to keep this 'progress' limited to your own part of the house."

"Maybe that can happen if we downstairs are also no longer bothered by that army of small ones running up and down the stairs."

Ten minutes later they exchange polite farewells and retire to their respective empires, muttering icy sedition under their breaths.

The greatest wars are fought over the mango tree. In season, fruit-laden fingers dip straight onto Shivalingam balconies, ripe mangoes press wetly against Shivalingam windows and splatter on their roof. When Sylvia Sunethra finds Shivalingam boys with their fingers sticky, upturning yellow pulp into their open mouths, she turns apoplectic.

Visaka, attempting to soothe, "But Amma, what are they to do? The tree grows straight onto their balcony."

"Doesn't matter! Stealing is stealing. This is our land. Anything that grows on it belongs to us. They should keep their fingers off our things!" She calls to unmerciful gods, "Bloody Tamils everywhere. What all have I done in another life to deserve this invasion business?" and hires little boys to skim up the tree to collect red, yellow, or even hard, pubescent, green mangoes, until the house reeks of them, first heady and pungent, then overripe and rotting, and Visaka faced with one more mango curry with mango chutney and mango sorbet must push fingers against her mouth and run for the toilet.

Perhaps it is this preoccupation with the mango tree. Perhaps it is her daily struggle to keep the family clothed and fed. Whatever the reason, at this time, Sylvia Sunethra's eagle eye is missing certain unforgivable breaches of propriety. Daily, Visaka on her walk home from school is followed by various schoolboys on bicycles who disperse when she reaches her gate. On the bus, there are always haggard, languorous-eyed young men attempting to drop notes promising eternal devotion into her lap. So far, none of these attentions has caused the slightest ripple in her slumbering biology. But now, the youngest Shivalingam boy, a few years older than her, nineteen or so, she guesses, loiters at the front gate at the exact time she arrives home. Most days she is unable to lift her eyes to his, but when she does, he is looking at her so intently that she must rush past, hurry into her room, throw herself on the bed, and wait until her heart has stopped thudding.

Because, after all, how is it possible that she feels this recognition? As if she knows him! So that despite his foreignness in so many ways, the oil shining in his hair, the scents of unfamiliar foods on his clothes, he feels intimate in a way that shocks her.

His name is Ravan. She learns this when his sisters call him for tea or his brothers for cricket in the lane. She writes this name in minuscule letters in her exercise books, then scribbles over it in dark ballpoint, tears out the pages, teaches herself not to repeat it, for fear of muttering it in her sleep. "Ravan," she thinks, "the name of the Lankan king in *The Ramayana*, brilliant strategist and warrior, abductor of Sita." She imagines being carried away by the Demon King, taken to his palace and seduced by a thousand courtesies. She smiles into the darkness, while inches away, Sylvia Sunethra turns uneasily and utters small, wounded noises in her sleep.

It buds with infinite slowness. A romance of glances and tiny signs doled out over months. The slide of a glance as they cross paths and that night she lies in her humid bed, wondering where he sleeps in the rooms above her, pictures his blossoming lips. What would it mean to press a fingertip against them? Would they spring back? Would he bite with those perfectly white, slightly wolfish teeth?

She learns the routines of his day, the hour at which he leaves the house, pushing his bicycle, schoolbooks in a satchel. She watches for his return, wet furrows under his arms, dark against the white shirt. The sound of his bicycle in the lane gives her vertigo. She listens, breathless, to the creak of the steps until he is swallowed by the unknown spaces overhead.

She starts to find presents on the windowsill of the room she shares with Sylvia Sunethra. A sprig of bright fuchsia bougain-villea left amid the flurry of white jasmine, a curving pink sea-shell. She runs her finger along the rim of it, holds it to her ear to hear the sea roar and mermaids call.

One day, as she passes the dark outside staircase, he is wait-ing. A whirlwind of limbs, like getting caught in a cyclone, being pulled and pressed against his hard, slim body. Madness, desire, his lips so close and then a sound and he is gone. She wonders if this has actually happened and knows it did by the pressure of his fingers still alive on her skin.

The next time he is gentler, pulling her against his chest, where she shelters, wondering at the density of him, the solidity of his sinew and muscle. She inhales the unfamiliar surface of his skin, flavored with spices she does not know the names of. His lips, by her ear, whisper her name, Tamil-inflected, so that it sounds foreign to her, the name of an Indian princess in a fairy tale. The sound of it makes her bold, makes her want to wrap her arms around him, cradle his face against her throat, but even as she decides to do this, there is the slightest sound, Alice in the corridor, and he has pulled away like the tide receding into that other, alien world.

One day at the gate, he says, "Come with me," takes her by the hand, and half drags her along the wall of the house. He whispers, "I have to show you something. A secret." A delighted edge to his voice and she lets him take her, like Sita being abducted by the Demon King, trepidation and exhilaration beating in equal measure along her throat. At the very back of the house, he pushes away jasmine and reveals a step leading down. He enters first, holds out his hand for her, and then she has stepped into a small, perfectly square room, the floor made of dirt, blue walls revealed by the tiny oil lamp he has placed on the floor, the thick fragrance of flowers. His voice next to her ear, "It must be from when they were building. A place for the workers to rest. I don't think anyone knows it is there."

For months, there are kisses by her ears, the corners of her mouth. They whisper in English, their only common language. Haltingly, stumblingly, learning the unfamiliar contours of each other's lives. He tells of the land his family has left, far up in the north, a place of dry soil and palmyra trees, lagoons that reflect the hard blue bowl of the sky. He wants to go to the university, he says, study, become a doctor maybe. It makes her remember her own dreams. Maybe they could be doctors together, he says when she tells him that she, too, has wanted this. A dim outline of a shared future reveals itself while the ghosts of their ancestors, her newly dead father, and others, similarly unseen, quake in rage.

It is in this small, square blue room that she learns the intimacy of another's heartbeat. The almost unbearably tender way in which his perfectly rounded shoulder falls into the hollow of her palm. It is here she learns the contours of her own body, its boundaries and spreading pleasures.

She learns how easy it is to deceive those who do not expect deception. Learns that Sylvia Sunethra, unable to imagine the possibility of her daughter trembling in the arms of the upstairs Tamil boy, perceives threats only from the men on the street, the male cousins at parties, the usual avenues by which deception may be enacted.

Over the months, they become ruthless, disappearing often into their jasmine-shrouded den. Held within the blue walls, they can hear the diverse workings of the house. The faraway-sounding calls of their various families, his brothers and sisters, Sylvia Sunethra and Alice. It is like being submerged underwater, lying on the ocean bed listening to the voices of a different world.

He takes away the necklace of her teeth marks on his shoulder blade like a prize won in battle. A bruise blooms on her inner arm, and she almost flaunts it, spinning an elaborate story concerning a cricket ball when asked to explain. The deception easy to spot, if anyone were looking closely. But no one is, and there is in her this demon that wants love to be acknowledged, wants to claim the slim, handsome boy as her own despite the punishments that such claiming would entail.

. . .

It has been six months since they first found the room. While upstairs Sylvia Sunethra works hard to manipulate the marriage market in favor of her youngest daughter, Ravan holds her head in his hands, the thumbs pulling very slightly at the corners of her eyes, staring into first one, then the other. She tries to pull away, his gaze has become so intense, so demanding, and she doesn't know what he is asking for. He says in a rush, "Let's get married. I have an aunt who married a Sinhalese. There'll be an uproar for some time, and then they'll forget." She stares at him with those enormous and uncomprehending eyes as she realizes what he is asking for, the whole of her life, the weight of her entire life. This is what he wants. Then she is shaking her head violently. Pulling herself out of his hands. Pushing past his reaching arms. Such madness he speaks. As if the differences between them could be blown away like dusty cobwebs. As if Sylvia Sunethra, brokenhearted dawn-beach walker, could survive the idea of one of her daughters wedded to a Tamil. She runs from him, bursting out of the room, both hands held out to push past heavy jasmine, but not before she has seen the thing that is smashing open in his eyes.

He will not speak to her. He ignores everything, her frantic, whispered pleas at the gate, the notes left in their various hiding places, her hours of waiting in their small, square love nest. Icy claws squeeze her heart, jab needles deep into the muscle of it. Such pain. When she takes to her bed, Sylvia Sunethra hovers, but she mutters, "Cramps . . . monthly visitor." Then her mother leaves and she gasps huge, silent, shuddering sobs into her pillow.

Heartbreak, like an illness. The heavy limbs, the aching head, the pain across her chest, akin to nothing so much as childhood malaria. Only Alice seems to know the truth, comes to stroke her head, pull long fingers through her hair, mutter, "It is alright. It had to happen. This is the best thing." And she realizes that Alice has always known, since the beginning, that nothing in the house escapes the woman's cat eyes. She realizes that perhaps Alice, too, has experienced this sickness, been bereft of love and heartsick sometime in the past, that they are united by the knowledge of loss. She buries her head in Alice's lap, inhales the scents of garlic, cumin gathered there, cries her eyes out. When she falls asleep, it is in exhaustion, like losing a wrestling match or drowning.

Three months of slow despair, and then the upstairs servant girl comes dancing into the kitchen. There will be sweets and music! The youngest son of the house is getting married! The old man has chosen him a bride from a northern village and now after months of stubborn, inexplicable protest he has agreed. She hears this and has to clasp her hands tight between her clenched thighs to arrest their uncontrollable shuddering.

At the gate, his gaze slides over her. He strides away into his again-unknown life and a hatred throbs along the passageways of her body, a ferocious, furious blush. She hates him and also the bride being prepared for him. At night she dreams of her rival's face, round and innocent. She rakes claws along the girl's skin, tears across belly and breasts, bites into flesh like dining on fruit. Hate throbs on her tongue, courses through each tiny vein of her body. She thinks that if hate glowed, they would all see her entire circulatory system, exposed like the veins of a leaf, surging with green envy, bright yellow rancor.

"Ravan," she thinks. "The name of a demon."

She grows careless with her heart, and worse, her reputation. She climbs upstairs, ignoring various Shivalingams who stare, openmouthed. She stands at the door knocking, and when the servant comes, she says, "Tell Ravan I'm here to see him." The woman scurries away, her eyes enormous, and then he comes, buttoning his shirt. He has been awakened from his afternoon rest. She stares at the disappearing triangle of his narrow chest, that space where she has placed her hands so many times, her fingers against the fluttering of a pulse in his throat.

His voice steady, he says, "Miss Jayarathna, right? What is it? What can we do for you?"

She, breathless, "You were right . . . we could . . . like your aunt and . . . Be together. After some time they'll forget, they'll leave us alone . . ." Her arm extended, describing a wide circle to indicate who would forget, the whole world, everyone except him and her. This is what she wishes for now, only them alone together, as they had been.

Fingers close tight around her elbow, the end of a sari thrown over her as if she had wandered up here naked. She is borne away in an iron grip, Alice come to rescue her, but not before she has heard him say something in Tamil. Not before she has heard the resulting giggles and the rising waves of laughter.

four

In the Hikkaduwa house, the whole family watches Beatrice Muriel slowly scan the newspaper lists hoping desperately to find her son's name among those who have passed the national examinations. When she lays the newspaper on the table, pushes tired fingers against her eyes like she does when she has a migraine, and it is clear that his name is not among the chosen, Nishan feels himself drop into a deep pit of shame and guilt. He makes his way to the door, hoping to slip quietly and calmly to the well and thereby drown himself, when Mala calls, "But look, there is a R. W. Rajasinghe on the Arts list. Could they have put you in the wrong column, Aiya?" And then he is shaking and laughing and jumping about and so are his mother, the Doctor, and Mala, because he has done it. He has changed all their lives. He has changed the course of their history. He has won himself a university seat. He will be one of the fifty engineers trained that year. When the jubilation has subsided, it is noted that Mala, too, has passed.

At university, Nishan hangs suspended between exhilaration and anxiety. He lives in crowded, disheveled rooms full of books, clothes, trays of tea, and snacks bought from vendors. Young men walk about the campus with their arms draped around each other's shoulders, their easy teasing and virile comradeship foreign to him. He worries about the stain of village in his speech, about his ill-fitting clothes and cheap new shoes. When the ragging starts, strapping seniors break into the dorms and exact all manner of humiliations. He is deposited on his bed each morning, aching in every soft place of his anatomy. On other nights, long examinations take over his dreams so that he awakens from a few hours of sleep further exhausted.

But Peradeniya is also the site of newfound freedoms. The campus spreads around him like the verdant pleasure garden of an ancient king. He is enraptured by the enormous trees that lift branches like cathedral roofs overhead, shoot roots like polished ballroom floors underfoot. In the hot afternoons he leaves the crowded rooms to study under the protection of these spreading giants. Escape from Beatrice Muriel's domain and the sensation of hours that are solely his, to fill as he wishes, are pleasures he had not anticipated.

In the women's dorms, Mala too is transformed. She lives in a room with three other girls, their clothes draped on the back of chairs, books opened on every surface. They sit on the balcony and share tea and ideas. It is close to dawn before they sleep. In her happiness, she blooms like a forest orchid. Her skin retains its dusky hue, but unhindered by Beatrice Muriel's ministrations, it gleams in the sun, polished ebony. There is a new voluptuousness in her. Young men notice her hair, not its kinkiness, but the curling vines that flee her bun to linger about her throat.

The campus has turned rebellious. Students read Lenin, Marx, Trotsky, and debate with their teachers, taking on the plight of the common man, class inequality, corruption and nepotism. Old separations and prejudices are dropping away. The struggle brings young men and women suddenly elbow to elbow. Never before have most of them been so close to men and women not related to them, and mere access to the opposite sex proves more intoxicating than rousing rhetoric. Eyes are allowed to meet at inflammatory speeches. Fingertips graze in the passing of revolutionary pamphlets. As the rhetoric of equality gathers steam, romances of all sorts bud and blossom.

The sway in Mala's waist, the curve of her hip beneath the folds of her sari, have caught the eye of many young men, each of whom is secretly willing to denounce the colonial prejudice of skin color by falling in love with her. For the first time in her life, history and circumstance have conspired to make her a desired commodity. She is granted the heady power of choice. And despite her lack of experience, she chooses wisely.

He is an engineering student, a friend of her brother's. She likes the way he looks at her, not appraisingly like some of the others, but as if he actually desired her opinion, and he trusts her judgment whether the question is mathematical or where they should have tea. There is, in him, a slowness of movement, inherent in the way he twirls a pencil while thinking. But also she likes the plane of his stomach under the thin, white shirt, the slimness of it, fanning out into his widespread shoulders. She has seen it once, as he came into Nishan's room, toweling his hair, water still dripping down the muscles of it. He had been shy, turning immediately on his heels when he saw her. Apologetic, when he reappeared, appropriately dry and shirted. But the memory of his skin comes back to her at the most inopportune moments, when she is opening an examination copy or writing a paper on Matisse, making her bite her lip and inhale sharply.

In Hikkaduwa, during the December holidays, Seeni Banda comes to the surgery door to announce visitors. Drying his hands, the Doctor is confronted by two young men, both stiff shirted and sweating.

One says, "Sir. I am C. K. Suraweera. This is Anuradha Munasingha. We are, both of us, in the engineering batch at Peradeniya." The Doctor notes their nervousness, the trickles of sweat running down their necks, is perplexed but says, "Aha . . . You are friends of Nishan's. Only . . . he is not here just now. He is in Colombo."

The first young man says, "Actually, sir, we have come about your daughter, Mala." And Mala, hiding just behind the curtain, pushes her hand against her fluttering heart.

When they leave, Beatrice Muriel stamps her foot, shouts,

"Madness! This boy comes on his own! No family members, no proposal, nothing at all? Only that sweating, sweating friend of his. Who does he think we are?" Pausing for breath and shifting the direction of her ire, "Mala, what do you have to say about this boy? If you have done anything with him I will skin you alive."

And the Doctor, "Shhh, wife, let her explain. Duwa, tell us, who is this boy? What are his intentions?"

And Mala, looking at the floor, a toe tracing designs on the polished red wax, "His name is Anuradha. We became friends at the university. He has done really well. He will take a degree and has a job already in Colombo."

Beatrice Muriel, wringing her hands, "Yes, yes, girl, but has he talked of marriage?"

"Yes, we have talked about it. If you will agree, he wants to get married as soon as possible."

There is silence and then the familiar smack of Beatrice Muriel's palm against her forehead. "A love marriage," she says. In her opinion, love marriages border on the indecent. They signify a breakdown of propriety, a giving in to the base instincts exhibited by the lower castes and foreigners. She believes marriages are far too important to be relegated to the randomness of chance meetings and hormonal longings. They must be conducted with precision, calculated by experts, negotiated by a vast network of relations who will verify the usual things: no insanity in the family, evidence of wealth and fertility, the presence of benevolent stars.

Now she is faced with the thorniest of dilemmas. Whether to hold on to her philosophies and see Mala a spinster, or succumb to impropriety and see her daughter married without the benediction of astrologers or a proposal.

Practicality decides the matter quickly. Anuradha is invited back to the house, installed in the best chair, handed a cup of tea and a slice of Beatrice Muriel's love cake. After he leaves, the Doctor tells his daughter, "A good boy. You will be happy," with moisture in his eye.

Beatrice Muriel says, "What a wedding we will have! With plumeria flowers and an Indian sari for you. We will put that Samaraweera girl's wedding to shame. These modern boys will marry even if the horoscope is bad, no? So why fight progress?"

While his sister is being spoken for, at a birthday party in a large white house by the ocean, Nishan is about to meet the seventeen-year-old who will be his wife. Around him, men swirl whiskey and politics. "God only knows what is happening in the north. Those Tamil buggers talking rot, oppression, separate country and what-not. Should just send the whole lot back to India. That's what I say."

Nishan juggles whiskey glass in one hand, cake plate in another. It is one of those rare occasions when he has been dragged away from his books by the uncle in whose Colombo house he is spending the university holidays. This uncle now steps forth to play his momentous though short-lived role in our story. "This," he booms, "is the youngest daughter of the house." Nishan looks, and observes the most delicate of features. The uncle continues, "Lucky boy who gets this one. She is studying now. Wants to be a lady doctor."

Witness Nishan. The sudden sweat that has broken out on his brow. He sees big eyes, sharp chin, fragile collarbones. He can only smile and nod, attempting to keep whiskey and cake steady.

Whereas she, object of his desire, what is she thinking? She, nursing a secret pain in her chest, her thoughts occupied by desperate plans. How to get upstairs? How to see him again? She sees and doesn't see the man in front of her. Much later, after the proposal has come, the marriage plans laid, she will cast back in her memory for this moment and burst out, "But he was such a mouse! Is it possible?"

In Hikkaduwa, Beatrice Muriel fumes and storms. She cannot believe her stars. First one child and now the other has made rubbish of her finely laid marriage machinations. The girl was fine. Lucky, even, to have the burden of a dark-skinned daughter lifted off her hands by a boy who doesn't seem to care much about dowry, hasn't even raised the question of what property or wealth Mala brings with her. But this, her son! An engineer! How to just give him up to the first girl who takes his fancy? Some Colombo girl of reduced circumstance, no less! How is it to be borne?

But histrionics make no difference. For once, the young man has made up his own mind.

On a September afternoon when the skies are liquid silver, Visaka comes home to find her mother in the front garden doing a sort of whirling dance, sari flying, fat arms shaking. She calls, "Come,

come quickly!" Draws Visaka under the wing of her sari, into the house and away from curious eyes. "Look, Duwa." She lays down an opened letter, the concentric circles of an astrological chart. "See who has sent a proposal for you. An engineer! From a far branch of the family. If we catch this one, all our troubles are finished." Sylvia Sunethra is smiling so broadly that Visaka can only arrange her features in a similar way.

The news flies. "The eldest son of the Hikkaduwa Rajasinghes! A qualified engineer, even!" Female relations gather at the Wellawatte house to offer congratulations. They drink tea, nibble Marie biscuits, and pinch Visaka's cheeks. They pat Sylvia Sunethra on the shoulder. "You have done so well for her. And all by yourself even. No father to help spread the word or negotiate the dowry. She's such a lucky girl." They scrutinize the girl, trying to ferret out the qualities that draw engineers to young, available daughters. Is it in the tilt of the chin? The delicate forehead? This girl looks like any other schoolgirl, painfully thin in her white uniform, heavy braids hanging on either side of her face. Her eyes are perhaps bigger than usual, her face a little more feline. But by what alchemy has Sylvia Sunethra produced such an illustrious boy for this perfectly ordinary-looking girl?

While relatives conjecture and theorize, Sylvia Sunethra sets the wedding machinery in motion. Astrologers confer with stars. Caterers are engaged. Small girls are measured for half sari.

On her wedding day, Visaka is awoken before dawn. She is bathed and dressed, her limbs are oiled, her lips and eyelids painted by careful hands. And all the while she is convinced of impossibility. She is not being dressed in yards and yards of white, this veil like sea mist is not descending over her head. These relatives are not gathered to wish her well, they are not placing her gently in a car adorned in jasmine. None of this is really happening, she tells herself over and over.

At the hotel, crowds of people. She is thankful now for the frothy protection of the veil, hiding her from their eyes, a filmy membrane between her and the real world in which Kandyan dancers twirl and flip and drummers pound her arrival. Her, the bride! This, too, is not happening. Then Alice is at her elbow whispering, "Be careful. He is here." She looks and sees a crowd of Shivalingams. Yes, they have come, too, honoring Sylvia Sune-thra's invitation. And there he is, Ravan, next to his wife, who wears a leaf-green sari. She must look away. Force herself not to look at that side of the room because she knows that if his eyes meet hers, she will sag under the weight of this sari, this blouse, skintight and constraining her breath.

On the *poruwa,* she is barely aware of the young man beside her. When she bends and unbends, worshiping at the feet of a long line of elders, he too bends and unbends so that it seems he is her double, her shadow, something without substance. It is only when their pinkie fingers are tied together, the water flowing over their hands, that she is suddenly aware that he is real, an actual man standing next to her, touching her.

She lets this man (her new husband! she thinks without comprehension) take her hand, lead her off the *poruwa* to a settee bedecked in pure white plumeria, the fragrance from the flowers so intoxicating that her head spins. She sits, she smiles over the heads of the people who come to wish them well. She offers first one and then the other cheek to lipsticked aunties who leave their mark on her skin, offers her hand to be grasped over and over by hearty uncles.

There are so many people, some she has never seen before, some she hasn't seen since the Judge's death. There are her new in-laws and their various people speaking to her as if from far away, their tones suspiciously reminiscent of some fishing village. She smiles, she nods, and is glad that this is all that is asked of her.

She sees him coming toward her. Ravan, as she has not seen him before. Confident, self-contained, not the boy she knew. She knows he has come to claim her. Knows he will lay his strong hand on her skin, those fingers will encircle her wrist, erasing the touch of all these others, she knows he will say to all these strangers, "She is mine. I'm taking her away now." She is rising from her seat. His eyes are vacant except for a sort of seething hatred. She watches his familiar lips move while he says, "Congratulations. All the best to you." He shakes her husband's hand. The green-saried wife kisses her quickly on each cheek and then they have moved away, into the crowd. Visaka sits down carefully. The edges of things move back into themselves. There is no more uncertainty in this world for her.

They honeymoon in the misty tea country where dark women in bright saris pulled over their heads bend over bushes, fingers twisting about the very top leaves like quick, busy insects. On cool hotel-room mornings she wakes to find her new husband, Nishan, bringing her tea. They spend days in the hushed lunchrooms of various hotels or wandering lush botanical gardens. At night there are awkward gropings. It isn't until the fourth night that she allows him to push hard into her. A completely new sensation, her flesh wrapped around this man. It is painful, frightening, the way his breath becomes tense, taut, until finally he shudders into her. She had not thought it would be like this. She had never suspected that this was the ultimate goal in all those long embraces in her hidden love-den. She realizes how carefully Ravan has kept this knowledge from her.

When afterward, her husband looks carefully at the sheet to find the splotch of blood that indicates her honor, she turns her head away. In the morning before they leave she strips it from the bed, folds it up carefully, and puts it in their bag so that he can present it to his mother. She knows that at the homecoming in two weeks it will be discreetly displayed in the proper way so that all the family will know that he has married a good girl, an unspoiled girl. Now she turns her head, settles it into the crook of her elbow, in her heart twin shards of gratitude and resentment.

What they both remember best: the rush and roar of an upcountry waterfall on the drive back to Colombo. The ferocity with which it poured into the pool so that they were only able to approach cautiously, slipping into the quiet edges of the water and wading in slowly. Extending first an arm, then a leg, and then their tentative heads to be beaten upon like drums, the sarongs tugged from their bodies leaving them half naked and laughing, exposed to each other for the first time in sunlight. For hours after, during the long drive toward the city, as the chill of the mountain water turned to sweat, the crash of falling water and each other's laughter rang in their ears.

They come together like misaligned planets and yet there must have been passion because after merely a year of wedded life, while people are still asking the usual questions about married life, the bride is starting to swell gently in the right areas. Sylvia Sunethra is delighted. The young engineer outwardly chagrined, but secretly proud. Visaka, herself, astonished at the rapidity with which her body transforms from that of an angular schoolgirl into the softness of maternity.

Upstairs, the wife of Ravan Shivalingam is also pregnant. The two women's bellies grow as if they had been inseminated at precisely the same moment. When Visaka sees her rival, swaying on the arm of her husband, her ire swells and surges so that I, nestled and suspended in the seas within her, grimace and twist my stubs of fingers into minuscule fists.

In more peaceful moments, I must have desired specificities because daily she longs for only one thing, that strangest of fruits, the spiky red rambutan. Every morning Alice returns from the Wellawatte market, her shopping basket full of every kind of delicacy. In the kitchen, she sweats over pots of lentils, fish curries, coconut sambal. Anything to tempt Visaka's appetite, but she is only interested in one flavor. She eats rambutan by the heap, splitting the bitter shells between her front teeth, feasting on the gelatinous white flesh until broken shells lie like shattered sea anemones at her feet.

And perhaps it is this glut of the scarlet fruit that brings on my birth, because one afternoon, two weeks before she is due, Visaka, sucking on a rambutan, feels me twist and turn and begin my headlong journey to light. Her screams summon the household. Nishan has taken the car to work so Sylvia Sunethra must ask Mr. Shivalingam if he will drive. In the ensuing commotion, the other pregnant woman, too, perhaps in sympathy with Visaka's shouts, goes into labor. The two are driven to the hospital, pain making them forget enmity so that they grip each other's hands white and scream in unison.

Shiva and I are born on adjacent beds in a large white room while the nurses stroke the thighs of our writhing, crying mothers. We enter the world on waves of our mothers' iron-flavored blood. First I, secretive and shy. I did not cry, they say, until he, too, had arrived. Purple faced, I had to be slapped into breathing. And then immediately after me, Shiva, as if he had been waiting for me to test the terrain. But when he does arrive, our crying fills the room, makes our tired and torn mothers laugh. Our fathers come rushing to claim us. They hold us awkwardly along the length of their hands, rest our slightly furred heads in their palms and look at us with shock while our mothers, to whom motherhood comes easily, giggle at their uncertainty.

Later we lie like replete kittens on our mothers' bellies and are taken separately to be blessed by the appropriate gods. Shiva to the temple of his namesake, where the *pusari* smears turmeric across his scrunched forehead. I to the Kelaniya temple, where the shaven-headed monk ties a white thread around my tiniest of wrists. It is here that my mother, still undecided about what to call me, looks carefully at the murals depicting the Buddha's life and pronounces with so much certainty that she cannot be contradicted, "Yasodhara."

five

Shiva and I grow up, twinned from birth, in some strange fashion, repeating the pattern of my father and Mala, the male and female twins that floated in our family history. In those early years our mothers take pleasure in each other. Who else can understand Visaka's bloated breasts, her ripped innards, her strange and unaccountable moods better than another woman who has just performed the same impossible feat? We are breastfed at the same time, our mothers nodding over our tiny heads, chatting in a mixture of Tamil, Sinhala, and English that makes them laugh often. We are patted to sleep, encouraged to burp, held and loved by two mothers. The strange timing of our birth allows us entry into each other's families in the most intimate ways since the two women, previously rivals, now seek out the comfort of each other's company. The result being that as a child I knew the contours of the upstairs as well as Shiva knew our rooms downstairs.

Three years after my birth, my mother swells again. When Lanka is born and brought home, Shiva and I gaze over the edge of the bassinet at this strange, alien creature and claim her as our own. We are a threesome from then on. Joined at the hip. A pyramid. A triangle. It is only in later years that she and I are taught the insurmountable differences between him and us.

Decades later and on a colder continent, I am fishing in my mother's desk for a recipe when a photograph tumbles across my hands. Wellawatte beach. Our delicate mother in oversized sunglasses and a minidress hefts a baby on her hip, grasps another child by the hand. Nothing physically maternal in her except the authority with which she holds my outstretched hand, pulls me to face the camera. Beside her, Alice, her hunch silhouetted by the setting sun, and then Sylvia Sunethra. In the corner a streak of motion, Shiva. I recognize him only because I remember the day. He had come with us, holding my hand, but tentative in the presence of our grandmother. We had been talking in our own shared language, that particular blur of Sinhala, Tamil, and English much like what our mothers used in the early days, when suddenly my grandmother, her attention telescoped on us, pins him like an insect. Her iced voice, incredulous, "Are you teaching my granddaughter Tamil?" Her hand smashing hard across his cheek. He rips his hand from mine, turns to run. The camera in my father's hand clicks shut.

I pass my hands over my face. I remember that moment so vividly. It was the first time we knew without question that we were different, separate, and that this difference was as wide as the ocean. In the other room my mother calls, have I found that recipe yet? She is waiting. I hide the photo back in the drawer, shut it resolutely. That was a lifetime ago. What came between us later was so much more painful, I have no desire to remember any more.

Our mother and our father then. She is cruel to him in ways we cannot understand. It is a subtle cruelty of unkind looks, pauses, and a way of undercutting his opinions in public so that he, the more educated, is easily rendered the fool. As children, we often resent her for it. It is only later that I understand her ferocious rage at the idea of being bought, of being wed despite the dictates of her own wildly beating heart.

But as children we are our father's pets. He takes us down to the beach, each of us grasping one of his fingers. Me and La, as we called Lanka almost from the beginning—that simple musical note that was exactly her, on one hand, Shiva on the other. My father liked it, I think, when people on the beach assumed he was the father of not just the two little girls, but also that slim-limbed boy.

He teaches us to dive, passing on fisherfolk lessons. Teaches us to plunge fearlessly into the surf, eyes open despite the rushing strength of the water. It sends us tumbling head over heels, swallowing brine. We emerge spluttering, almost drowned, dizzy. But in the ensuing years, all three of us learn to negotiate the waters until we are as agile as otters, as sinuous as eels, delighting in the suspended weightlessness of liquid.

• • •

In the smoky kitchen of the Wellawatte house, Alice is cooking. Between her fingers, garlic cloves slip out of their skins, naked and pungent white. Green chilies slit themselves lengthwise, fat stubs of ginger reduce themselves into paste. Spices perform fireworks in her frying pan. She teaches the three of us the precise engineering skills required to construct Christmas cakes, gingerbread houses, cream caramels. She makes us whip eggs until our forearms are aching and the eggs are transformed into stiff towers of frothy white. She gives us authority over the sharpest and cruelest of her tools, the flashing knives, the ridged coconut scraper with its stool. So that from childhood, we are intimate with these instruments.

Nightly, Alice still unfolds her mat outside Sylvia Sunethra's door. A small dark shack made of shabbily aligned walls and a corrugated tin roof behind the house holds her few possessions. This is also where her son, Dilshan, sleeps.

Some years older than us, he is our greatest playmate and ally. He lives barefoot and in a checked blue-green sarong. The soles of his feet are thick and black as tire rubber. He lets us poke at the deep, sunbaked cracks and laughs, "I don't need Bata slippers like you, Baby Nona. I have them already on my feet."

It is always easy to locate Dilshan in the house. The house cats congregate wherever he goes. Yet he is immune to their persistent mewing ardor and pushes them gently away with a pointed toe, an impatient foot. He is sinuous himself, winding his way about the house, fulfilling Sylvia Sunethra's various dictates for shopping or clearing the inner courtyard after the monsoon has ravaged the jasmine tree. If he is angry that his mother, one of our own, is now reduced by the trembling hump and his own illicit birth to this in-between place between aunt and servant, he does not show it. In later years, when he joins the army, it is the cats that mourn most openly, raising their whiskered faces to the sky and yowling outside the opening of his hut, refusing to eat even the fisherman's best tidbits for weeks.

Alice sits sideways on the coconut scraping stool. Her hands push the half coconut repeatedly over the rounded blade and a steady stream of fragrant whiteness falls into her bowl. The rhythm of her words matched to the back and forth of her body, she spins us stories of far-flung villages, mud, wattle, and coconut-thatched huts in roadless places, where life is ruled by the cycles of moonlight and sunlight, monsoon and drought. The jungle lies thick on the edges of such villages, and if it were not tamed daily by machete, it would burst in and reclaim its dominion. The night is always loud with jungle creatures. The gunshot ex-clamation of a crocodile's jaw cracking through turtle shell, the crash of a musth-dripping bull elephant, the yellow-lit eyes of a hunting leopard.

She heaves herself off the coconut scraper and inspects the day's vegetables. We beg her for more. More stories. We are ad-dicted as if to food. So she tells us of the demons that stalk these lonely places. The full-lipped Kalu Kumara, who takes on the as-pect of a seductive youth and emerges on moonlit nights, causing usually staid village damsels to tear at their clothes and utter long, moaning sighs. The other various demons that come creeping into the villages and cause mischief, illness, bad fortune. "When one of these demons enters a person, a child like you," she whispers and makes us jump, thrilled, "the village has to summon the devil dancers. All night long, they dance and drum, and spin and leap and flip in the air. They wear masks with bulging eyes and huge headdresses of human and raffia hair. They are six foot tall and the next morning the sick child, the child who was almost dead, is better, is laughing and walking. I've seen it with my own eyes," she says.

We are mesmerized. "But Alice," Lanka says, "can't you take us there? Can't we go and see?"

The onions she is chopping seem to break through her defenses. She flicks moisture from her eyes into a dark corner of the kitchen with a deft movement of the wrist. Her voice is suddenly gruff. "Too dangerous. There are worse things than the Kalu Kumara in those places now." She will not elaborate. Her knife moves through vegetable matter with purpose and fury.

Later, she boils water in her great earthen pot and Dilshan, called forth by the fragrance of heated milk and cinnamon, comes to squat on the back steps. She pours tea, steaming and frothy, into delicate teacups, takes them into the house on a silver tray for our parents, then comes back to reach for the metal beakers set aside for her and Dilshan. We have been warned away from these by Sylvia Sunethra. "Otherwise," she has whispered in our ears, "you will grow a hump as big as Alice's."

Alice pours long falls of milky tea. She takes the two beakers outside to her son. They squat on the back steps as the twilight falls and the reign of insects begins, talk in low, muted voices. And we, running inside after games, even in childhood, are always taken by the ocean of tenderness between them.

On Sundays, our father drives us all across the city to Mount Lavinia to visit his twin sister and her husband, our Mala Aunty and Anuradha Uncle. My father's parents, too, have left Hikkaduwa and come here to the house of their daughter. There are now two camps. In one our mother, in the other Mala and Beatrice Muriel, and between these two camps the sort of subtle rivalry that exists between women who lay claim to the same man. No harshness is ever uttered, but we sense animosity in the sugar-dripping words that pass with the teacups, the overly polite conversation so different from the familiar, bantering way our mother talks with her childhood friends, the laughing girls she was a schoolgirl with.

Eager to leave this unacknowledged battlefield, we press Mala to take us into her garden, where green things shoot out of the ground, thick flowers explode into fruit, ferns unfurl themselves like plumage. Even on this island, where foliage spills effortlessly from every crevice, her garden is exceptional. In later years, on a different continent, the sentence "On the island of her youth, one could spit and a tree would grow" makes me smile and remember Mala Aunty's garden.

Here, Colombo does not exist. It is the chattering of the

mynas, the conversations of toads, squirrels, and snakes that hold court. We play hide-and-seek, wade into her ponds to fill jam jars with writhing tadpoles, and cavort with her pack of dogs, named Brandy, Whiskey, Lager, so that just calling the pack makes one feel light-headed and drunk. Showing us around the garden with such joy that her face almost splits from smiling is our aunt's Tamil servant girl, Poornam. She is small and sprite, a few years older than me, but so much tinier

We all know the story, how years ago a Tamil woman came to my aunt's gate with the child. Rang and rang until Mala, annoyed, came to the gate and the woman thrust this little girl at her saying, "Please take," and our aunt saying, "No, I don't need any servant girl now," but then looking closely to see the bruises on the edges of the child's face, on her legs under the too tight dress, she opened the gate. The woman pushed the child forward and turned away to disappear. Our aunt was left with this malnourished, dirty little thing. In the bathroom scrubbing the child, she found bruises and lacerations everywhere, had to try hard not to break down and cry in front of the girl. Now Poornam sleeps on a pallet outside my aunt's bedroom. She wears dresses that Mala Aunty sews just for her on the machine. Every fortnight, her father comes to spew filth in Tamil at my aunt's gate. When Poornam hears his voice, she hides under the kitchen table rocking and holding her head. He screams outside the gate that our aunt is a bitch in heat, that she has stolen his child, that she conjures evil spirits and black magic. His breath is fiery with the local toddy. It is not until Mala has passed over an envelope of rupees that he leaves and Mala is able to extract the child from beneath the table, hold her while she convulses in silent terror.

But these days Poornam is our merry playmate. She shows us the varied delights of the garden that she and Mala Aunty have made blossom. At the back wall, a row of coconut palms waits to be plucked and in honor of our visit, Mala sends for the coconut plucker, Alwis. Alwis is taut, composed of skin stretched over long bones He smiles and flashes enormous gaps, bloodred betel-flavored spittle. He gathers up his sarong around stick-thin legs, wraps his limbs around the tree trunks, hauls himself up as quick as a monkey to send coconuts, heavy as bricks, bouncing on the lawn. His voice floats above our heads, suspended in the midday light. "Careful, Baby Nona! Only one of these will crush your head. Pattasssss! Like a smashed frog on the road. Then it won't be Baby cracking coconuts. It will be coconuts cracking Baby!" Laughter echoes as he slides down the rough trunk. Earthbound, he grasps a coconut in one hand, smashes down with the machete. A spume of liquid arcs skyward.

We drink sweet, fresh coconut water, cool as well water. Afterward, he hacks the coconuts open, fashions small spoons of husk so that we can scoop out the inner flesh, gelatinous as egg white, creamy as ice cream.

Alwis lives in the shanty colony behind our aunt's house. Sometimes leaving her house, we see him bathing at the single tap that spouts beside her front gate, his dark body glistening wet in the sunshine. Fingers deep in the snow white foam on his head, he gyrates precise parts of himself under the tap and waves a sudsy hand in our direction.

. . .

Lying in our shared childhood bed, I am awakened by the dawn that comes suddenly bursting into our room. A curl of her hair lies against my shoulder as if claiming me while she lay unconscious. La wakes, pushes me out of bed with her long curved toes, a finger to her lips. We tiptoe outside to find Shiva. Together we wait for the fisherman who comes bearing overflowing baskets suspended from the long pole across his shoulder. His resonating cry, "Maalu, maalu, maaluuuuu!" summons Alice, nudging away the cats with her slippered feet. The fisherman sinks onto his heels, his sarong pulled up to reveal thighs like dark muscled wood. He pulls aside banana leaves, displays the day's catch, silver sea creatures, small bundles of fat-armed squid, live crabs, with pincers raised in defense. Alice decides quickly and the fishmonger shakes his head in admiration. "Alice Nona always knows how to pick the freshest catch." There is a brief bargaining war, then our dinner is wrapped up in newspaper. We carry these bundles into the house like treasure. If Alice is in a benevolent mood, she will let us help her prepare the fish or crab curry, if not she will tell us stories as she does it herself. Either way these are magic mornings.

Rumor has always been the most trusted purveyor of news. Now the trade winds bring strange tales southward. In Jaffna, a city two hundred miles north of Colombo poised at the very top of the island, a city which has always been the stronghold of Sri Lankan

Tamils, a gang of Tamil boys is up to suspicious activities, it is said. Smuggling. Also bank robbing and weapons stockpiling. They are led by a youth with the fierce eyes of a true believer. He speaks of revolution, secession, independence; he speaks of splitting the island; he speaks of a Tamil homeland. People scoff, "Ragtag boys armed with sticks and stones. Uneducated Jaffna kids speaking big-big politics. What do they know of such things? Who does this kid think he is? A bell-bottomed King Elara?"

On a hot, yellow Jaffna afternoon, an old man sags and crumples at the gates of an ancient temple. It is the city's Tamil mayor, Alfred Duraiappah, the newspapers scream, shot sharp between the eyes by the upstart smuggler, robber of banks, and seventeen-year-old revolutionary secessionist, Velupillai Prabhakaran. He has killed the old man, he proclaims, because Duraiappah was a traitor to his race, a lackey to the Sinhalese oppressors. From now on the battle against Sinhala oppression will be fought by any means necessary. And in this way the nation hears the name of the man who will come to be called the Leader.

In the morning, the postman rings his bicycle bell and Alice, hunch wobbling dangerously, hurries to the front gate. She leaves the family's letters on the front table. But there are others she tucks into her sari blouse. These are from Dilshan, her son, who has been with our family from before our births but who has newly left us to enlist. He is in the north with his army battalion, together with entire generations of young Sinhala men hoping for new lives, better lives than those of their parents. The letters capture Alice's whole attention. We watch her read them, her lips moving slowly. But we are shut out of this part of her life as surely as if she had a door to close. The letters make her unattentive to us so that we are jealous of Dilshan, whom we too love, but who steals her affection so completely.

When he comes for leave, a tall, handsome stranger with a shank of thick, black hair falling into his eyes, it's hard to believe that he is the playmate we have climbed all over from birth. It takes us days before we are again easy with him.

Then he is again on the top balcony with us, throwing off our sandals to the ground below and attempting to hook them like fish with the fishing poles we have fashioned from sticks and large safety pins. We are on a ship, he says, tossed by the waves. He makes us see the water rising, the heaving horizon. We lurch about the balcony like ocean-tossed fishermen, drunk on the picture he has painted with his words.

His return causes strange reactions. Sylvia Sunethra comes into the kitchen. When he scrambles to his feet she says, "No, no, sit, Putha, you must have enough standing where you are stationed." She presses an envelope into his hands and hurries off. It is money, we know, we have seen her counting out the rupees just this morning. It is not easy for her to part with, but she tells us, "Poor boy. Might as well give him something to put aside."

On the last morning of his leave, he comes to the kitchen steps. He is dressed in his uniform, the khaki ironed, the boots polished. A different person. A stranger with hard eyes, he makes us suddenly self-conscious, shy. When he kneels to put his fore-head at her feet, Alice bends over, she runs her fingers over his hair, her hump quivers. She says, *"Budu saranai, putha."* After he leaves, she will not talk to us. She keeps her head down and serves us cold noodles and soggy fish for days.

In these years it is fashionable to cultivate seawater aquariums, so each house has great transparent rectangles perched on back porches and verandahs, glass cases in which live startlingly striped and painted, finned and ruffled sea creatures amid coral and sea-weed. When the monsoon comes, the fish tanks overflow, and the water gushes out over steps and into the gardens, carrying along the most exotic sea life.

Walking to market with Alice, our slippers are dragged im-mediately from our feet, our umbrellas are grabbed and thrown by the winds, so that in a few moments we are soaked from hair to toe, barefoot and exhilarated. In the churning roadside gut-ters, fluttering sea fish gasp and slowly drown in the onslaught of fresh water.

During the monsoon months, all distinctions between land and sea are lost and it feels as if we are swimming through the air. The cats walk into the house with the kicking back legs of frogs hanging from their mouths. They must be given chase and persuaded to dislodge their sleepy, disgruntled-looking prey. Ponds form along the back wall and soon are crisscrossed in miles of gelatinous strings beaded with ebony seeds that burst into a mil-lion squirming commas. We fill jam jars with tadpoles, balance them on our desk as we do homework by kerosene lamp (electricity goes out often in the monsoon). Magnified in the flame, the tadpoles rise and fall, rise and fall while we labor over numbers and letters. Outside the rain smashes down. Under the table warm, wet canine tongues lick hopefully at our bare soles, impatient for dinner.

This is our shared childhood then, marred only by certain memorable moments. Once, for example, my grandmother's eye, pulled from her various concerns, fixes on the three of us. "Boy, don't you have a place to go? Huh? A family of your own?" she asks. When Shiva, eyes averted, leaves, she puts her twisted hand on my head and says, "Don't get too fond of that one." And I at that age, bold, say, "But Achi, why not? What has he done?"

She: "He hasn't *done* anything. But they are Tamil. Not like us. Different."

I ask, "How different?"

She: "Can't you see, child? They're darker. They smell different. They just aren't like us."

Her voice, cajoling. But I am already anxious to get back to the kingdom of our friendship, and slipping away before she can catch my arm in those tree-rooted fingers, I say, "Anyway, he's not as dark as Mala Aunty, so that dark-skinned thing can't be right."

I am ten and Shiva is at my window, holding an unlit kerosene lamp. "You won't believe what I've found!" he whispers. When I climb out, he pulls me along the side of the house, pushes aside jasmine vines to reveal a dark crevice. He jumps down into it and in the moment when I am deciding whether or not to panic, his slim wrist appears to pull me down into the darkness beside him. I am suddenly blinded, claustrophobia clawing at my throat when he fires up the lamp, and blue walls spring up around us. Such a color! Cerulean, turquoise, flashes of emerald, like being swept underwater. "Look, someone left a radio!" he says. "Do you think it works?" We are laughing with the discovery of this secret place.

It becomes our hideout, of course. A place to shelter from adult whims, taking with us the various pleasures of childhood, Asterix comics, packets of biscuits, board games, jacks, cushions. It was our retreat and sanctuary.

It is around this time that watching our aunt Mala and her husband, Anuradha, La and I realize how different they are from the other adults. At parties they don't part, him to drink whiskey in the garden with the men and her to sit in the living room with the women sipping tea. Instead we find them in the in-between no-man's-land of darkened hallways, laughing together and touching often.

When she rejoins them, the women tease Mala, "Can't leave that handsome husband of yours alone for even one minute, no? He must really be something. The way you are always after him like a puppy dog." And, "My God, married for so long and still so much hot hot passion." They smooth the knife-sharp pleats on their saris, balance teacups on their knees, and pat their carefully elegant heads. Behind the good-humored teasing, we sense the jagged edge of jealousy. Lanka grasps my hand. "Big, fat, stupid aunties," she whispers, "why are they so bad to her?" And I, with the infinite wisdom of thirteen, am able to hit it exactly on the head. "Because she had a love marriage. But they had to marry whatever smelly uncle was chosen for them."

But despite their gnawing jealousy, there is one matter in which the aunties may legitimately pity Mala and for which she must endure the barely concealed glee of women who say, "Oh, poor thing. No matter. You can't imagine how annoying it is to blow up like a balloon and then always have children crying and pulling at you." Because, despite more than a decade of happy matrimony, her belly remains as stubbornly flat as on her wedding day.

Unable to conceive, my aunt delves into the sex lives of plants. Pulling apart tender flower lips with pollen-dusted fingers, she exposes fleshy stamens, produces hybrids and variations never before seen on the island. Her dahlias are as big as our heads, her orchids monstrous in their size and hue. Every year, she walks away from the Colombo Garden Show with the biggest trophies and the envy of other horticulturally minded ladies.

Across town, Anuradha's mother, a lady we take pains to rarely encounter, smites her forehead. "All this nonsense! Prize, schmize! What is the point of making plants grow when nothing is growing inside of her?" Refusing to be consoled, she repeats these words in the presence of the most surefire gossips, ensuring their passage through an intricate web of mouths into Mala's burning ears.

. . .

In 1981, in the northern city of Jaffna, Sinhala policemen and para-militaries storm the old Tamil library, rip books from the shelves, set fire to the mountains of paper. The conflagration shoots high into the sky, a funeral pyre visible for miles, a warning to all who can see. For weeks afterward, torn, blackened pages fly over the lagoons and salt marshes, the onion and chili fields. They lodge in the branches of palmyra trees, float into houses and buildings, entangle in the barbed wire fences and the limbs of gods soaring over the *kovils*. The storm of words finds its way into cooking pots and outhouses. The ground is littered with fragments of angular Tamil.

In Colombo on television we watch a Sinhala politician. He shakes his head to and fro, his double chin swaying. He says, "If there is discrimination in this land which is not their Tamil homeland, then why try to stay here? Why not go back to India where there would be no discrimination? There are your kovils and gods. There you have your culture, education, universities. There you are masters of your own fate." From upstairs we hear nothing but silence. When I see him next, Shiva is brusque, his usual high spirits deflated. When I ask him what is wrong, his voice is cold. "They burnt ninety-five thousand manuscripts," he says. "Your people burnt up our history." I stare at him, not know-ing what to say, but already he has turned from me and is running up the staircase.

SIX

It is January 1983 when an impossibility occurs. Mala's perfectly synchronized body refuses to bleed. Mystified, she waits and wonders if she has hit some early menopause, her body rejecting even the charade of fertility.

In his examining room, as she repins her sari, the doctor waves flippant fingers. "What nonsense, of course it is not menopause. Young, healthy thing like you. It is only the most obvious thing. You have conceived. You are expecting."

"But, Doctor, this is impossible."

"Why impossible? Are you not having relations with your husband? Is he not able to perform?"

A deep beetroot blush further darkens Mala's face. "No, Doctor, nothing like that."

"Because if that is so, perhaps you should be looking for more virile companionship, no?"

Mala slaps away the wandering hand. "No, Doctor, we have just been trying for so long."

The doctor sighs at the ignorance and, worse, silly morality of these Colombo wives, says, "Well, now the most mundane thing in the world has happened. You have succeeded. You are pregnant."

Mala hums as she reaches to pull dead leaves off the airborne bromeliads. One hand is curved around her belly, which swells under her sari skirt. Her breasts are heavy. She feels full of sap, like a plant with a seedling buried deep in the intricate unknown passageways of her body. Her feet are swollen, tender. The thongs of her rubber slippers stretched painfully over her arches have made her forswear footwear.

It is dusk, but feels like dawn. There is a freshness in the air, a chorus of bullfrogs singing from among the mud-rooted, sky-reaching purple lotuses of her pond. Only the silken whisper of bats' wings across the darkening sky give evidence of day's end.

Close by, Poornam pulls the garden hose over her shoulder, heavy as an anaconda, showering the thirsty foliage. Loamy earth mixes with water, mud rises between their far-spread toes. Mala exclaims, "I think the baby likes that! She pushed. Just here. I felt it!" She takes Poornam's wet hands and places them palm flat on her belly. The girl laughs, shakes her black curls. Yes! She, too, feels it! That unexplained, unexpected life unfurling in the cave of Mala's body. Poornam's hands leave small prints on the stretched skin of Mala's stomach. They look into each other's eyes, a sudden aching devotion between woman and girl.

Yet at this time, there are also strange signs and forebodings. A lifelong vegetarian, Mala is now taken by the fierce longing to taste the unknown flesh of animals. Anuradha is sent forth. He drives across town to where the imam recites the call to prayer, passes men in white skullcaps, women looking out from under the ends of their saris. He follows the thin stream of glinting blood to the butcher shop, where the skinless hanging carcasses assail his senses. Covering his nose with a handkerchief, he bargains for the flesh of animals he has never tasted. The sharp-eyed Muslim tugs dripping red organs off the hooks behind him, bounces them on the table, wraps the various pieces in newspaper and hands them to Anuradha, who, arms full of sodden newspaper, stumbles out and homeward.

Mala consumes these organs with curiosity and at night cries over the unfamiliar guilt of eating animals. Yet as the baby grows, she longs for even more intimate slices of animal flesh. She dreams of consuming the kidneys and hearts of chickens, the eyeballs of goats, the thick-skinned and slippery livers of cows. In the kitchen, Poornam cooks the offerings, her own Hindu aversion to flesh buried under a mountain of love for her mistress.

Fed to repletion, Mala's belly grows rapidly, but the rest of her stays as sharp as ever, like a thin child wearing a pillow under her dress, playing at being pregnant.

When Anuradha comes home, there is dinner. And then bed, where enclosed in the frothy kingdom under their mosquito net, they conspire their baby's future.

He: "Doctor, lawyer, engineer!"

She: "No! Nothing so boring as all that. She will be an artist."

He: "Like Keyt?"

She: "No, not modern. More in the style of whoever painted the Sigiriya maidens."

He laughs, delighted: "You mean completely unknown and unsung?"

She: "No, fabulously talented, able to make the rock breathe and live."

They giggle. Hands reaching for each other. Outside on her pallet in the living room, Poornam stirs in her sleep, mutters indecipherable words and unconscious prophecies.

July, a month of stifling, breathless heat. Heat that radiates as if the powers-that-be have dropped a woolen blanket over Colombo, attempting to muffle the screams that are coming. We stay inside, watch rounded drops of sweat run like mercury along our skins. Only the circulating rumor of impending disaster causes the slightest of breezes.

I slip away into the blue room to meet Shiva. We throw jacks. He goes first and I watch him, unaware that the fluency and fluidity of that motion will stay with me for years, will become the mark by which I measure all masculine movement. When it is my turn, I throw with a like accuracy, but his fingers suddenly steal out, wrap about my own wrist. "Not like that," he whispers. We are each stilled, silent. We have touched rarely, especially in these past few months when we have become somehow aware of each other in a different way. A way that makes me watch him secretly as he plays cricket or bends over his books. I have seen him watching me, too, with the breath caught in his throat. Now I see his pupils expand, the black space blossoming into the mushroom-like brownness. It makes me instantly breathless, as if I had swum far out and looked back to see no land. And then his lips are by my ear and each hair on my body stands upright. The shotgun crack of breaking glass. Screaming rising from outside the gate. We are torn apart, fleeing from the room, each to our respective families.

In the house, Amma grasps me hard across the upper arm, shakes me. "Where were you? Where?" she hisses. But there is also relief in her breaking voice. And then, the inhuman sounds coming from outside take away her attention.

We lock ourselves up in the house. It is impossible to know what is happening outside the wall. We are just grateful to be together, to be at home and not out on the streets. We don't know what is happening until much later. But this is what happened. First the streets were full of open-bedded trucks carrying red-eyed men who sang rude songs at the tops of their voices. They passed sloshing arrack bottles from hand to hand like riotous university students on a class trip. But in this case, other things also were passed from hand to hand. Knives, metal poles, machetes, dusty hoes, large white cans full of incendiary gasoline Hundreds of men stalked the streets, headed arrow straight to the residences of Tamil families. They dragged out fathers and mothers, girls and grandmothers, ripped clothing, shattered bone, and cut through flesh. They burned homes and houses, bodies and businesses. They set fires on front lawns, threw in furniture and children over the wailing of mothers. They committed the usual atrocities in the usual ways, but here was something unexpected and incongruous. In their earth-encrusted, calloused fingers, they clutched clean white pages, neatly corner-stapled. Census accounts, voting registrations, pages detailing who lived where and most important, who was Tamil, Burgher, Muslim, or Sinhala. And in these lists was revealed precision and orchestration in the midst of smoky, charred flesh–smelling chaos.

In the Wellawatte house, we huddle in the back bedroom as twice the mob comes to slam its heavy fist against the front door. Each time, a fiery-eyed Sylvia Sunethra flings it open, fixes the men with her wrath. Unquavering, as if blind to the machetes and broken bottles, she shouts, "What is this knocking and knocking to break down my door? Such shameless behavior I have never seen."

The foremost man, white pages clutched in one hand, a curving fish knife in the other, steps forward. "A Tamil family is living here, no?" Sylvia Sunethra fixes him with a gaze that does something to him, reminds him that before this business with the Tamils, there were other, older differences, distinctions of blood and caste that would have made his ancestors drop their eyes before her.

"Tamils. What nonsense. This is a Sinhala household. Only I and my family are here. No bloody Tamils."

The men, shamed by the righteous old Sinhala lady, turn away. They will pursue their dark deeds in other, more convivially acquiescent households.

Sylvia Sunethra closes the door, leans against it. We, her terrified family, emerge from our hiding places. "See? What did I tell you? You only have to talk to these idiots with a little chili powder on the tongue. Put them in their place." But her fingers running through La's curls are quivering, her bosom rising and falling. "Now I must go and talk to those Shivalingams."

She makes her slow, wobbling way up the back staircase, uses her key to enter a kingdom she has not seen for years. Inside, the late afternoon light lies indolent; there is silence and a thick cloud of fear. "For a moment, I thought they had already fled," she tells us later. "But I stayed there very quietly and then slowly they came out." Shivalingam men and women from behind the heavy furniture, Shivalingam children from beneath the dusty spaces under beds, until Sylvia Sunethra is surrounded. Then she makes promises, gives reassurances, returns to us and for three days turns away the mob by the sheer force of her will.

When night falls, she sends Alice creeping upstairs, bearing rice and dhal, some okra pods, the last of the coconut sambal. For these three days, no cooking smells drift down to us, no film songs fill the air, no jabbering of Tamil is heard. It is as if the rooms above us lie empty and haunted already.

If we could have entered the dead telephone lines that day, followed them across the burning city, down to our aunt's quiet bungalow and into her bedroom, this is what we would have seen. As smoke rises over Galle Road, as muffled screams make their way over her gate, and though there are still two months to go, our aunt Mala's belly is wrenching and twisting. It is the third day of twenty-four-hour curfew and Anuradha, white faced, fingernails bitten past their quick, has been watching his wife writhe for the last two days. He says, "The hospital. We have to go." And Mala, gasping, "No Anu, please. It's only the heat. And the baby kicking." He says, "Alright. I'll go and bring the doctor here." But she can't allow this. Has terrible visions of what could happen to him out there, in the unseen nightmare beyond their gate.

He carries her to their old yellow Volkswagen, the tight, battered Bata slippers dangling off her feet. She worries about this, the impropriety of leaving the house in her house slippers. But then Poornam has pulled open the gate and it is too late to ask for other, more appropriate shoes. They drive into the lane. A lull in the faraway shouting, the street festooned in sunlight and birdsong, foliage spilling everywhere, and for a moment there is normalcy, the sense that they are leaving the house for a walk along Galle Face Green or Mount Lavinia beach. They turn onto Galle Road; drive into thick, rolling smoke; glimpse armed men, abandoned cars, looted shops. Mala, the aching of her womb momentarily shocked still, presses a knuckled hand against her mouth.

Anuradha whispers, "God," as the clearing smoke allows them to see. He is wrenching the wheel around, homeward, when the hand smacks, splay fingered, against the glass next to Mala's head. A teenage boy in a torn, stained school uniform. Behind him, the mob congeals, and the boy, in his terror, scrambles onto the hood of their car. Through the garnet smears on the windscreen, they see the glint of knives, broken bottles, machetes. The mob surrounds them completely now and though she cannot see the men's eyes, Mala knows that they are expecting sacrifice. Knows that this Tamil boy in his school uniform, his face squashed against the glass so close to her own, the open fish mouth, the wide eyes, and that terrible gushing cut on his head, has been chosen as sacrifice for years of deprivation, broken governmental promises, failed examinations, and decades of relentless physical labor. And the boy himself, knowing this, his hands raised to protect his delicate face, does not even beg for mercy.

She hears the door slam. She sees Anuradha push through the men, pull himself onto the car, his body in front of the boy's.

She hears his words through her own shuddering sobs. "This child. He has done nothing. He is no problem for you."

Her fingers struggle on the lock. She will jump out. They won't hurt a pregnant woman. There are greater human laws they will abide by. She is sure of it. Just outside her window through the dirty glass, a machete is raised, hefted from hand to hand. She sees the silver gleam of it, sinks low in her seat.

Anuradha negotiating, "I can give you money. Anything. Just let me take this boy and go."

The voices, "What have you got to do with this Tamil bastard? These motherfuckers ruining this country. Think they can take over. Time to teach a lesson they won't forget. Crack some heads before they murder us in our beds. Move aside."

Anuradha turns, wraps his arms around the cowering boy.

His eyes search for hers through the blood-smeared glass. She sees the blade raised and brought down. The flutter of his lids so familiar. His body jerking and then sagging as it has innumerable times over hers in the sanctity of their bed. But this time, it is the unnamed boy who receives his weight, who shrieks the ear-shattering screams of an animal in terror. More blood than she can imagine, running onto the bright yellow paint of their car. Then a hundred hands reaching out and pulling him and the screaming boy into their midst.

She is huddled on the floor of the car, arms wrapped about her belly, when the door is eased open. A voice in Sinhala whispers, "Come, Nona, come with me." She looks and sees Alwis, the coconut plucker, slum denizen. "Nona, let us go home now." His calloused hands pull her onto the seat and then out of the car.

The mob is gathered in front of the car, a blur of limbs, and the metallic arc of weapons, but Alwis's sinewy, coconut tree–clasping arms will not allow her to break away, throw herself in the midst of the mob, beg for her lover's life. She is hurried away. When the smoke has cleared for a moment, she struggles loose, looks back to see men on the upturned car like flies on a day-old catch, white cans upturned, gushing gasoline. A roar as the spark ignites, catches, bursts into flame. The men's voices roaring and falling in time to the jumping flames. A dancing circle of men. Those on the periphery pushing forward, curious to see what the center holds. A louder shriek as a sarong catches a flying cinder and the circle scatters open. And what is it that my dark aunt sees at that moment? Too grotesque to be revealed surely. Too horrific to be imagined. But in the name of veracity it must be told: two vaguely human figures, lurching in an almost comic fashion, garlanded, each, with a flaming tire. Hands bound, black rubber melting onto skin, red flames dancing skyward, funnels of smoke obscuring wide open mouths, a glimpse of damaged eye. The swirl of men closes ranks. The scene is closed off from Mala's eyes like a book of naughty illustrations slammed shut. So fast that she almost cannot accept what she has seen. A soft rain of ash is falling, settling into her hair and skin. At her ear, a steady stream of words. She knows she must concentrate on this to avoid losing herself. She knows she must walk home now without allowing what is sheltering within her to pour out like water onto this smoky street.

Alwis's lips, close to her ear, whisper, "Look down. Glass, madam, all over the road." She trains her eyes on her swollen feet in their tight rubber slippers. Watches them curiously as they step carefully over broken glass.

They move with a will she cannot recognize as her own. She marvels at these feet, at their earnestness in moving away from loss. At the biology in her that has so assuredly chosen her unborn child over her dying husband.

At the head of their lane, a bus on its knees, front tires exploded, hemorrhages thrusting, pushing passengers. At the far side, a particularly jovial mob gathers. Reaching high above their heads the men pull a woman out of the small side window. They catch her sari pallu, pull, jumping and climbing on each other's shoulders. Mala has stopped in the street, turned to salt, Lot's wife, despite Alwis's panicked urgings. She sees the woman's open

mouth, her arms flailing in this most exposed and air-bound uncertainty between the bus and the men. A long streak of red bi-
sects her forehead, and then like a cork out of a bottle the woman
is dislodged. She falls into the circle of men, streaming to earth,
sari fluttering like a parachute. A roar of delight drowns the woman's screams. Then, again, the sound of gushing gasoline. And finally Mala allows herself to be pulled away, down the street, into
the quiet of the lane. Her red gate within sight. The scent is rising again, the thick fragrance of charred flesh like that which
wafts from the Muslim quarter during Eid, the festive roasting
of animal flesh.

She whispers to Alwis, "Not blood. On her forehead. It was
her *pottu*. She must have tried to rub it off so they wouldn't know
she was Tamil. It wasn't blood. It wasn't blood." Her mind turns
over the image. The woman falling, the *pottu* streaked across her
forehead, the waiting men. She knows this fixation is just another trick of her biology to keep the other images far away.

Later that day, Mala lies writhing in her bed. Poornam's delicate
hands attempt to soothe her mistress but Mala cannot be soothed,
is muttering through clenched teeth, "Nonono, no." Her breath
coming in jagged panicky gasps and sobs. Because something
catastrophic is unfolding and Mala is feeling the thick cold fingers of it caressing her calves, moving upward along her thighs,
into the secret places of her. The large cruel knuckled fingers of
fear and grief are forcing apart her labia lips, reaching into pink,
then breaking into red, tearing through her smooth curved cervix

into the sealed chamber where her forming child lies dreaming. Cold fingers wrap around a tiny ankle, start tugging. First gently, then insistently, so insistently that she kicks frantically at the sodden sheets, and despite Poornam's desperate attempts to still her, falls heavily to the floor. She holds her contracting belly, willing it to remain peaceful, patient. But she is gushing salt water and other hands are pulling downward and now she must tighten up, grow rigid, all energy and attention focused on keeping herself inviolate, unbroken. Her knees locked together, thighs clenched because she will not allow the child to emerge because it is too soon, too soon, and there is still time for hope, for birth. But relentless gravity is pulling, legs are kicking in blood, knees are parting, thighs are being pulled asunder and slowly she feels it sliding, slipping out of her. So small, yet so painful, and in a final rush she has delivered something minute and malformed.

Knees slipping, she rocks the amphibious creature as it gasps for air, tiny eyes blinking, a deep-sea fish hooked and dragged too quickly into light. Its gills fluttering as it drowns in air. She holds it until dawn, the girl's arms tight around her.

When the light comes, she feels Poornam's hands pulling at the baby. "Under the plumeria, by the pond," she says, and Poornam is gone, bearing away the tiny corpse.

And then, it is all over. The mobs, red eyed and weary in the manner of holidaymakers at the end of a vacation, head home to the villages as if they, too, are waking from a dream, returning to human form after a brief demonic possession.

Behind them, they leave burned cars, shattered glass like ice on the streets, looted textile factories from which bolts of cloth lick the sky like dragons' tongues, towers of garbage, bodies blackened beyond recognition, orphans, torn women, and destroyed men.

Arteries, streams, and then rivers of Tamils flow out of the city. Behind them they leave: looted, soot-blackened houses, the unburied or unburned bodies of loved ones, ancestral wealth, lost children, Belonging and Nationalism. It is a list that stays bitter on the tongue, giving birth to fantasies of Retribution, Partition, Secession. They flee to ancestral villages abandoned decades ago, and it is in these northern places that the events of this July will make them the most militant and determined of separatists.

As the smoke clears, we realize we have lost more than we thought possible. In the midst of these nightmare days, the Shivalingams have packed their few bags and scattered far into the wide world, leaving the house, above us, empty and echoing.

In those first months, I wander upstairs, listen to my footsteps ringing through the haunted rooms, and am inconsolable with the loss of Shiva. His voice comes to me on the staircase. I spill hot, angry, secret tears. It is impossible to breathe in this, our shared atmosphere, without him. I lie awake at night wondering where they have gone, that large and riotous family who shared our lives so intimately. But then my attention is taken because Amma has started agitating for leave-taking and exodus. I hear her and Thatha in their bed. "I won't bring up my children here," she whispers. "What sort of place have we become that grandmothers and children get burnt in the street?"

"But where to go?"

"America," says Amma with finality. "My brother can sponsor us, give us jobs, put us up."

I turn to La lying next to me, whisper, "Amma wants to move to America."

"Ammmerica," La sighs as she slips into sleep. I know what she means. We have seen its glittering image in countless movie versions. But how can one actually live inside it? Like moving into a dream. Unreal, impossible.

The following days are eclipsed in white. The white of flags flapping across front gates, the white of mourning saris and of shrouds wrapped around the bodies fed to the funeral pyres.

Our uncle's broken, burnt body is brought to the Mount Lavinia house, enclosed in a tight-shut coffin. La and I huddle together, wearing saris for the first time. Unsure how to move in the yards of cloth that engulf us.

"Inauspicious. Wearing a sari for the first time to a funeral," Amma muttered as she dressed us that morning. But what to do? These are the dictates of the time.

Mala, somnolent, leans on our father's arm, her stomach noticeably smooth. La grasps at Amma's own white sari, asks, "What happened? The baby?" In a hiss she is told to be quiet, not to ask rude questions. People gather in Mala's darkened living room.

They sit cross-legged against the wall. The row of saffron-robed monks enter in single file, line up against the opposite wall, hide their faces behind their splayed fans, and begin to intone in a deep-throated rumble. The coffin sits in between the mourners and the monks, a dark rectangular presence. It absorbs the light in the room, a single hideous reminder of what we have all gone through, the price that some of us have had to pay. The mirrors are turned to the walls so that Anuradha Uncle's spirit will not linger here, see itself, and become attached to this place. This is stupid, I remember thinking. If Anuradha Uncle's spirit was here it wouldn't be his own ghostly face in a mirror that would keep him, it would be Mala Aunty's heartbroken sobs.

The back of the room spills commotion. A sharpened finger points straight at Mala Aunty's heart and like an uninvited fairy, Anuradha Uncle's mother lurches forth, screaming, "Bad luck woman from somewhere!" Shocked relatives look up. Everyone suddenly wide awake and alert to scandal. "This happened because of your ill-fated stars." A vast intake of air and then, "I should have locked my son up when he came to me with stories of falling for a black-black *yakshini*. Some witchery you did to catch him. Yes, don't think that we don't know about you! No one would even look at you! Only my so innocent son, and now your evil stars have killed him!"

And Mala, breaking free from our father's grasp, eyes spitting fire. Now she does resemble the dread demoness Kali, hair flying, a dance of wrathful limbs and stomping feet. "My fault! Hag! Old woman from nowhere. Did you see what happened that day? Did you see the men pulled out of their cars? Did you see the women being burnt? Is that my fault also? Did I give the mobs their knives and hoes and machetes? Did I give them the burning tires? Did I gather up the men and put knives into their hands? Me and my bloody stars! If I had the power I would have burnt you up, not your son!"

Thick spittle splatters across the old woman's face. Mala is pulled away. She goes quietly limp in our father's arms. Gentle hands draw the old woman the other way but she breaks away, throws herself on the coffin, gasping for breath, crying in such huge heart-shaking sobs that it's painful to watch. I remember my father whispering to Mala Aunty, he must have asked if they should try to take the old woman away. I remember Mala Aunty shaking her head against my father's throat, him stroking her hair. I remember Amma's arms around us, sheltering us from the sound of those two broken women. It is one of my last memories of the island.

A few months later we are packed and flying across the world to start a new life, our hearts thudding fearfully in our mouths. As the plane takes off, I rest my forehead against the window. Below me the island glistens verdant green. I imagine all that it holds. Such things of horror and exhilaration as are seldom gathered together. The striated lands of the north stretching into the sea; the lonely lagoons; the creeping, fearful soldiers; the firework explosions; the villagers on bicycles; the gleaming Colombo towers; the high-rise hotels of the tourists and expatriates; the clubs that boast signs reading NO LOCALS; the leprous beggar on the streets, his fingerless palm spread forth in supplication to the slick fashionistas, the half-naked European women, the foreign men grinding over the buttocks of brown boys; the serene-faced Buddha statues; the rock fortress of Sigiriya, with its ancient long-eyed, swan-breasted nymphs; the black shape of a water buffalo with its ubiquitous shoulder-riding white egret; the jade spread of paddy; the deep green of tea; the lonely village roads; the dark forests; the wild elephants; the stick-thin stilt fishermen poised over the surging water, praying for their next meal while the cameras of tourists click away; the tired housemaid, newly returned from the Middle East; the spired churches; the scent of jasmine so potent, it catches the attention of traveling poets and writers, lures them here and will not let go. And always, always, the ever-churning sea, returning on itself, wiping away every footprint. These are the things I am saying good-bye to. I turn my head from the window as fear and liberation beat in equal measures through my bloodstream.

seven

We fly away from the island and twenty-four weary hours later, Los Angeles lies framed below us. A dry-as-salt landscape marked by rectangles in every shade of blue: cerulean, navy, baby, aquamarine, turquoise. A desert city of swimming pools.

In a dry-eyed, hyper-vigilant, vertigo-prone state of jet lag, we confront America. We had expected Amazon blondes and hatchet-jawed cowboy types. Instead there are uniformed Vietnamese men, Indian security guards, Malaysian Salvation Army workers all speaking an incomprehensible form of English.

Bored black women glance at our passports. They ignore our staring eyes. We have never seen black people except on television, and then they are usually stealing things or running away from white policemen. Perhaps they are used to this kind of racist scrutiny, the openmouthed curiosity of the newly arrived, because they quickly wave us into the arrivals lounge, where Ananda Uncle with wide-open arms awaits.

He herds us into his vast, cushioned car. California in December is colder than anything we have ever experienced. Our teeth are chattering, we cross arms over the thin cotton clothes we have flown across the world in. Yet, more than the cold, it is the dryness of the air, a sense of moisture abandoning our skins we feel most immediately and profoundly. The air is thin; it stretches endlessly blue and parched into the sky. We shiver and start as if exposed to hoary ice-frost and Ananda Uncle says, "Wait until it is summer, then it will be hot enough to turn you into dried fish." He laughs and in the backseat next to me, La sticks her tongue out at him, pulls it back in quickly before Amma sees.

He drives through streets as wide as rivers, passes other cars, each a silent moving island. He calls our attention to various sights. "There over the hills is Brentwood. And on those hills, the Hollywood sign. But can't see that now. Too much smog. When the air clears, eh? On the other side is Disneyland." He drives with one hand on the wheel, the other gesturing expansively. "This country. You can be anything here. You can become president, you know. Here anything is possible. When I came, years back, I slept on the park benches outside the hospital, made friends with the nurses. Had them call me in when I was needed. That way I saved on bus money, didn't have to go home." We are mesmerized by the purring embrace of soft leather, his endless narrative, the blue city unfolding outside the windows. The car eases onto the wide gray roads, and we fall asleep, exhausted and caught in the octopus coils of freeways.

I dream of the Wellawatte house, of dropping down into the blue room where Shiva waits for me. "I'm going to America," I say. "Los Angeles."

"Don't be crazy," he says. "That place doesn't exist. It's only in the movies." I'm trying to tell him that he is wrong, that I am going, that I am already there, when he throws his head back and starts to laugh. He's right, I think, it doesn't exist, it's only in the movies.

I wake to La's head slack on my shoulder, her mouth dripping into the cloth of my T-shirt. It is evening now, the sun setting in dramatic purple and orange hues all around us. The light different from anything I have seen, making me aware suddenly that I am exactly on the opposite side of the world from where I have spent my life.

We have pulled into a neighborhood. There are tall, graceful houses, square lawns of glistening neon grass, empty streets that make me wonder where the people are. Surely there must be people. But I see only a car here or there unloading a mother and a few children. There is no one walking, no shops spilling into the street. There is no music, no car horns. It is all profoundly quiet, profoundly lonely.

We curve into a driveway. In front of us, a mansion with ornate fairy-tale turrets rises out of lush greenery. We stare and stare. Does he live here? In this enormous house that could hold twenty, or more? Ananda Uncle parks still talking, unaware of our silent awe or perhaps just not commenting on it, perhaps used to the struck silences of all the newly arrived, all the shell-shocked souls he has similarly rescued. Pulling our suitcases out of his trunk, he says, "Just hard work and some luck, and all doors are opened." He flings open his own door and we are greeted with the most unexpected of scents, cumin, cardamom, chili frying. We had expected more exotic odors, perhaps hot dogs and hamburger meat, pizza. Whatever we expected, it was not the scents of Alice's kitchen. The disorientation is overwhelming. What is this place that we have landed in that looks so foreign and smells so familiar?

Ananda Uncle sweeps us around his house. In each enormous, soaring room, we are greeted by carved ebony furniture, ceiling-tall almirahs, peacock-feathered fans, gaudy batiked women and flowers, carved elephants, coconut shell turtles, posters of palm-swept beaches: pieces of island nostalgia thrown up like flotsam on a foreign beach. I hear Amma whisper to Thatha, "My God, it's like a handicraft shop." It is our first experience of immigrant nostalgia. A force that we will all succumb to, more or less, at various times.

At six o'clock Ophelia Aunty comes home. She is Ananda Uncle's beautiful Burgher wife. The one for whom he risked Sylvia Sunethra's wrath. The one for whom he moved, as his mother said, to this "bang-bang, shoot-shoot country." We are shy in front of her tailored suit, her efficient heels and lacquered face, while she looks the four of us up and down, taking in our unavoidable otherness. But there is also a gentleness radiating from her, a certain tenderness that makes it clear why our uncle has chosen this woman over all others.

She takes us into the kitchen where a hook-nosed imp stands on a stool and stirs steaming curries. Ophelia Aunty says, "Rosie, these are Sir's sister and her family. They will be staying for some time." The tiny woman waves her hand, mutters something into her pot. By Ophelia Aunty's deference we can tell we are in the presence of a culinary genius with skills akin to Alice's. The scents she stirs make the tears prickle behind my heavy, sleepy lids. America is exciting but already I miss Alice, Mala Aunty, our grandmother, the house cats, Shiva, everything familiar that we have lost, with a sudden sharp tearing in my chest.

In the room Lanka and I are to share, a brass cutwork lamp casts broken shadows upon posters showing the plump breasts and faces of Sigiriya maidens. We lie down on the soft beds, kick off the thick blankets; we have never slept under anything more than the thinnest cotton sheet or in separate beds before. We lie awake for hours, our thoughts bucket heavy with this new place and the strangeness of time moving in an unnatural rhythm. It is almost dawn, a grandfather clock somewhere in that huge house booming four before I fall asleep, and then I dream of the island as seen through clouds, the pain in my veins as it is pulled away farther and farther until swallowed by the frothing ocean.

When I wake, La is curled around my back in that narrow bed, both of us shivering despite her hair, which lies upon us like a silky duvet of the purest black. The light flowing through the window is tepid amber. We go downstairs to learn that we have slept into the twilight of the next day, carried forward in jet lag through two revolutions of the planet.

For some time, we flounder between time zones, somnolent

and sagging in the afternoon, wide awake at 3:00 A.M. Amma
goes to work with Ophelia Aunty, leaving before we wake up.
She is a preschool teacher's aide at Ophelia Aunty's school, tying
the shoelaces of white kids, wiping their noses, learning to sing
nursery rhymes in a new accent so that the children don't complain that they can't understand their teacher. "What is she speaking, Mommy? Make her speak English like you." She comes home
exhausted and gray so we learn not to bother her with questions
about this place, with all our curiosity and need.

Ananda Uncle takes Thatha to work with him. Our engineer
father is now the parking lot attendant at the clinic that bears
Ananda Uncle's name on a wide golden-lettered sign. All day he
sits in a cramped shelter handing out tickets, getting back dol-
lars, making change as quickly as he can with the unfamiliar
notes and coins. "Why is the five-cent coin bigger than the ten-
cent coin? It makes no sense," I remember him saying. He comes
home just before we go to bed. He, too, looking shell-shocked,
as if trying to make sense of what he has seen.

It is still Christmas vacation at the school we are to attend,
so we must stay home with Rosie for a week. Guardian-less, we
wander that house of trinkets and mementos. When we find
Rosie's lair-like room under the stairs, she waves us in absently,
her whole attention latched onto the synchronized bevy of hip-
thrusting, bosom-shaking Hindi film heroines on her diminutive
TV screen. She pulls a tall bottle from under her bed, cackles
through whiskey fumes, "This is my friend, Johnny, do you know
him? Johnny, Mr. Walker?" We race away, back to our room, wonder whether we can tell anyone, decide not to. Clearly Rosie is a

force in this house, whatever sins she commits overlooked by dint of her culinary sorcery.

On the third day of house arrest, Lanka says, "Let's go outside." I am apprehensive; we have been warned to stay within earshot of Rosie. But between drunken viewings of Bollywood's finest and long hours in the kitchen, it is clear that she has zero interest in us. Lanka stamps her foot. "What is the point of coming to America? 'The land of the free,' they say, and we can't even go outside!"

And as always in those days, I acquiesce. We slip past Rosie's room, down the stairs, through the heavy front doors into the wide, tree-lined street. Grand houses rise out of the earth, their roofs caressed by the branches of graceful trees, every perfectly shaped leaf in place. It is like a picture postcard or an illustration in the children's books we learned to read English with. La says, "It's so quiet," and I, too, hear the roaring silence. She grips my hand. "Don't people live here?" We are used to voices, car horns, vendors, radios, the constant wash of other people's lives over ours. This soundlessness, punctuated only by birdsong, feels ominous. We walk along, the perfectly paved road hard beneath our feet like a long, winding gray ribbon. The houses are so huge it takes minutes to walk past each one. La says, "This one is so big. Who can live there?"

I shrug. "Someone really, really important. Maybe a movie star or something."

"Maybe it's Michael Jackson!"

"Don't be stupid."

"Maybe it is—you don't know."

"Okay, so why don't you just walk up and say hi, does Mr. Michael Jackson live here? And then maybe you can marry him and live here with him."

"Okay, maybe I will."

A police car glides up behind us, giving us no time to panic or run. The blond policeman approaches with a gunslinger's walk, says, "What you girls doing out here?" We are silent. On the island, we knew to act demure when faced with men in uniform. The cowboy-policeman says, "Do you know what could happen to two little girls all by themselves?" His eyes glint turquoise as he takes in the insect bites on our legs, the dresses Amma sewed that reach past our knees, Ophelia Aunty's oversized cardigans on top, the cheap rubber slippers. I had not realized our out-of-place-ness was so insistent. He says very slowly and loudly, "You were reported. Someone called about you."

This is when we realize that there are eyes behind the curtains, that the houses are not empty but instead hold people who look out but do not reveal themselves.

In the backseat of the police car, we grip each other's hands, terror throbbing in our throats. The policeman says, "Okay, where do you live? On the other side of town? In Monrovia? Altadena?" But neither of us can speak; we are lost, disoriented by the litany of unknown places he has named. The policeman sighs. "Well then, I'm just going to have to take you into the station. What are you two anyway? Runaways?" I meet his eyes in the rearview mirror, they are a terrifying empty blue, blank as the sky beating overhead.

As we pass Ananda Uncle's house, Lanka cries, "There! We live there."

The policeman stops, looks, his eyebrows rise high into his forehead. "You live there? In that house?" He points at Ananda Uncle's mansion, we nod violently. He shakes his head. "You better not be lying or pulling some kinda trick."

"We aren't lying. That's where we live." He takes us to the door, keeps his thumb on the doorbell, until Rosie appears, the irritation in her eyes at being dragged from bottle and film quickly replaced by deference before this blond giant.

"These children are yours?"

"Oh yes, sir. They are belonging to the Master's sister." She grabs us and pulls us into the house quickly. "Thank you very much, sir. I will be feeding them now. Thank you." She closes the door on his face, locks both locks, turns to us. "Where did you go? Don't you know that you can't just go walking anywhere in this country? There are people, men who like to take little girls and do all sorts of dirty chee-chee things to them."

Lanka says back, "This is a free country. We can go walking if we want."

Rosie's face contorts into a sneer. "Right. Little children just off the airplane. Where will you go, huh? This place isn't like some tiny village at home. There are no buses everywhere. There are no people who know your family everywhere. Here you are alone, you hear?"

Later, in our shared bedroom, we play cards for hours, until our fingers stop trembling, until the silent streets, the hidden eyes of neighbors, the cowboy-cop, seem far away. La says, "I bet that was Michael Jackson's house."

"Maybe, maybe not," I say. We promise never to tell Amma and Thatha. We know it would just make the bags under their eyes even darker.

"Where is the market?" Ophelia Aunty repeats my mother's question and giggles behind her polished nails. "There is no market. We are going to the supermarket." It is Saturday. Both our parents are home and rested. We pile into the gigantic car and Ophelia Aunty steers through the behemoth streets. At the supermarket what riches greet our eyes! What mounds of dew-dripping, perfectly formed vegetables! There are carrots without blemish, beets without a trace of the earth in which they grew, fruits of the most gleaming perfection. Mountains of tangerines, sparkling red onions, bloodless meat. We had not imagined such munificence was possible, that there were so many ways one could clean a countertop, so many specialized ways of wiping an ass. How is it possible to choose amid such extravagance? We wander the aisles overwhelmed, unable to make decisions.

At home Alice shopped at the market. Sometimes we went to the supermarket, which we had thought was clean and modern and well stocked, but how paltry it now seemed. Ophelia Aunty wheels the cart with precision, drops item after item into it while she talks nonstop.

Thatha shakes his head in wonder. "In this country, they have thought of everything," he says, gripping a loaf of packaged sliced white bread in his hands and squeezing gently.

We learn that in America even the most familiar objects have previously unimagined manifestations. Rosie presses a bowl upon us. "What is it?" I ask.

"Aligeta pera," she says, the Sinhala term for avocado. We survey the proffered dish. The coloring is familiar, but into this have been mixed various things, including, is it possible, a tomato? She says, "Try, try—you will like." She pushes a bag of tortilla chips at us. "Eat with this."

Back home, avocados dropped from the trees like a blessing. But we ate them, mashed with condensed milk, solely for dessert. It was creamy delicious, while this looks completely alien. To be polite, we taste Rosie's offering and, repulsed, must wait until she turns her back to spit it out, the difference between what our tongues expect and what we are tasting impossible to reconcile.

But there are also unexpected pleasures. Drinking water, for one spectacular example, now comes gushing straight from the tap. You could fill a tall glass from the faucet, sparkling cold, and drink, not having to wait for the long process of boiling and filtering and then refrigerating that we were used to.

Oranges, too, are a revelation. On the island, they were meager green orbs, sour and full of pips. They had to be mixed with water and great quantities of sugar to make what was optimistically called orange juice. Here, oranges are a marvel, fat and bright as sunlight, their juice sparkling, their skins falling away into swirls and curls. For a time, we revel in oranges, consoling ourselves for the loss of mangoes and avocados in condensed milk.

Six months after landing in the desert city, we leave Ananda Uncle's mansion and move into a one-bedroom apartment where the carpet is a worn gray-green. In these close quarters the tension between Amma and Thatha boils and swelters. Each little room becomes disputed territory. Amma takes over the bedroom, spreading her few clothes, paltry makeup, and costume jewelry everywhere. Her perfume colonizes the air, her photographs are laid out on each flat surface. Thatha takes over the front room, sleeping on the couch. His clothes spill like the guts of a disemboweled animal from a suitcase on the floor. In these months, he is purse-lipped and preoccupied with studying for the Professional Engineer Exam. His books, broken-spined and covered in scribbled calculations, lie all over the floor and front table.

We negotiate these territories carefully, striving for neutrality like the Swiss or the Norwegians. We sleep in the bedroom, piled together around Amma. We watch cartoons with the sound turned low while Thatha studies at the table. Ananda Uncle has been true to his word, moving him out of the clinic's parking lot and into the office where he now answers phones and directs patients. But his dissatisfaction is apparent in the determination with which he studies. At dawn, or on breaks, during meals and on the bus, at whatever moments he can steal, he studies. When he falls asleep on the couch, a book clutched to his chest, we see his lips moving in the secret language of engineers. He has contracted the recent immigrant's fever. He wants more, so much more. He wants to conquer this new country. Make it recognize his talents, his abilities, make it see him. When he falls asleep on the couch, we learn not to wake him. When even our muffled whispers rouse him, he is angry and disoriented, furious that these brief moments of respite have been stolen from him.

On weekends, the tiny apartment is as tense as a war zone. Amma and Thatha circle each other, testing terrain, pushing the pulse points that are most tender, most vulnerable to injury and cutting word. Some days, we must duck smashing dishes like rapid machine gun fire. When the crash of plates takes over that of voices, I make La change into her bathing suit. We go out quietly, making sure we are not heard above the recriminations and the accusations. Outside, the apartment pool is loud, the voices of kids like those of seabirds echoing across the water. They cry "Marco" and "Polo" to each other from opposite ends of the pool. We don't understand the rules of this strange game, so we stay aloof, each of us slipping into the water with a relief akin to that of long exiled mermaids allowed to reenter their native element. In the water, sunlight quivers like cobwebs of light. We swim with arms arching overhead, eyes open to the curved bottom of the pool, the long ribbons of our breath released in streams of silver-spun bubbles. We pass each other in streamlined motion, each of us frustrated at the rounded edge that comes far too soon, flipping legs against the hard surface that propels us the other way. We remember the ocean that we have lost. Those morning walks down to the beach. Our father's swimming lessons inherited from the fishermen of his own youth. We are used to water without cease, water that stretches warm and endless to the very rim of the world. This glorified bathtub cannot satisfy our desire for water. We swim to exhaustion, lungs threatening to burst, our just developing biceps and thighs quaking, sinews stretched and lengthened.

Afterward, I want to read with my elbows flung over the side of the pool, wet thumbs cleaving to pages, rivulets running down my skin until half of me is submerged and the other half desert dry. But La wants me to tell her stories. She wants the stories Thatha used to tell when we lived in that white house by the railroad track. The ones that he has no time for now. She wants the one about the foxes' and hens' wedding, the one that he used to spin for hours, full of details, the hens' wedding clothes, the slavering foxes, the farmers at the very end scaring away the furry bridegrooms from their plump feathered brides. She wants me to tell her about Mala and Alice and Achi. She is forgetting their faces, she says. So I tell her stories while she floats on her back, her hair spread weightless like a dark waterweed. We stay until the other kids leave, claimed by parents or older siblings to various meals of dim sum or tamales. We stay until our hands are wrinkled like pink mice and the setting sun lights the tired little pool a tepid apricot.

When we return to the apartment, a sort of peace reigns. Thatha is at the table, his pencil skimming quick sums and calculations, worry on his forehead. Amma is in the bedroom, sorting through her photographs, touching her fingers to beloved features, ourselves as babies, Alice hunched and scowling into the sun like a fairy-tale villain, all of us at Wellawatte beach, our hair thrown about by the sea winds, the colors startlingly vivid. We had forgotten that such colors existed. For a moment we, too, feel the sea breeze. But Amma holds the picture, gazes at it for so long, that we are uneasy. For all her determination to build a new American life, we can see her longing to return to that lost weave of women.

But there are also the triumphs, as when Thatha, answering an advertisement in a newspaper, buys a car, a battered brown station wagon, a decade old. Our very own car! The space of it! The backseat that folds down! The windows that slip noiselessly away at the push of a button! To celebrate, we drive seaward. That afternoon there is a sort of affection lingering between Amma and Thatha, her fingers grazing his arm as he drives and he returning the attention even as he stops to consult the map, tells stories about the clinic, the impatient patients, the homeless drug addicts who gather in the parking lot. La and I are quiet, willing this peace to last, to expand into our other, everyday life.

When the beach swings into sight, it is as glorious as celluloid promised, long and sun drenched, the sand peppered with people in various states of undress. Thatha carries a large cloth bag into which Amma has packed careful containers of rice and curry, plates, a flask of tea. She shelters under an immense black umbrella as if from the most potent of thunderstorms. She will not allow herself to get dark even in this mad country where people actually lie in the sun turning obscenely brown and black.

The Pacific. That farthest western ocean. It churns and seethes, dark blue flecked with diamonds. The sight of it makes me realize how much I have missed salt water. La throws off her T-shirt. In shorts and bathing suit she rushes to the water's lacy edge. I run to her. We step in and instantly the water cuts at our ankles like a hundred shiny silver blades. We leap out shivering, icy drops splashed across our skins. The ocean we grew up with was as warm as bathwater, pulling you in to hold you tenderly; you could fall asleep in such water, lulled and embraced, the temperature at one with that of your own body.

We retreat to Amma and Thatha, shivering, chastised. Amma says nothing, but her look is triumphant. It says that we are stupid to trust this place, to expect its rules to be the same as the ones we were born under. She hands us heaped plates of rice and curry. We eat with forks (we are, after all, Americanized now), shivering in the bright sunlight and wondering at the various bodies that sport and play, at home in the icy water.

Amma has never really cooked before. "It wasn't necessary," she says, "Alice was always there." But now there is the necessity of feeding us, and so the recipes come, transcribed on onionskin-thin blue aerogrammes. Alice's words transcribed through Sylvia Sunethra's hand to our mother's ear. She reads them, frowning, her mind fixed on the intricacies of substitution. What can she use in place of gotukola, jaggery, coconut oil? The myriad things that do not grow in this foreign soil. She must learn the skill of appropriation. To use spinach when the recipe calls for gotukola, brown sugar for jaggery, olive oil for coconut oil.

On weekends she takes us in search of potent spices and fresh vegetables. We brave Mexican markets where quivering brains, coiled intestines, and the enormous scarlet hearts of bulls lie in piles, while we look for red chili and turmeric. We buy exotic vegetables we have only seen in shiny foreign cookbooks, serrated broccoli, hard and cool white cauliflower. We bear these treasures home, heavy brown bags on our laps in the lurching bus, ignoring the curious sideways glances of other passengers.

In the apartment, Amma roasts curry powder in the oven. La and I crush mustard and cumin seed with a mortar and pestle. Vegetables pile on the counters, carrot and beetroot greens trailing off the edge like the blue-green plumage of tropical birds. Pots boil, spices fry, oil sizzles. The room is shrouded in steam, which wafts into the hallways and makes our neighbors, those erstwhile Mexicans and dutiful Chinese, glance up curiously, inhale sharply and deeply. But they are only curious. They have their own foody witchcraft to remind them of various homelands. It is only the envy-eyed landlady, her hair cut short, arm fat wriggling out of her sundress, who wrinkles her nose as she walks by our open window. She drags her equally overweight dachshund on the end of a leash and gossips about us to the dog. "Ohhh, are they making your nose twitch, my Wogums? These Indians. Always cooking with their onions and their curry. How can they breathe in there? Must be used to it. Where they come from, it must seem like a palace."

Inside, La and I stifle giggles. She thinks we are Indians. We have never even been to India! Amma pushes a sweaty hand against her forehead and frowns. This landlady is the bane of her life, coming often to complain about the smells coming out of our windows or the noise we supposedly make. Amma is always sweet and courteous on these occasions, but now inside the sanctity of her own crowded and tiny kitchen, she whispers, "Ooo, my little Woogums. Why don't you just come over here and kiss your mommy on the mouth with your dirty little dog breath, your filthy little doggie teeth. Come here, little Woogums! Mmm-mmuuuahhhh . . ." She pantomimes the fat woman's swaying elephantine walk, the way she holds the poor squirming dog high in the air, bringing it down to her lipsticked mouth to kiss passionately. Thatha, too, has come into the kitchen now. The three of us hold our hands tight against our mouths to hold in the giggles, but it is no use and outside the landlady stands nonplussed listening to the gales of laughter floating out of our window into the sunshine.

In these first years we learn the lesson of our inadequacies. In school we learn quickly that the smell of our bodies is shameful, and must be dissipated by perfume, deodorant. That the hair on our legs, the fine down that we had never noticed before, must be daily shaved to smoothness. That certain kinds of clothes are acceptable and that these do not include the ones we have brought with us from the "old country" or those that Amma makes for us, no matter how painstakingly, on her old, beaten machine. We learn that acceptable clothes can only come from stores, and for

this reason we become adroit shoppers at the local bargain base-
ments, the Salvation Armies and the Goodwills, looking for
shirts, jeans, sweaters that will mark us as normal, as acceptable
and undistinguished in the crowd. We learn also that hair condi-
tioner comes in bottles and must be bought separately from
cooking oil. We learn that although we have been speaking English from birth, people cannot understand the crispness of the
Queen's English mixed effortlessly with the roundness of Sinhala in our mouths. We have singsong accents, they say. A ten-
dency to substitute V's when W's are called for and vice versa, so
that "veil" comes out sounding like a large sea mammal. Various
conversations are thus rendered incoherent.

These are lessons about shame learned by watching eyes: by
noticing the way the other kids wrinkle their noses or pretend
not to see us when we sit next to them at the lunch table or on
the school bus. By careful observation we realize that adaptation
and emulation will be necessary if we are to survive in this new
place. So quite quickly we learn to shed our old clothes, our old
manners. We say "cookie" now quite effortlessly, knowing that
the word "biscuit" will be answered with blankness.

On our second Christmas in America, Ophelia Aunty gives us
ribbon-festooned presents. I forget what La's box contained, but
for me there was a tray of colored oil pastels arranged from the
deepest midnight to the purest moon. I am uninterested, but
Lanka is enraptured, in love with each hue. Suddenly she is playing with color, testing and mixing shades so that our brown

paper–bound schoolbooks become orgies of violet, rose, scarlet. All surfaces become her playground. Thatha's notes and Alice's letters bear tiny sketches in the corners, bits of mural appear on the wall behind Amma's bed. She asks for drawing paper and pads, but Amma says these are too expensive, so I take grocery bags, slit them along the seams, and smooth them on the table for her. These are her first drawing books, grocery bags carefully stapled together at the edges.

In these days, it is always dark before Amma and Thatha get home. We let ourselves into the apartment, heat the food Amma has left in the freezer on the stove. We are supposed to be doing homework, but La is drawing faces, her tongue against the roof of her mouth. I can see the curl of it between her slightly parted lips, her forehead wrinkled in concentration. I should play big sister, bring her back to her schoolwork, but I let her draw instead. She mutters to herself, "No, no, not like that." She says, "Look, Akka, a lip is like the petal of a hibiscus flower. The way it curls over." She draws for me a set of the most luscious curling lips, and I know that the colors have released something inside her.

In later years, Lanka's paintings will cover entire walls. She will paint fluorescent green paddy fields stretching into sapphire skies, mangosteens split and glistening with erotic plumpness, tumescent green plantains bursting off the canvas. She will paint ferocious forest orchids and elegant five-petaled plumeria. From her brush will spill forth all those we have lost. Mala in the garden, surrounded by a whirlwind of dogs, Alice smiling her crooked beaming smile, Alwis's gap-toothed grin. The entire island will burst from her brush, so that entering a room containing her paintings, one will feel the air suddenly wet, the hair will stick to one's forehead. "I can remember it all this way," she will tell people, "only when I paint."

If La's particular obsession was the precise moment at which blue becomes green, mine had to do with books, words, paragraphs, and the ways they fit together on a page, nestled next to each other, waiting like time bombs. The greatest thing about America to me was the constant availability of books. The first time I walked into an American library, bells rang and cherubs sang about my head.

I wandered about in rapture, borrowed books by the armload, and became known to the librarians. I liked to inhabit books, devour them. Reading seemed so similar to eating, to consumption. I didn't like to eat now unless there was a book open by my plate. A habit Amma hated and shouted at me often over. If I could get away with it, I would have written in the margins of my favorite books, drawn diagrams, arrows, and small pictorial commentaries in direct conversation or argument with the writer. Instead I read in the bathtub, at the dinner table, on the bus, leaving a trail of books behind me. Amma and Thatha revered books. They read carefully without bending pages or breaking spines, bent to kiss them if they fell on the floor. They were aghast at what they saw as my irreverence, and I in turn could never understand the politeness with which they read.

. . .

Three years later we leave the combat zone of the apartment for that most cherished slice of the immigrant dream pie, our own piece of land. The house sits on a quiet street, long rows of houses stretching on either side of it like carefully set dominoes. These are houses painted in innocent pinks and peaches, with silver basketball hoops and green-green lawns in front. Oh, the sanctity of that green! We had not realized before with what pride the American suburban family tends its lawn. The shade of its greenness indicating all manner of propriety and belonging. We, too, tended our tiny bit of the North American continent with care. Every weekend we watered and weeded and manicured. It was supremely important to ensure that our lawn was the same color as those of the other houses stretching into the far distance.

Amma has a proper kitchen now. There is counter space, quickly multiplying pots and pans, a large collection of knives. "There is nothing like a good knife," she tells us, drawing a sharp blade along the leg joint of a chicken, pulling it apart effortlessly so that there is only a thin trickle of blood through the pink flesh. "Keep them sharp and they'll never betray you." She plunges all the bits of the chicken into the pot, cooks it with dark roasted curry powder and red chili powder in coconut milk, so that hours later it is succulent and dripping off the bone. We eat it with coconut sambal and white rice. We eat with our fingers. Here inside the house we don't have to use forks, and yes, it does make the food taste so much better.

The house allows La and me those prerequisites of an American adolescence, bedrooms of our own. Mine, a flushed creamy pink. Hers, phosphorous blue-green, the shade of deep water just beyond the surf, so that entering her room felt like falling into the lair of a mermaid. I remember her head on the very edge of the bed, her hair spilling onto the floor in swirling eddies and whirlpools. In those years, I almost expected a silver sequined fishtail flashing among her bedclothes. In this room she is free to experiment with paints, pastels, colored pencils. She tapes white sheets on the walls, no longer limited to the brown paper bags of our first immigrant days, and paints. She fills the walls top to bottom with scenes of other places, huge portraits, fruits and flowers, so that soon the blue-green walls are not even evident anymore. Meanwhile I, in the next room, build towers of books, fortresses of words, scribble into the night. In this way we are each claimed early by the muses who will stay with us through our lives.

By the time she turned fourteen, it was confirmed. La was going to be, indeed . . . already was . . . a beauty. Skin as smooth as creamy plumeria petals, eyes as big and lashed as extravagantly as a cow's, and that heavy mass of hair. So much beauty that I witnessed all the clichés. The old men reading their newspapers who looked up like bloodhounds on the trace when we walked to the drugstore for ice creams, the love notes that appeared wedged in the crevices of her locker that made her sigh and crumple them up in her fist, the phone that rang in the middle of the night only to click off when picked up by our irate parents.

And I, how did I feel about all this one-sided bounty?

I, finding myself that comic figure, the plain older sister? I can't lie. It broke my heart. To be confronted in my mirror with a plainness that suited Jane Eyre, the flat listless wall of hair, the dull eyes and round figure, while just a bedroom away slept my sister who evoked spasms of desire. How tragic! How unfair! How could it be that some beautiful long-ago ancestor had revealed herself in La's features and not in mine? I was the older by those all-important three years, and yet it was for her the phone rang, it was she who was invited out on weekends and Friday nights. Of course my parents made her refuse these invitations. No daughter of theirs would go out with boys or even groups of girls at night. Who knew what could happen to young girls in this country? There would be no "dates," they declared, except the type that could be eaten, an often-repeated joke that invariably made them giggle. But at least La had the satisfaction of being asked, while I was never invited out at all. The few friends I had were book-hungry nerds like myself, held back by thick glasses and myopic stares. And the worst of it, La had no use for it. She threw her beauty around like an old shoe, wearing the baggiest of our father's shirts, the most unflattering of men's pants, the strangest combinations of colors and patterns. It drove a wedge between us, of course. I retreated behind my books, behind an impenetrable wall of studiousness. La knocked literally and figuratively at my doors. I think she was astounded by this distance. We had always been so close. But I was angry with her for her sudden beauty, and I kept myself closed from her.

Only years later did I understand the carelessness with which she dressed. It was, I think, an attempt to reach over the walls that had sprung up between us. Her need to tear up the labels that had us pinned like specimens under glass.

"Yasodhara Rajasinghe: dusty, brown-winged bookworm. Lanka Rajasinghe: luminous, blue-green, glitter-winged butterfly." That carelessness, it was her attempt to claim me as sister and ally.

Then, too, something else profoundly painful has begun. On the island when we left there had been stirrings. Now there are outright bloodlettings. There is a new group. The Liberation Tigers of Tamil Eelam coalesced around the Leader, who is ruthless, unafraid of death. They are calling for secession, for a separate homeland. They desire a long curving slice of land along the northern and eastern coasts of the island. They call it Eelam. They are willing to kill and die for the maternal comfort of this homeland, for the possibility of belonging. The government, too, is willing to send Sinhala soldiers to kill and die to protect this sliver of contested homeland. I don't remember the first time I heard the term "civil war" in reference to Sri Lanka. Civil war? How was that possible? We could not fathom what this term meant or the implications of what would be.

When a bomb detonates, our first indication is a phone call from our grandmother Sylvia Sunethra. She tells Amma about the explosion that has happened a half mile from the Wellawatte house. She reports the numbers of wounded and dead, the state of the suicide bomber's body. Amma hangs up the phone, leans against the wall as she recounts these details to us. She talks in her most sedate voice, attempting to alleviate our fears, soothe our anxiety. She knows that if we are to survive watching this war from a distance, as spectators, we do not have the privilege of indignation or anxiety.

Once I walk into a room I had thought empty, to find my entire family, silent, eyes riveted on the television. On the screen, the chaos of a just detonated bomb. The camera bobs between running feet and bleeding bodies. It comes to rest on a round object lying on the steps of a building. In the instant that the camera focuses, we see that this is the decapitated head of a woman. Her eyes and mouth agape, hair streaming down the steps and with it the various sinews and octopus strips of flesh blown from her neck. Her blood drips quickly before the camera pulls abruptly away and a newscaster fills the screen.

We never talk of this. But I dream of that head every night for a week. I know it must have been the suicide bomber. Only an extremely close detonation would pop a head off a body like that. It makes me ponder this woman, girl really. What could have led her to this singularly terrible end? What secret wound bled until she chose this most public disassembly of herself? Just moments earlier she had been just another nameless woman in the teeming crowd; now, blown to bits, she was either martyr or mass murderer, according to one's taste. Either way she had attained instant immortality. But what had led her to that moment? This is a question that haunts me.

We never talked about that woman. But there were images like this around all the time, casual reminders of what was happening just outside the stage of our lives.

. . .

Another adolescent memory: Thatha driving Lanka and me to school, each of us caught in our various concerns.

I have a physics test I'm not sure I will pass. I comb the pages over and over attempting to make sense of the symbols, this incomprehensible language that our teacher assures us will be necessary to navigate our adult lives. I am not convinced of this necessity, but this coming test is tying tight sailor's knots in my stomach. Thatha drives carefully, reaches for the radio, and suddenly a reporter is informing us of bloodshed on the other side of the world. "Suicide bombing in Colombo, Sri Lanka." The words fall like perfectly pronounced shrapnel around us. We hear the crash of bodies, a voice crying out in Sinhala, picture instantly the dark bodies pierced by ball bearings, the chaotic swarm of strangers, the intimacy of damage under the fierce May sun. Thatha turns the radio off. We drive through silent streets. The scenery incongruous with the images that flicker behind our eyelids.

I remember the moment when I knew that we were all involved, that the island was not some vague and distant memory, but vivid and alive. Most Sundays, we went to Ananda Uncle's house, where La and I were always sequestered in a back bedroom with the other kids. All of us had been threatened with all fashion of misfortune if our homework remained undone. And yet ignoring these threats, we entertained ourselves according to our various proclivities. The boys paying tribute to a pre-beach-strolling David Hasselhoff in deep philosophical discussion with his car Kit, Lanka at a table, immersed in the drag of her brush on new canvas, her forehead furrowed, every now and then indulging that disgusting habit she had then of sucking the point of her brush into an ever sharper point. I lay on the bed, reading *Wuthering Heights*, wondering at the cosmic unfairness at which, instead of wandering the moors with fire-eyed, uncouth rapscallions, I was stuck here with these particularly unsympathetic companions.

End of book. Enough of Heathcliff and his Cathy. I bounce off the bed, go searching for food and parents. Loud voices burst like fireworks from the living room. The servant woman Rosie lurks in the shadows, listening. She grabs my sleeve, pulls me close to her, whispers in a fiery, fumy snarl, "Baby, better not go in. Sir is very angry. Listen." A chink in the door, and I see Ananda Uncle stomping about the room, the other adults slouching in their seats like guilty children.

He shouts, "What are you going to do? Sit here and let these Tiger bastards take the country? How many of you are here because you got a free education in Sri Lanka? All of you buggers! Otherwise you would be in Colombo watching the Tigers ride in. You owe it to help stop them. The government can't fight these bastards without our help."

He mops his streaming face. Someone raises a tentative schoolboy hand. "But should we fund the military? What about the reports that they are killing villagers?"

Ananda Uncle's voice gets quiet, drips venom. "You and your bloody principles. You sit on your arse in America and have principles. Meanwhile, rich Tamil bastards here, and in London,

Canada, Australia, fuckers who haven't been home in decades, all of them send money streaming, pouring, overflowing into the Tiger coffers. They're not crying about Sinhala villagers. They're not worried about principles."

There is a stirring as people reach for their money. Wallets are opened, checks are written.

Ananda Uncle says, "That's better. That island is our motherland. We owe it to her to help her in her time of trouble. This money will help keep kids from becoming orphans. It will keep people alive." In his voice the reverence of true belief.

Beside me, Rosie's whiskey breath stirs the hair beside my ear. I yank my sleeve out of her clawed grip, run back to the bedroom where Lanka lies on the bed, flopped on her stomach, the soles of her feet gently cupping each other. I clamber on the bed to be close to her. I wish I hadn't left this room. Wish I hadn't heard what I did. But the words stay with me. The implications of complicity impossible to ignore even at that age.

At Christmas we gather at Ananda Uncle's. Every year there are more new families looking lost and speaking in thick accents. The women have forests of hair on their legs and armpits, they wear cheap skirts to the ankle and unflattering haircuts. Their husbands wear tight suits and rubber sandals. Their children are clad in either frothy pink or light blue, according to the appropriate gender. They waft a certain specifically island odor, a suggestion of sweat, coconut oil, and turmeric. Every year they come looking more and more shell-shocked. It is impossible to tell what they have seen, what they are escaping. They do not ever talk about these things. They seem so foreign to us, they have not yet learned to suppress their smells and moderate their voices. They are surprised by too much and too easily impressed by America.

In a few years, these children will be wearing jeans, their mothers will be perfectly coiffed, and their fathers will smell of cologne. But for now we keep our distance lest the aura of foreignness so laboriously shed rubs off on us.

In these myriad ways, we carved out our lives in Los Angeles. Yet falling asleep was often an act of travel, taking me quickly by the hand so that I am instantly surrounded by verdant foliage, the ocean's emerald roar, the voices of Alice, Mala, our grandmother. Those most familiar and beloved of women.

But there are also nightmares. Over and over I dream of a small house, a glittering lagoon, a mango tree, and a young girl. She stands before me and her large bruised eyes do not leave mine. When she unpins the sari fold at her shoulder and pulls it away from her, I see sunset-colored bruises on her delicate clavicles. When she undoes her sari blouse, I see the grenades tucked like extra breasts under her own. It is grotesque. I wake trembling, and her eyes stay with me for hours.

part two

eight

SARASWATHI, NORTHERN SRI LANKA
It is the dry season here in the northern war zone of Sri Lanka, and the lagoon reflects sunlight like the shards of a thousand broken bottles. The village children used to gather here to play, but I come here alone now. So many of them are gone, whisked away in speeding white army vans or torn from the sides of dead fathers and bleeding mothers by the Tigers. The other, "lucky" ones have run away to the Internally Displaced People's camps. You can tell where the camps lie from miles away by the smell. Thousands of people without running water or toilets, there is bound to be this terrible smell. So even when the gunfire echoes, I am glad that Amma and Appa refuse to leave, that they keep us here in this small house by the lagoon.

There were seven of us before. Amma; Appa; my brothers, Krishna, Balaram, Kumar; myself; and like a tail at the very end, my sister, Luxshmi, who was named for the goddess with the long and lovely eyes, Luxshmi, who provides all things material, a stream of golden coins pouring from her open palm. Whereas my little sister was named for the butter-skinned goddess of plenty, I was named for Saraswathi, the serious-eyed and studious goddess of learning. When I complain to Amma, she only laughs and says, "Look how wisely we have named you," and it is true, because there is something in me that loves the glide of pages between my fingers, the stroke of my pencil across paper, the hush of the village classroom. Even now I am studying for the teacher's certification. Next year when I am seventeen, I will take the exams, and one day maybe I will be the village schoolteacher.

But these are big-big dreams for somebody living inside a war, so I don't speak of them often. Sometimes I get this breathless feeling that the war is a living creature, something huge, with a pointed tongue and wicked claws. When the tanks rumble past in the far fields, I feel it breathe; when the air strikes start and the blood flows, I feel it lick its lips. I've grown up inside this war, so now I can't imagine what it would be like to live outside it. When Amma and Appa tell stories of before, it is that world with plenty to eat and no air strikes that is alien to me. What would it mean to live without the soldiers in their sandbagged checkpoints? Without the barbed wire? Without the giant photographs of martyred Tigers?

When the war first stroked its nails across the hearts of my brothers Krishna and Balaram, they were older than me, but only little pieces of the men they longed to be. The Tigers had come to our schoolroom. They showed us videos of what the Sinhala do to our people. How they murder and kill us Tamils without mercy. They spoke of the Leader, his lifelong struggle for Eelam, a homeland where we would be safe from the Sinhala. What determination shone on my brothers' faces! They wanted so much to help save our people, but also to be known as brave and valiant fighters. They came home quivering with hate, the war shining in their eyes.

When they ran away to join the Movement, Amma didn't cry. She kept her back straight and her eyes glistened only with pride. And I, convinced by her strength, hid my own tears. I was proud of their fearlessness.

Sometimes, Amma takes Luxshmi and me to the martyrs' cemetery. We search through that forest of headstones until we find Krishna and Balaram's names and then Amma cries over her sons. But I don't, because these graves hold only rust-colored earth. My brothers' bodies were torn apart over the disputed territories, leaving us no fragment to mourn. It is outside of the cemetery that my brothers haunt me. When the earth of the onion fields is made ready for planting, I wonder if this was where Balaram's blood splattered onto the ground. The lagoon in a particular light makes me hear a quiet splash. Then I see Krishna's face floating, his mouth open, his uniform sagging, the water tinting rose and then scarlet around him.

Sometimes I am certain it was easier, a quiet click underfoot, and then, instant incendiary light. The swiftness of the land mine. I hope that is how they went. Much better, faster and sharper, than bleeding in the onion fields or a heavy boot into the lagoon.

This is what happens when you don't know the way someone died, all the other possibilities come crawling in until your head is packed full of death. But I'm getting better at pushing away these thoughts with both hands. The last time we saw either of the boys was about three years ago. They had been granted leave from the camp and for days before they came, Amma bought lentils for *vadai,* stirred batter for *appam,* and fried a whole fish. I don't know where she got it, the market had been empty for weeks, but the scent of it made us all weak-kneed. We hadn't eaten like that in so long.

When they came, they ate and asked for more, but they kept their guns strapped to their backs while their fingers moved through the food. When they smiled, only their mouths moved. They looked to the left of me, to the right of me, but their eyes slid off my face like water. They didn't praise Amma's food. They didn't speak of the weeks we ate unsalted rice so that they could feast. They talked only of Eelam, of their weapons, and how many bastard Sinhala soldiers they had killed. When they left, Luxshmi and I fell upon their banana leaves, scooping up the last bits of *appam, rasam,* the precious bits of fried fish into our mouths; we gnawed on those bones until they were sharp dry splinters. That was the last time we saw them, and now their faces have grown dim. I can only picture them in their uniforms, not as they were before, when we were children together, playing by the lagoon, the slap of our slippers echoing across the bund in time to our laughter.

Kumar, my youngest brother, had eyes like a girl's, dark as a she-cow's with great curling lashes. When Amma brought out her dancing saris, he'd run his palms slowly over the silk as if they were the pelts of animals. He would put on her silver ankle bells and dance the gopis or Radha so skillfully that Amma laughed and called him her favorite daughter. We fought over those bells, each of us, determined to dance most like Amma.

After Krishna and Balaram were killed, Amma kept Kumar close to her all the time. She couldn't bear to lose her last son, she said. She had given two sons to the cause, she wanted to keep one for herself, for the time when the war was over, she said, clutching him to her even though by that time he was taller than her and didn't want to be held. She kept him in the house all the time. But that year, in the malarial months after the monsoon, we all had shaking, dripping fevers and there was only Kumar to go to the market. The soldiers came for him then. Kanahamma, the old market woman, saw it, the white van swerving to a stop in a cloud of red dust, the nose of a gun glinting through the open doors. We have not seen Kumar in two years. He would be eighteen now and I don't think I would know his face if I saw it.

Amma never cries for Kumar. This is because she thinks he is still alive. At the end of each day, when the sun is falling quickly over the water, the bats starting to stream over the violet-dusk sky, she stands at the door waiting for him. She never says his name, but I know she is still waiting. Stupid Amma. Every time she does this, I must fight myself not to grab her shoulders and hiss the truth into her face. He is never coming back. He will never walk through the door, with Snowy at his heels, a bag from the market over his shoulder, smelling like Kumar, that particular mix of boy-sweat and dust. There are soldiers everywhere and when they take you, you do not ever come back. But I can never say such things to Amma. One day she will know that her youngest son, too, is gone and for him she will not even have an empty grave to cry over.

When she was young, before the war came, Amma was a dancer. She has danced in all the halls and temples of the island and even across the seas in India. When she is in the mood, she tells us how she met Appa. He was a drummer. But old even then, she says, his beard already white. Now he is bowed and bent. His left leg drags behind him and his fingers are always atremble like butterflies. But these are lucky things, Amma says, because these days, only the very old or the very young are not taken.

On the evenings when the fighting sounds far away and there is no rumble of tanks or aircraft, Amma's students come shyly in twos and threes. A few small girls, they gather in rows, barefoot under the spreading branches of our mango tree. I make sure that their muscles have not forgotten the stance, that their limbs are well stretched and pliant before Amma comes. I arrange their arms as she used to arrange mine, curl or clench their fingers to imply the blooming of the lotus or the ferocity of a warrior grasping his weapon. I push their shoulders downward so that they must dance from an even lower squat, their thigh muscles quivering, and the sweat beading on their upper lips.

When Amma comes out, there is no music, only the rhythmic slap of her hands and her quiet voice calling out the steps. Sometimes there is also the echo of faraway gunfire. But those sounds only pull at a small part of our attention. We are caught in the desire to please Amma, to perfect the placement of our feet on the earth, the tilt of our chins, and the flash of our eyes. I dance so the girls can follow my feet. But more than that, much more, I dance for the thrill of it, the way the movements flow through me like water pouring over my skin, the way my arms move through the air, winged creatures. In these moments, twirling, stamping, arms extended, fingers curling and uncurling, in the midst of movement, I feel the air become very still, very quiet, as if all the attention in the world has descended into this small clearing in front of our house, as if Krishna with his flute, Luxshmi on her lion, perhaps even Shiva Nataraj himself, drum in hand, foot poised in mid-stride, frozen in the midst of destruction, have descended to watch the magic in our limbs, our eyes, our fingers, as we dance under the mango tree.

In the darkness just before sunrise, there is a sound like thunder shattering my dreams. Amma leaps awake, drags me and Luxshmi off the mat and out of the house, sweeps us into the trench that is next to the front door, and then the whole earth is moving, bucking and pushing against us as if it rejects us, wishes to spit us up into the air where the low-flying planes will see us and narrow in with bombs aimed at our heads. Amma pushes us against the ground so that my cheek rubs against the indigo earth, the tears running off the side of my face making a sticky red puddle. In a few minutes, Appa will crawl to us. We know that when the bombings start we must run with Amma and let him come in his own time. But Luxshmi cries and cries for him. He comes slowly, dragging the useless leg in the midst of the world being destroyed, and then the four of us hide, the taste of dirt just under our mouths, the scrape of it under our clawing fingernails while the bombing goes on and on and on.

After the bombings, Appa begs Amma to take us and leave this place. When he says this, she gets very angry. She says, "And go where? To the IDP camps? And then what? Live there for years? With no food and a shit-filled toilet? What will happen to me and the girls in such a place?"

Appa says, "If you stay here, one day, either the soldiers or the Tigers will come."

Amma's voice gets shrill. She says, "No. It has to end. Someday they will all get tired of it." But there is no certainty in her voice. Appa is sad, but he cannot fight with her. He is too old and sick to leave. His cough in the night sounds like a hundred soldiers tramping on his chest, and he knows Amma will never leave him alone with no one to find food or cook for him.

Some days a heavy, ugly smell rises from the fields. Then we know that someone has been out at night, maybe a child, or an old man. They have stepped on a land mine that lay buried like a subterranean fruit and now they are in pieces, rotting and raising this terrible smell. We walk past this place quickly, with a piece of cloth covering our noses, swallowing our bile, angry at this person who has forgotten the obvious rules: never step off the roads, never forget what is buried just underfoot.

There are roofless, bombed-out houses with bullet-splattered walls and empty eyeless rooms everywhere. I hate these houses;

they look like dead bodies or like mad people, laughing through their openmouthed doorways. I want to know what this place looked like before, when all the houses were whole, when people lived in them and cared about them and grew vegetables in front of them, flowers even. It's a time I can't remember except for Appa's words. He says, "Balasingham Uncle used to live there next to the old post office. He had three sons and a daughter. In the corner house was Ponnambalam with his wife and children. We used to go there when you were small and play cards until the sun came up. You were great friends with his little daughter, Janaki. Do you remember?" I nod my head. But I remember none of these people. I remember nothing from the time before people started dying.

I haven't tasted fish for so long that when I remember Amma's seerfish curry, the chunks of fish swimming in the creamy, fiery coconut milk, my mouth waters and my stomach complains like Snowy with the tree squirrels. The fishermen no longer go to sea because the soldiers arrest anyone found in the water; they are afraid of Sea Tigers, who load boats with explosives and ram into the navy boats, so there hasn't been sea fish in the market for years.

Amma used to scrounge money to buy us lagoon fish. These were thick-fleshed and rubbery bottom feeders, but Luxshmi and I didn't care. We just wanted a little fish with our bit of rice. But these days there are so many bodies rotting and bleeding into the water that whoever eats lagoon fish gets sick and vomits for days.

When we meet relatives from a far village Appa says, "This is

Saraswathi, my eldest daughter. Clever girl is studying for her teacher's certificate. A pride and joy in my old age." He looks at me with such love that I must look away. The relatives also look at me, but their eyes are full of weighing and appraising. They have all had children taken from them by the Tigers or the army or the southern cities. They will go back to their village and say, "Old man Balakumar is training his daughter to have airs. Just because their family has had three sons taken. He thinks they will leave him his daughters?" I beg Appa not to boast about me. But he laughs and says, "If I can't be happy about my clever daughter, what is there for me to be happy about?"

Luxshmi and I walk to school, our uniforms glowing in the slanting light, skirts swinging in unison, the white tip of Snowy's tail like a flag leading the way. At this hour, there is a freshness in the air, the day still blooming, a blushing pink that will unfurl into garnet, amethyst with the sun. High in the sky, the crescent moon hangs suspended for a few moments longer. Women in saris ride their bicycles along the dirt road, skillfully swirling their front tires around potholes. I want a bicycle! How wonderful it would be to ride to school, Luxshmi balanced on the crossbar, both of us laughing with our braids streaming behind us!

A truck rumbles by. The loudspeaker on its roof listing the virtues of a recent martyr. She sold her life dearly, it says, taking with her dozens of the enemy in the midst of Colombo along with a beloved Sinhala politician. No one much listens, we are used to the death-defying exploits of the Tiger suicide martyrs, their faces tower over us on billboards, and in posters along the bullet-peppered walls.

Kanahamma sits by the roadside, selling strings of jasmine. I don't like to pass her. She is the one who saw the white van come for my brother Kumar. Her wrinkled lizard face makes me see it, the half-concealed gun, the squealing tires, blood, so I hurry Luxshmi past her. But as we walk by, we both inhale, catching the fragrance of the jasmine garlands that unfurls, celestial in our nostrils.

At the junction, a small crowd has gathered. Snowy is growling, urging us the other way, but Luxshmi, that naughty girl, runs ahead to see what has happened, and I must push against the hot mass of bodies to find her.

I am overtaken by the smell of shit and death before I see it. A man's body sagging forward, held against a lamppost by arms tied behind and a thin piece of wire that bites into the mottled scarlet skin of his neck. Popeyed, openmouthed, as if he had been taken by surprise last night, while eating with his family, or maybe later while walking outside to the toilet.

A wooden tablet balances sideways on his stomach, hung from the knotted black string around his neck. It lists, in careful chalk letters, the crimes for which this justice has been enacted. Under that, his intestines burst forth, like an intricate and exuberant flower. Flies buzz within the coils.

Voices in the crowd: "Bloody traitor, got what he deserved. Must have been informing the soldiers for a long time. That must be how they knew about the ambush in Vavuniya."

A woman's voice calls back, "No, that's absurd. This man wasn't an informer. He was my neighbor. I would know if he was doing such things."

"Shhhh . . . stupid woman."

Luxshmi pushes through bodies to stand next to me. She puts her hand in mine and says, "Come, let's go." But my feet won't move.

"It's Yalini's father," I say.

I hear her quiet gasp. I make myself look more closely at the slightly squashed tomato face. It is my friend Yalini's father. Yalini, who has sat next to me in school since we were both smaller than Luxshmi. I know that I won't see her ever again. That even now, she and whoever's left of her family are running, out in the open land, like animals scrabbling for whatever shelter they can find.

Luxshmi grasps my arm, pulls me. We walk away, fast now. As we pass Kanahamma she calls, "Girls, what is it? What happened over there?" I say nothing, but Luxshmi bursts out, "It's Yalini's father. The Tigers tied him to the lamppost and cut him. Here and here." She draws slashing lines with her palms across her stomach. "Because he was a traitor. He told the soldiers where the Tigers were hiding.

"So the Tigers cut him . . ." Her voice trails away.

Kanahamma sucks air between her teeth. She gestures at the small pile of flower strings. "Take one," she says. "Have something sweet to smell today." I start to say something, to explain that we have no money, but she waves away my words. She says, "Take, child. You must learn to take what is given." And already Luxshmi is searching for the freshest, most fragrant string. She holds one up triumphantly and we take turns burying our faces in the creamy blossoms, inhaling slowly so the thick fragrance drives out all other thought, a miracle entwined around our fingers.

The schoolroom sits under the banyan tree. I am the oldest girl left. When Miss Rajasingham comes down the steps from her little house, we fall quiet. She is Colombo returned, with a university degree. There is nothing I would not do for her.

She walks around the classroom, between the rows of desks. Her braid follows the curve of her spine and spills down past her bottom. As she moves it sways to her particular rhythm. In the noon heat, the small hairs escape to snake along the side of her nape.

Today she is wearing her long red skirt, her white short-sleeved blouse, tiny drops of molten gold in her earlobes. When she is in a particularly good mood, she wears a light pink sari that I do not like. That color belongs on some pale woman with yellow hair in a foreign film, not on Miss with her long sharp eyes and the fat black *pottu* between her curved brows.

Sometimes she wears a sari the color of the emerald onion fields, it has a thin gold border in the shape of swirling peacocks, and then she looks like well water on a hot day. Some days she wears a chili powder red sari. This is my favorite. It is most perfectly her.

She lives with her husband in a small house behind the school. On the days she wears the red sari, he comes often to the school. He comes to check if we are alright, if there is anything we need. But really he comes to see her. I see him looking at her, stealing glances from the corner of his eye, and I watch her bend her head, trying to pretend that she does not notice, but when he goes away I see her turn in his direction searching for him.

Miss is training me to take her place in front of the blackboard. When I get my teaching certification, I will live in the small house behind the school, and maybe I also will have someone who looks at me the way he looks at her. In practice for my Maths paper, Miss sets me complicated equations. They take a long time to solve, but I love the long columns of numbers, the need to proceed logically and patiently as the numbers lead you to the final and inevitable answer. It reminds me of dancing. The way my shoulders, the tilt of my arms, and angle of my knees must stay within precise formations, yet also lead where I take them. A sort of freedom that can be attained only within strict rules.

After school, Amma has made us promise to hurry home. There are soldiers everywhere. They look at us from under their rounded helmets with eyes that are filled with hate, but also with fear. They think any of us, man, woman, child, may be bomb strapped, jiggling with flesh-tearing ball bearings secreted under skirts and shirts. It is always better to avoid their fearful eyes, to walk quickly past, trying not to betray our own palpitating terror. I have learned to keep my eyes averted when Luxshmi and I pass the checkpoint closest to the house, but the soldiers always lean over the sandbags, call to us in halting Tamil learned on the battlefield.

"Why always in such a big hurry?" they say. "Come and talk to us, we won't bite," and smile, baring their wolfish teeth.

If you are a girl, there is always the chance that the soldiers will spoil you or that people will say that they did. I don't know what "spoiled" means exactly, but it must be something truly terrible. It happened to my friend Parvathi. She was coming home from school when a soldier grabbed her, dragged her into the chili fields, and spoiled her. People stopped talking to her as soon as it happened, but they never stopped talking *about* her.

"Did you hear?" they would press close and whisper when she passed, silent as a ghost on her mother's arm, her head drooping like a heavy flower on a fragile stem. And I wanted to say, "No. What happened to her? Tell me, please." I wanted them to explain, because I never understood what it was, what terrifying thing had happened to her that made everyone so afraid of her. As if she had a disease we could all catch. She was my friend before. But after it happened, Amma wouldn't let me go to her house or even talk to her on the street. One day last year she jumped into a well. When I heard this in the market after school, I didn't go home, I went straight to her house. Her mother was outside making a noise like a wounded dog. Her father, too, was there, but he was silent, his face a kind of gray that I had never seen on a person's face before. There were lots of people standing everywhere, but I pushed through and I saw her.

They had laid her on the ground. Her face was bloated and waterlogged so that I barely recognized her. I thought they must have a different girl, a stranger. Her arms were bent at crazy angles. I realized later they must have broken from the impact of hitting the sides. I felt something breaking in my chest, a sound rising in my throat, something inhumane like the sound her mother was making. But then before it could escape from my throat, Amma was there pulling me to her, pulling me along the road home. Later when they burned her body, only her mother and two sisters were there. Even her father refused to go. She was my friend. But now, I dare not even speak her name.

On market days, Amma goes to haggle for what she can get. She sends me to look after Luxshmi as she plays with the other children by the lagoon. In the sand lie many things left by the dead: shreds of uniform, ripped flak jackets, hard round helmets like buried skulls. Sometimes our toes catch on sharp fragments of bone.

I watch them play. They comb the beach for rags, dress themselves in shreds of Tiger stripes or Army camouflage, don ripped flak jackets that reach their knees and helmets that cover their eyes. They tie long branches across their backs and crawl along the sand. Small soldiers fighting small rebels. They lift sticks to their shoulders, make loud machine gun *rattttatttttatttt* sounds before dropping and rolling away. When I get tired of watching this, I get up, dust off my skirt, and call to Luxshmi. She doesn't want to come so I must drag her away, my fingers around her upper arm. These cannot be good games for children to play. But what else is there now? They are only acting what they have seen.

We sleep with Amma and Appa on either side of us, a deterrent to bad dreams and what might come in the night. To drown out the machine gun fire in the distance, Appa tells stories of the time before the soldiers and the Tigers came. He says, "The prawns in these lagoons were as big as my arm." He holds up his arm and with the other hand, between pinkie and thumb, he measures a length from wrist to elbow. "This big. With huge heads and long falling whiskers. So big, they used to walk along the banks like tame dogs. In the mornings we used to spread our nets and bring back baskets pouring over. The export men from Colombo would come to buy. They would send our prawns abroad where the white people were mad for the taste." He shakes his head. "Those export men were crazy. They would drive up from Colombo all night to get the freshest catch. Sometimes they would stop the cars and fight in the middle of the road about who should have the first pick." He laughs at the memory. "Appa would sell most of his catch, and with the rest Amma would make prawn curry with red chili."

We lie wide-eyed in the darkness, empty stomachs rumbling. Appa is quiet, suddenly ashamed of himself for calling forth the ghosts of the lagoon. When we fall asleep, it is to the imagined fragrance of prawn curry, the fat white flesh, sweet as fruit, spilling from the hard crimson shells between our grinding teeth.

One day there is an uproar in the schoolyard. Trucks and motorcycles raise clouds of maroon dust and Tiger-striped men and women flood the classroom. They carry a television and video, run cables to the generator in their truck, give us sweets wrapped in little pieces of colored paper. Then they show us videos of what the Sinhala soldiers do in the villages. We see bodies, burned red and black, beaten into shapelessness, hung by the feet. Men slashed across the neck, limp women with babies crawling on them. An old man with a flap of skin, pink as a dog's tongue, hanging off his scalp, white bone underneath.

They show us burning houses, burning kovils, burning churches. This is what the Sinhala soldiers do, the men say. This is the way they enforce their brutal domination over our Tamil people. The images make last night's food rise in my mouth. I, too, hate the soldiers, but I cannot bear to look at these piles of bodies, the blood staining the earth like spilled chili powder, the faces that look like broken masks.

The Tigers say, "It is your duty to fight for your Motherland. Only by taking up arms can we save ourselves. A separate country, Eelam, is the only answer."

From my desk, I can see Miss's face. It is twisted up, her knuckles pressed against her mouth. There are big tears in her eyes about to fall. She looks my way and makes the tiniest of gestures, an almost imperceptible shake of the head. It comes to me that she is afraid of these men. I want to speak to her, reassure her that despite their hard eyes and their guns, these are our boys. They are my brothers who went away to fight, they are the boys on the street, the boys that she teaches now. They are forced to fight because of what the soldiers are doing. They are standing up for our ways, our lives, our culture. But Miss has been away in Colombo. She doesn't understand these things, the way the soldiers move in and treat people worse than animals, bomb us, and set us on fire.

After they leave, Miss tries to calm the children. She tells them that they should study harder, try to get into university, help their people in other ways. But she knows that by morning, more of them will be gone, gathered up in the trucks that wait in the shadows just beyond the schoolyard.

I sit cross-legged as Amma's deft fingers rake my scalp. She lets my hair fall across her arms, says, "So beautiful. Like the new monsoon clouds that the poets sang of. It will bring you a husband who will want to wrap himself in it." I imagine this, a young man, as straight and slim as a sapling, the taut muscles of his arms wrapped in the winding tendrils of my hair, thick ropes binding him to me. A man who will hold me and keep the terrors outside far away as I rest my head upon his beating heart.

But we both know that in this place an eligible son-in-law is rarer than gold, as precious as clear water. I say nothing as she spins beautiful lies for me.

One night as we unroll the sleeping mats, Snowy, staring into the night, bares his eyeteeth, makes deep wounded noises in the back of his throat. The hair on the back of his neck rises in a sharp porcupine row as twin Tiger women materialize out of the darkness. They are dressed in striped shirts and baggy trousers, their waists cinched in belts. They wear their hair cropped short, close to the skull, a little jagged as if they have taken knives to it themselves. They are not like the other women of the village. They walk with a different rhythm, their backs straightened by AK-47s. Their bodies betraying a certain muscularity brought on by years of training and fighting.

Appa rises slowly, reluctantly. He calls to Amma, "Make tea, visitors have come." Under his breath, he hisses at Luxshmi and me to stay inside. But the women know we are here. They sit in the low chairs and ask Appa how things have been, whether he has had any problems with the soldiers, if they may help him in any way. They tell him that the present campaign is going well, that major battles have been won. They say that it is only a matter of time before the military forces concede defeat. Finally they say what we have all been waiting, breathless with fear, to hear. "Uncle, bring out your daughters. Let's see how they have grown."

When we come out, slowly, cautiously, they cast their eyes up and down our frames. The taller of the two says, "Uncle, you have been withholding from us! This girl is old enough now. You must send her to join the Movement." She is looking straight at me. My skin turns suddenly cold.

"The other one you can keep for a small time. But this one, your elder, she is ready." Appa looks at the floor.

He says, "I am an old man. Already I have given three sons." He wipes the corner of his face with his cloth. Amma brings steaming tea in the two steel cups. Cardamom dances in the air, making us inhale sharply; Amma must have used the new tea, her precious store of spice. The women reach for the tea, the tumblers catching and throwing the lamplight. They are used to tea this rich. Everyone knows that the Tigers are well fed.

Appa's voice in the dark, "Please, let me keep this daughter of my old age. Maybe she will marry, give me grandchildren for the sons I have lost."

The other woman says, "No, Uncle. This is old-fashioned talk. Women are good for so much more than getting married and having babies. Our Leader teaches us that women are as brave as men. We, too, can fight as fearlessly, as ferociously. You must have greater goals for your daughter. What bigger aspiration could you have than for her to fight for her people?"

Appa moves his head in small, conciliatory gestures, twists the cloth in his lap. "Let me keep her for a few more years. She is so small. Only sixteen. Next year I will bring her to the training camp myself."

The women laugh. One says, "Sixteen! I joined when I was fourteen. There are martyrs who joined at the age of twelve. Don't worry. Just send her to us. She will have a glorious future. She will help us secure Eelam for the future of our people."

The other says, "Cut her hair before you bring her. She will not need it when she is fighting."

Appa nods. "Yes. We will do as you say."

The women look placated, they get up, stretch their sinewed, muscled bodies as if they have been sitting too long. Turn and disappear into the darkness.

When they leave, Amma wraps her arms around me, pushes my head against her chest, mutters in a choked voice, "What do they want? I gave my sons. Now I must give my daughter also?"

Appa hisses, "Shhh, woman. They will come back and take not only this one but the other as well."

Amma strokes the top of my head. "I won't let them take you. I won't," she mutters, fierce against my ear.

I am alone. Amma, Appa, and Luxshmi have gone to see Maari-yamma, whose youngest son was bundled into the back of a speeding van last week. Now she lies unmoving on her bed. If left alone, she makes her furtive way to the well. She has been pulled away from its dark open mouth, fighting and screaming abuse, twice.

Amma had wanted me to go, but I can't bear the smell of Maariyamma's dark room, the picture of her son in her quiver-ing hands. The sounds of that house remind me of Parvathi's house after she died, the weird keening sounds that mourning people make.

So Amma left me here alone. She didn't want to but I told her I had schoolwork to do, the dinner to cook. That way she won't have to come home and cook for us after the sun has already gone down. By the time they get home I'll have finished cooking, laid the food out for us. It's nice sometimes to be alone. It hap-pens so rarely. When everyone is gone, there is a kind of peace.

I'm behind the house, squatting over a pot of raw rice. I like the roundness of the earthen pot in my palm, the harsh scrape and heft of the grains in my other palm, the coolness of water on this sweating afternoon as I swirl my fingers through it. With each stroke of my fingers and as it is poured out onto the thirsty waiting earth, the water in my pot is rendered less cloudy. I like watching the rice settle into the cleaner water, the white of the grains held in the red of my pot.

A sort of quietness has fallen. My ears open wide to it. It is an unexpected respite in this place of many loud and unrelenting sounds. I stand and tip my head, hold the pot against my hip, listening. The hairs along my neck are rising. Somewhere Snowy breaks into hysterical panicked barking, a shriek of animal pain, something horrible happening to our sweet, sweet dog, then the crashing of boots and the pot is falling, smashing, cutting my feet as I fly into the dark house, eyes popping, heart hammering, desperate for a hiding place, but there is nowhere and I am crouching in a corner of the back room, arms raised to cover my head, when the soldiers break in.

I leave bloodied footprints on the deserted road in front of our house, the rifle butt digs like an animal into the small of my back. Through windows and doors shuttered against the noon glare, I see the flash of curious faces. I beg with my eyes as I am hurried past, but no window is opened, no door is cracked, no one shouts and screams and stops these men from taking me. At the junction, they push me into the yawning maw of a white van, slam the doors shut, and I am alone scrabbling on my knees, thrown from side to side on the cold hard metal. They drive for a long time. When the van stops, I huddle in a corner as the door opens, the sudden sunlight blinding. Two soldiers come for me, they grasp my upper arms, pull me, my legs and feet dragging useless against the earth into the burned-out carcass of a house, into a back room with bullet-riddled, broken cement walls, no roof, overhead only a perfectly framed square of sun-lit sky.

They encircle me, shouting questions that pound against my head. "What is your name? Where is your training camp? Where are your brothers? How long have you been a Tiger?"

I see the rifle butt coming before it smashes into my face. Gushing red, teeth spilling, I fall hard onto my wrists, then they are upon me. *Tiger bitch.* A many-clawed, many-toothed beast. I try to fight but the dress Amma sewed so carefully is ripping, exposing knees and thighs, my breasts, my nipples. *Tiger bitch.* The ribbon she tied into my plait is yanked hard so my head snaps, the braid unravels like a serpent across the cement floor, and hair falls about me like that of the mad woman in the market. My wrists and ankles are caught in their iron grip. *Tiger bitch.* I am pulled apart, uncovered, exposed. They hold me down. Their sweat falls in shining drops and they will not let me avert my face. I am drenched and soaked. Their mouths come down upon me like the salivating tongues of dogs. They tear me open with their nails, bite me with their fangs, their spittle falls thick across my breasts. They break into me. Break me. Break into me. Break me. Burying their stench deep inside my body while they pant like dogs over me. Until I no longer smell like myself. Until this body is no longer mine. Until I am only a limp, bleed-ing, broken toy. *Tiger bitch! Tiger! Bitch! Tiger! Bitch!* I pull my eyes onto that perfect square of sky. High above, a crane passes slowly.

Luminous white against the blue, winging her way across the air. I watch her flight across that square of sky until she is gone and then I, too, am high in the sky winging my way across space. So high and so far away, reveling in the freedom of air against my body, cavorting in the pleasure of it, while far, far below, far away, unimaginable things are happening to the girl I used to be.

I lie on the cement floor, slick with their juices, saliva, sweat on my breasts and face, liquid seeping slowly from between my legs, the smell of decay rising from my body. I hide behind the tangled wall of my hair. This is what it means, then, to be spoiled. It means this thick horrible smell rising from me. It means to be broken. It means forever.

The men attend to their other needs now. They build a fire in the front room, prepare food. They are quiet, their anger spent. They speak only occasionally, and then their voices drift to me from very far away. Sunlight moves slowly across the room, illuminating first one bullet-splattered wall and then another. I know other people have been hurt in this room. Many have died.

An older soldier comes and nudges me with the tip of his boot. He says something in his language, points at the remnants of my dress, pantomimes dressing and then makes a shooing motion with his hand. I focus beyond him on the sunlit sky.

Later, another soldier comes. He brings food. I lie unmoving. He puts the food on the ground, leaves. It stays there until the flies come, their buzzing loud, their wings blue-green and myself, huddled in the corner torn and bleeding, reflected in their hundred-faceted eyes. I watch them burrowing in the rice. Imagine them mating, laying eggs, dying. Blood flows from between my thighs, I wonder if the ants and flies will find this trail, follow it to my flesh, take small bites and then big ones. I wonder if I will feel it.

It is evening when the soldiers leave. When their footsteps have faded, there is a rush of pain, a knife stabbing repeatedly at the soft, broken, battered center of me. I come to myself from far away with great gulping sobs, and then I am shaking, crawling across the ground, feeling with trembling fingertips for cloth. The bits of my dress are thick with the mud off their boots. I pull the tattered pieces across my body. Fumble onto the bullet-splattered wall and stand on shaking, nerveless legs.

The sun is sending long rays across the earth as I leave that dead roofless house, my hands clutching the ripped dress together. The smell of the men is buried deep inside my skin, burrowing into my head. If I can only get home, I will be alright. Amma will take care of me. She will wash away the smell, put me to bed, and then this pain will go away, the sound of the men over me, their grasping hands and teeth, it will all go away. If only I can get home.

I walk and walk. Through fields and over bunds. It seems like hours, every muscle in my body feels ripped. When I come into the village, there are people on the streets. They look at me with wide staring eyes. A man on a bicycle swerves as I walk past, his front tire falling into a pothole. Someone calls out my name. I stumble along the lagoon toward the house. From inside the house, Amma, who has known the sound of my step since before I was born, calls out, fear in her voice, "Who's there?"

. . .

There is sound and silence. Amma beats her breast and hurls curses. Appa wears silence like a cloth pulled over his head. From the moment I staggered into the house, lame, bleeding, wild-eyed, he has not talked to me. He has avoided my eyes and also those of Luxshmi and Amma. His gaze skims over us all as if we are not in front of him. In the mornings, he limps from the house although we know there is nowhere for him to go. When he returns at night to this house of grieving women, we hear the lagging reluctance in his step.

At night, I lie with Amma on my left, her heavy arm stretched over me, Appa on my right, his back turned on me. I lie trembling, teeth gritted, eyes wide open, staring into the impenetrable dark. I will not sleep because then the soldiers return. As soon as my eyes close, they climb all over me. Their smell drops over my head, pushes its way into my nostrils, deep into the caverns of my skull, until I am full of it, fighting, kicking, and scratching, and then I wake, limbs thrashing, teeth grinding, fighting Appa, who has climbed over me and is holding down my wrists, his face a crumpled mask from which tears drop onto me, making me fight even harder, remembering other shining drops falling.

Luxshmi's voice, small, terrified, "What has happened, Amma? Why is Akka like that?"

"Shhhhh, little one. It is nothing. She is only a little sick these days."

I lie, rigid, while they fall asleep around me. My hands clutched into fists, the nails ripping into my flesh so that the pain keeps me from falling back into that pit of men.

I lie on the mat for weeks, my head turned to the wall. Amma spends the last of her money to buy fish, greens, spices. She spends hours in their preparation. When the food is ready, she feeds me, mixing the curries with her fingers, talking to me of people in the village, of the bird's nest in the mango tree, the possibility of fresh fish in the market, anything to keep me from remembering. But the smell of food turns my stomach, and everything she puts in my mouth tastes of blood.

Visitors come to see whether there is truth in the rumors. I stay hidden in the back room, but I can hear them talking. When they ask about me, Amma says I have been sick, that I caught a fever and am resting, that I will soon be well. They say, "A lot of fevers this time of year. The mosquitoes have been so bad. Cases of dengue are up." From behind the curtain, I hear the curiosity in their voices like open fish mouths just under the surface of the water. I cover my ears with my hands and turn to the wall.

Amma keeps Luxshmi home from school now. She sits beside me, strokes my head, and brings me bright tumblers of well water. I am parched like a fish stranded in the paddy fields after a storm. I drink and drink, but always, my throat is dry. There is such terrified curiosity in Luxshmi's eye. She wants to know like I wanted to know. What is this thing that has happened to me? What is it that makes me broken, makes me fight and scream in the night? But I cannot meet her eyes, cannot explain to her the shame of what has happened.

She brings me jasmine strings from Kanahamma. The old

lady gives these to her and says, "Give this to your sister. She must have something good to smell." I hold the flowers against my face, their scent rises, sweet and pure, driving away the smell of the men. I fall asleep, the blossoms crushed in my fist.

In Amma's cloudy mirror, I catch a glimpse of a girl. I know she is me, only because there is no one else in the room. She is big eyed, bruised, with a wounded, torn mouth. Thin as a bone ravaged by the street dogs, her shoulder blades as sharp as knives.

The flesh has dripped from me. The hair that Amma combs every day hangs limp like oily curtains on either side of my face. I want to draw them shut. Close off the view of this terrified, wide-eyed creature who looks out of my eyes.

Some weeks later I hear a familiar step outside. Miss's voice. I hear the chair creak gently as she sits. I see her in my mind's eye. Miss in her deep red sari, the molten drops of her tiny gold earrings catching what little light is there in the darkness of our front room, her hands carving elegant gestures and the long thick braid shaking as she asks Amma if I am alright, if anything has happened to me, if she can help in some way. I hear Amma say, "No. No, of course nothing has happened to her. What could happen? The girl is fine. She has just been a little sick. But soon she will be fine." Miss isn't convinced. She says even if something has happened, it is alright. I must return to school immediately, start studying for the teacher's examinations that are coming fast. She will help me catch up on the weeks of lost work. She says she has brought my books with her.

They send Luxshmi to fetch me, but I push away her small desperate hands. I don't want Miss to see the deep shadows beneath my eyes, the dark blossoming marks on my wrists and neck. I can't bear to have her smell the men on me. She thought I was like her and I believed her. I thought I could take her place at the blackboard, live in her little house. But I'm not like her at all. I've slipped into some other place that exists alongside this one, a place no one else knows about where men can take girls, rip them open, and bury a kind of corruption in their flesh. I feel it now, this other thing buried in my flesh and marked by the smell of them. I know this thing will not go away, so I lie with my head to the wall, waiting for Miss to leave.

She stays for so long that I start to think maybe she wouldn't mind so much about the smell. I am willing my legs to move, my head to rise when I hear her say, "Okay. Well, make sure you tell her I was here. Tell her I'll be waiting in the school for her. She must come back. She's a very talented student, you know. One of my best. Here, let me leave these books for her . . ." I hear her steps on the verandah, and then she is walking down to the mango tree where she has leaned her bicycle. I see her ride away in my mind's eye. I watch her until she is only a streak of vermilion against the green banana trees and tall, waving palmyras, and then she is gone and I am truly alone.

Luxshmi brings the books into the room. They lie in the corner for days, calling to me in first soft, and then strident voices. When I can no longer ignore their summons, I crawl to them, insert a finger into one, flip it open. By the dimpled afternoon light, I survey the numbers, wait for them to cast their usual spell over me, to enmesh and submerge me. I stare at the page. It is easy material I mastered years ago. My own precise and neatly rendered solution on the right side of the page. But now, the long rows of numbers are a foreign language, a blurring, messy heap that will not disentangle into order. I try to control them, but the numbers look like bits of debris fallen across the page, accidental and lacking order. I know then that the Teaching Certificate has slipped through my fingers. I leave the books in their corner. Sometime later, they are gone and I do not ask after them.

I wake to Amma's fingers on my forehead, casting away my nightmares. Slow tears are following the curve of her cheek, falling into my hair like the first drops of monsoon. Panic rises like gorge and I struggle upright, instantly awake. She says, "My girl . . ." I stare at her, waiting for her to speak, watch as she pulls herself together and then says, "You have to go from here, my daughter. We can't keep you with us anymore. You must go to the training camp. Learn to fight. Become a hero." And realizing that this is not the trailing end of a nightmare, I grasp her hands, "Please, Amma. Please. Let me stay with you."

"Think, my girl. What will you do here? What man will take what the soldiers have spoiled? Who will give their son for your sister? If you don't go, you will ruin us all."

I beg for my life. "Amma, please. Please. Let me stay with you."

She shakes her head. "You must go. Show people that you are a good girl. If you don't go, no one will believe that you were taken by force. They will say, she is not even angry. There is a checkpoint close to the house and she must have encouraged them in some way. We will lose face with everyone. You must go. It is the only way."

She gets up, shakes off my clinging, reaching hands. "I have packed your things. Appa will take you to the camp after you eat."

In the other room, Appa and Luxshmi are eating. Bits of roti, the crunch of an onion. They will not meet my eyes.

I stagger outside. It is half dawn, the sky swathed in night-chilled ribbons of pink. I look into the blind open mouth of the well. There is one way out, Parvathi's way. I drop the bucket into the well, hear it boom against water, pull it up, hand over hand, heavy and sopping, rough rope cutting into my fingers. I splash cold water against my gasping face. Lift the bucket, pour water through my hair, molding my sarong to my skin. Shivering, my bare toes digging into this wet bit of earth. My ears open to the cry of the water birds high above, the stir of the mango leaves, Snowy barking somewhere . . .

She is sending me away. . . .

When I go back inside, Amma is waiting with scissors in hand. I sit on the ground in front of her and she takes them to my head. Appa and Luxshmi watch silently as ropes of wet hair fall all around me. She cuts until my nape is bared. Until my head is suddenly light, suddenly airy, the weight of all that hair, sixteen years of it lifted off my head, my shoulders. Behind me, Amma is crying, but I am tearless now.

nine

yasodhara, los angeles

In 1989, we take the oath, exchange our maroon Sri Lankan passports with the sword-wielding lion, the pages upturned by exposure to sweat, humidity, sea air, for crisp-paged, clean blue ones. We have become the most privileged and God-blessed persons on the planet, Ameri-cans, thank you very much, not Ameri-can'ts.

When I tell Amma and Thatha that I am going to study literature at university, there is less consternation than I had expected. Of course they see no evident future in the study of books. The truth is, neither could I. But at that time I could see nothing more desirable to do with my life than to spend it burrowing in words. Possibly Amma and Thatha could see no other possibility for me, either, because beyond certain mumblings of "Well, at least you might be able to get into law school afterwards," they let me go.

At university I read mountains of text, argue philosophy, write into the dawns, and study without respite. I lose my virginity, drink too much, chew on fibrous mushrooms, and dance in unknown but tender arms. I make love that feels like war with ivory-skinned or ebony-hued boys, but never with the shy brown ones who remind me painfully of certain long-lost fingers grasping my pulse.

I learn that the plainness of my face, the roundness of my figure, are not deterrents to desire, that even the ugly sister can be adored. And then I fall hard into love. He is green eyed, smooth muscled, caramel toned. We tumble and twine, lips and hips joined through two years of college. He reads me Heidegger and Byron, introduces me to the Mexican grandmother who brought him up, shows me secret watering holes and hot springs deep in the California desert until I am sufficed and sated. Despite his declarations that marriage is a trap, a grotesque prison, his inability to understand why anyone would willingly castrate themselves within it, I dare to dream secretly of forever, imagining emerald-eyed, brown-skinned children, somewhere to nest. I know that I would have to risk Amma and Thatha's wrath. They would never understand me falling in love with a "foreigner." Especially Amma, I know, will never forgive this breach of etiquette. But for his kiss, I could face her anger. When he leaves me, suddenly, unexpectedly, for a poetry-spouting freshman with ugly glasses, I learn that the tearing of the heart muscle is far more painful than the tearing of the hymen.

After graduation, I stumble home, ripped open by heart-break, unsure of what to do next. I hide my anguish from Amma and Thatha with excuses about studying too hard for final exams and am relieved when they seem to accept this. One morning Amma comes to me while I am still in bed. Her fingers stroke my forehead like I'm a little girl. She says, "Duwa, is there someone? You know, someone that you like? A special friend?" I shake my head. She nods, pleased. She says, "Maybe it's time that you thought about it. Thatha and I can make inquiries, you know, just see what is available. Who is out there. It's a good thing for a girl to marry young. That way you can grow up with your children like I did with you. You won't be an old mother like these foreign women." I listen to what she is not saying. The fear that I will grow old and bitter with my books, while other, younger girls get married. I lie in bed thinking about it after she leaves. My whole body throbs with the loss of love. What do I have to lose?

At breakfast, heart in my throat, I tell Amma and Thatha that I am ready for them to start looking. Suddenly all is parental bliss. Amma and Thatha in ecstasy embark on what La will call The Great Husband Hunt. Whereas before there had not been an e-mail account between them, now there are multiple accounts, Internet advertisements, online horoscopes. A digital camera is purchased. I am outfitted in various clothes, a pink sari, a black suit and heels, a white "party dress." In these various personas, I am posed on the front lawn. Thatha takes photos while Amma calls out directions, fixes the pleats of my sari, the fall of my neckline. "Just a little lower," she says, giggling. "Not a bad idea to show a tiny bit of skin for a husband—no?" They are giddy with anticipation, imagining wedding cake, grandchildren, real estate to be purchased. Only the face beside mine in the framed wedding photograph remains blurry, a space to be filled.

They write advertisements using words such as "pretty," "fair," and "educated" to describe me and post these in newspapers in cities around the world where Sri Lankans congregate. A few weeks of silence, and then envelopes bearing exotic stamps start arriving. They are thick, thin, and everything in between. Out of them spill horoscopes, land deeds, resumes, pictures, bank statements, letters from parents, sisters, cousins looking for "good girls" for their various menfolk. Sometimes there are letters from young men with no intermediaries to conduct their romances for them. It is daunting, that capsizing pile of letters. So many lonely men dreaming in Sinhala, moaning in their chilly beds, wanting American green cards and perfectly cooked eggplant curry. So much palpable need, such archaeologies of desire, that I am suddenly afraid. I had started this venture in defiance at my lost lover, but now there is such hope shining in Amma and Thatha's eyes that I cannot walk away and let them drown under the weight of the still arriving letters.

At this time, La is at university, enrolled up north in Berkeley as a business major, she says, but learning instead the secret language of color, how to wield her brushes with steady and precise hands, how to mix shades most effectively. She is lost so deep in these studies that we don't hear from her for weeks. When she does call, she cuts off my arranged marriage narratives to tell me about the long, languorous origins of pigments, duplicitous ochers, poisonous cadmium, murderous scarlet.

She comes home for Christmas and picks up letter after letter saying, "Better than TV! Look at this one, he wants a 'homely' wife." Her brow furrows, "Why is he calling Akka ugly?"

Amma shouts, "No, you silly girl, 'homely.' He means a good homemaker. Not 'homely' like you say here for 'ugly girl.' These Americans. They don't know how to speak English." She holds up a picture. "What about this boy?"

"Well . . . he's not really a 'boy,' is he? Considering the hair loss and paunch the size of Texas?"

"You girls want everything! He has an engineering degree, a house in San Jose, a good family. He has to also look like Tom Cruise?"

"Okay, Amma, with that one she can rub his tummy and it will grant her wishes." They cackle like witches. The sound of it makes the tight fist of my heart unclench.

Later La comes to my room. She lies on my bed next to me, both of us staring up at the ceiling, and says, "Why are you doing this?" There is a catch in her voice. I decide to tell her the truth. "Because it's safe and now more than anything I want safety. I can't go through another heartbreak. I just want to be with somebody safe. Somebody who won't leave." She nods slowly, as if the movement causes her pain. We fall asleep together, her hair swirling around us like when we were children, her fingers clasped in mine.

A month later they have found him. A doctor, of course, handsome in his photograph, something earnest in the eyes. His name is Siddharth. He is named for the Buddha and I for the Buddha's wife. The ancient intimacy of our names is impossible to ignore. Inquiries are made, horoscopes compared, long-distance phone calls placed to his parents in Sri Lanka.

When we meet, it is disarmingly easy. We go to an Indian restaurant and he breaks the naan, uses his fingers in the island way, mixing to the second knuckle and no higher. He talks of Galle Face Green when it was still green, the kite sellers and peanut men, the spray dashing against slick, mirrored, black rocks, the daredevil drive up to Kandy through mountain passes in a minuscule bus clinging to the silver-ribboned road, the granite cliff face rising on one side, falling into clouds on the other, the sudden startling darkness of tunnels. On the way down, flower boys racing barefoot, their arms full of upcountry blossoms, scarlet and crimson clutched against their own flushed and panting faces. A waterfall of words. Forgotten images flaring up like lit matches in the huge dark space of America. I see that falling into this man could be as easy as regaining a childhood. How could I not be seduced by my own lost memories?

We are married in a hotel in Los Angeles under a *poruwa* of plastic instead of palm leaf. I wear a white sari with a gold border and hold a bouquet of white roses trimmed to look like lotus buds. Girls with American accents attempt to sing the Jaya Mangala Gatha accompanied by a scratchy, much-used tape. The *kapuwa* hacks a coconut and lets it fall. When the two halves stop spinning and come to rest right side up, the whole hall breathes a sigh of relief.

. . .

I had not expected marriage to be such a homecoming. I am in graduate school now, slowly working my way up the tortured mountain that will afford me those three treasured letters at the end of my name. I am going to teach university English, this is the goal, but I had not expected marriage to be such a boon on this journey, had not expected to know his scent as well as my own so quickly, to feel such pleasure when he hands me a cup of tea with the precise measure of milk and sugar that I desire. In the solitary seclusion of sleep our bodies are in the most perfect unison, turning at the same moment, his head resting on my shoulder, the tender smoothness of his sole against the top of my foot. Talking often into the night, I realize that we are unconsciously tapping our feet against each other, some tender staccato language of the body.

In darkness we learn each other's contours and textures. The velvet expanse of his belly, cream to my roving tongue. The shape of him in my mouth luscious and rounded as fruit. I move above him and he slits his eyes to watch me with the most rapt of concentrations. I know he is listening for the slightest gasp in my breathing, the quiver of my wetness holding him. I see the shine in his eyes about to spill, an admission of the enormity of this thing that is between us, the whisper of his ragged breathing.

Sometimes waking earlier than him, I am startled by this stranger sharing my pillow. I must look and look into this face and come away with no greater understanding or knowledge of love. When he goes on his first conference trip, I realize I cannot sleep without the weight of his thick thigh thrown across my hip, the very thing I had complained about, and pushed away so many times. It is only in absence that the true weight of love is felt.

But I also know that this marriage is an intimacy forged in a scarred place. It rests at least partly on my ability to recognize a certain sort of despair in his eyes. A despair that I know is caused by reports of bombs, bodies, spilled blood, the only type of news from that other place that reaches us here on the far edge of the world. On those nights we make love as if dying, our two bodies rafts in a tumbling, turbulent midnight sea. The succor of mouths and skin sliding on skin driving away the images. Each of us climbing a mountain to that single shining moment when the images are shut out.

While I am falling in love with my husband, La is falling in love with her dreadlocked art history professor. During the day, she sits in his seminars, arguing her point, presenting papers and being lectured like any other student. At night she waits for him outside the dorms, watching for his stealthy black Audi, hoping that friends or roommates will not happen upon her getting into his car. In his wood-paneled bedroom in the hills, far above the dorms, they tumble and toss in his large white bed. She calls me in rapture. "He's so beautiful. I am in love, love, love."

Newly legitimized by matrimony, I am scandalized. "What will Amma and Thatha say?" I ask.

"Nothing if you don't tell them." The note of irritation at the edge of her voice razing my skin.

Six months later she says, "How will I tell Amma and Thatha? He's African-American. He's so much older than me. . . ."

"But is it permanent? Why tell them at all?"

"Yes, of course it's permanent. We are in love." She stresses the word as if speaking to a child.

She calls me from his house. "We're going to the wine country. We are going to drink wine until we fall into a haystack somewhere and make love all afternoon."

She sends me a photograph. She has taken it in bed, her arm outstretched with the camera, the sheets pulled up to her chin, her smile open and teasing as if she is cajoling her partner in crime to pose. The man next to her, heavy limbed, throws an arm across his eyes, as if he wishes not to have his image captured, but his lips twist into an exasperated smile. He is annoyed, but he also wants to please my beautiful sister.

I know it is my duty to warn her, to tell her that such happiness calls forth the demons, that the very sound of her laughter will draw forth pain. But I cannot find the words.

Then there are long days on which he does not call. She says, "He must have gotten mad busy. It's the end of the quarter, there are papers to grade." And then, "Maybe he's lost my number?" Finally, fury when she sees him flirting with another student, a nubile Thai girl who gazes at him with devotion and licks her cherry-red lip gloss with a pink-tipped tongue.

I pick her up at the airport. Her eyes are swollen, red veined but dry. In the arrivals lounge, she buries her head in my neck and stays there, trembling. I take her bag and walk her to the car; she is heavy against me, moving slowly and silently. In the car, the words break free, a torrent. "He doesn't want me anymore." There is a note of incredulity in her voice. "He's with her now." She turns to me. "What's wrong with me? Why doesn't he want me?" I feel my heart tumble, I had not wanted her to learn of the pain that shifts between men and women like a tossed ball in this way. I had hoped it would be gentle and come in time, but now she is broken, split wide by it.

She lives on our couch. She wears large shapeless clothes and cries so that her long eyes are constantly swollen, her hair limp as if it, too, were deprived of energy. I make her help me in the kitchen, put her to work chopping the onions as I prepare curries and sambals, the foods of our childhood. She cuts slowly, asking unanswerable questions. She doubts herself now. Sees herself as discarded, unwanted, unlovable, easily replaced. The fierce strength that I have admired since childhood is gone, like an animal suddenly spooked into forest darkness. She cuts herself easily, not noticing the blood that trickles from the side of her thumb onto the eggplant and onion slices. She keeps talking while I run her fingers under the tap, the water swirling away, ruby and then pink tinged. "It hurts," she says, laying her uncut hand on her chest. "It hurts, here. All the way from my throat to my groin, a constriction. It's hard to breathe. I didn't think that lovesickness would actually hurt. I feel ill. Literally." In her voice a tone of discovery.

I come home heavy with grocery bags, she says from the couch, "Should I call him? Maybe it was just a misunderstanding? Maybe he lost my number here and has been trying to call. Maybe he misses me. Maybe it was just a whim with her, something forgettable and he's sorry." She looks at me with pleading eyes, willing me to say, "Yes, maybe that's it. Why don't you call him and see?" I can see it in her eyes, the need to hear his voice on the phone, laughing, talking to her in the low throaty voice he had two months ago. I feel like the executioner standing by the block. The heavy ax handle in my gloved hand, waiting for the delicate neck to be lowered onto the slight sway in the wood.

I shake my head. "No. No calling. It's over. You have to let him go. He's with her now and even if he's not, he would have called you if he wanted you." Her face crumbles like a sand castle kicked by a vindictive child. She cries in gasps as if the wind has been knocked out of her, as if she is choking.

We give her Siddharth's office to colonize. She haunts art stores buying up whatever bargain paint, canvas, crayons, turpentine she can on the remains of her student money. Back at home she paints copiously, her brushes moving over the canvas in a fury, as if her life depended on it, as if her pain were dripping away with the flow of scarlet and turquoise. I don't understand it, but it must be some way in which she speaks to herself, battles the love demons that have moved in so swiftly, taken residence in her skull, taken over her voice. In the evenings she invites me in to look at her efforts. I am blown away, slowly realizing the extent of her talent, the skill in those long-digited hands. When I try to tell her she brushes away the compliments, says, "It's nothing. I could do so much more. I will do so much more. In time." There is a certain new ferocity in her eyes now. A certain new thing that was not there before. I recognize it as scar tissue.

When a bone breaks, it heals stronger in the cracks. I realize this is what is happening to her heart.

I find her in the bathroom one morning staring into the mirror. There are trailing snakes of hair on the closed toilet seat, piled on the floor, dripping off the sink. She has cut it all off with my kitchen scissors, close to the scalp, so that there is only an angry spiky stubble left. I am ready to make a fuss, but she is dry eyed. She looks at me, her eyes still red but no longer dull, they mirror the shine off my butcher knife. She says, "Okay, I'm ready to go back to university." I take a fist full of hair off the sink, bring it to my nose, inhale and nod. She continues, "But I'm not doing business anymore. That was bullshit. I was just trying to please Amma and Thatha, make them happy, you know."

"What will you do?"

"I'll paint, of course," she says. "It's all I really want to do."

Later I will remember this as the moment that I knew her work was going to be serious, even lauded. But in those later years as she was painting, making her name, appearing in New York galleries, San Francisco galleries, I really wasn't paying attention, because by then, after several happy years during which I had thought I was the happiest woman in the world and we the most blessed couple, my marriage was falling apart like a house with ill-constructed foundations. Fissures and cracks appearing in the walls as if earthquake rocked, tsunami washed.

. . .

It is years before I learn my husband's lover's name. First there is only a vague distracted look that flits across his face when the phone rings. A hurried click when I answer. Later a longer pause and I know that someone has called only to hear my voice, that someone driven mad by curiosity wants to know what I sound like, what I look like. Someone desperate and yearning wants to tell me what I already know. When I hear that breathless silence, I slam down the receiver before she can detonate the bombs buried just under my skin.

In the beginning he was discreet. I thought I had that old wifely disease, a case of jealousy and overactive imagination, but increasingly there are days when I hear him in the other room on the phone, his voice throaty and sweet. When I enter, he raises his voice, says things like, "Okay, Andrew, I'll see you at the office." He hangs up quickly. Looks at me, frank admission in his eyes as if daring me to say the words, ask the questions. But my throat is constricted by love and I say nothing.

He gets more and more distant; he spends more time away, more nights at far conventions, we drift away from each other. Now I'm used to sleeping alone. I don't even miss his presence in sleep, the way we used to shift and turn together perfectly synchronized, the weight of his thigh on my hip. It is a busy time after all. I am teaching, writing, reading. There are conferences I, too, must attend, papers I must write and deliver, professors to cajole and students to encourage. When we do meet it feels like being with a stranger from a world I do not understand. I watch his eyes. "Coward," they say. "Coward who allows this thing to happen and says nothing about it. You deserve it."

One night lying back to back, oceans of silence heaving between us, I can't stand it anymore. I whisper, "What is she like?" and the words are suddenly pouring out of him. She is tall and blond, slim and svelte as a Prada model, all sharp lines and efficiency, poreless perfection in tailored clothing. He cries and says it is no use, he's in love with her. He reaches for me and I let him hold me as he tells me everything. After that I imagine them together endlessly. Not so much the mingling, her golden hair falling over him, the rise of her body over his—these images too, of course, come to rake nails across my heart, but it is the other moments when perhaps they are in his car, singing along to a song on the radio. Or eating together, some rushed meal out of boxes. The tenderness of it, the closeness, these are the mundanities that make me sob.

He holds me as I weep. He is kind, solicitous. "We have so much together," he says. "It would be stupid to throw it all away. After all, this kind of thing happens in all marriages. We must be realistic about it. We couldn't have stayed the way we were forever."

"But why?" I shout. "You had her before we were married. Why didn't you just go on fucking her, marry her, whatever. Why did you have to marry me?"

"My parents. They wanted so much to see me with a Sri Lankan girl. Wanted to see me settled down. Having children and all that. Then they started looking for a wife for me and I just couldn't stop them."

"So you just let them look until they found me. Lucky me."

"Yes, and then they found you. I was going to make them stop but I thought I'd just meet you to make them happy. But then when we met . . . We got on so well, didn't we? I didn't think we would. That it would be so easy."

"So you married me even though you still loved her."

His voice is shaking. "I tried to break it with her. I thought once you and I were married it would pass. You and I have so much in common. . . ."

I realize that the similarity that I thought would sustain us, the shared language and culture and history and food, was never enough. Not even the ways in which we have held each other through that long, faraway war have been enough. Now it is difference he desires, while similarity is constraining, cloying.

These are the moments I despise him most, trapped as he is by the cultural dictates of a small island a million miles away. Living his life according to tradition, denying love, denying passion. So cowardly. *So cowardly!* But I can't hate him. He has the shreds of my heart caught between his teeth. "But I want this also," he says, trying to hold my hand, pull me toward him. "It's good, isn't it? We don't fight much. I love you. We are creating something together here, aren't we? Isn't it bigger than this thing?" He gestures with his hand, dismissing the "thing" as irrelevant, unimportant. These are the moment I almost believe him. Maybe he's right, maybe it'll work out and she is only some bright shiny golden thing he is playing with for a moment.

We go to marriage counseling. The therapist asks us to make a mission statement for our marriage, to read certain books, to have regular dates and hold hands. I dress up for these dates. I ignore important deadlines for conferences, stop reading and writing so that I can buy dresses, makeup, shoes, and stockings. These things feel like talismans: if I could just figure out how to use them the right way, I know I could win him back. I paint my eyes and lips, I pull silk stockings along my legs and slip my feet into unfamiliar high heels. When I meet him at the movie theater his eyes run over me, taking in these changes. He says, "Oh wow. You look so good." But I know he is taking measurements, making notes, comparing, and that I have come up short. When he slips away claiming to go to the rest room, I'm sure he is calling her, laughing at my efforts.

He greets my jealous tirade with incredulity. "Of course I wasn't calling her. I was using the rest room!"

Jealousy has made me insane. "Then let me see your cell phone."

"No, are you crazy? This is too much!"

"Just let me see it."

"No, I'm leaving. It isn't working, but that's because of you. I'm doing everything I can."

"Let me see your phone."

When he turns and leaves the lobby, I go back into the theater, sit in the dark, and watch without seeing. Later that night I dig his phone out of his jacket pocket while he is showering, scroll through the numbers, and see that I was right.

When I call Amma, she tells me to be patient. "Don't worry, Duwa, he will come back to you. It will blow over. He's not going to leave you for some blond bimbo."

I splutter through my tears, "How do you know that? He loves her."

"Love-schmove. It won't last. You're his wife. He's a good Sri Lankan boy. He will come back to you, don't worry. I'll call his mother, have a good talk. They will set him straight. In the meantime you must do everything to tempt him back. Are you dieting? Might be a good time to lose a few pounds, you know, make him notice you again."

I hang up, my heart muscle tearing in even greater rips.

La calls one midnight. It has been months since I've heard from her. She is giving up her studio, her blossoming success, to go back to the island. Her agent is livid, but she wants to do this. She will teach art at a school for war orphans, children brought to Colombo from the villages where they have lost their parents. Most are amputees, she says. Their legs neatly cut off at the knee by land mines. I can't imagine this. What good is it, I argue, teaching art to these kids, they've gone through incredible trauma. They need professional help, not messing around with paint and paper. She grows angry, says, "What else is there to do? It's what I know. It's what I can give. We each have to give what we can." Then she says, "Come with me," and for a moment her words hang in the air like possibility, the sudden scent of jasmine and sea air swirling in the room

But there is Siddharth's voice in the next room. If I go, he will belong completely to her. She will have won. I cannot abide the thought. La says again, "Akka, come with me." There is a

beseeching in her voice, as if she knows exactly what I am thinking, the depths of my impotence, even though I have told her
nothing of the situation. I suddenly realize that Amma has prob-
ably told her everything. La never really liked Siddharth. She has
always found him pretentious, artificial. She is offering me a life-
line. I hang up, angry at her, angry at myself for not going with
her, for not being able to imagine leaving my life, my marriage
with all its tyrannical love, to go across the world and teach am-
putated children to play with color.

A few months later her voice over the international line is disembodied, at 4:00 A.M. She can never keep in mind the twelve-hour
time difference so that I am always dragged out of bed, heart racing, tragedies of all sorts enacting themselves in my head before
I clutch the phone to my ear and her sunny and broken-up voice
travels across oceans to me. She says, breathless, "I've found him!"

"Who?"

"Shiva." Instantly I am surrounded by that particular shade
of blue, the whisper of his fingers about my wrist, a rustle of
breath by my ear.

"Shiva?"

"Yes, him." She and I acting as if the name belongs only to
this one.

"They went to England, after the riots, settled there. He's
back here working at the hospital now. Doctoring."

"Where? How did you find him?"

"I went to the Wellawatte house, just to look. Told the people there that I grew up in it and they let me in to look around. They said someone else had come. Someone who had lived there around the time we did. They said he was a foreigner, too, like me, but with a different accent. They gave me his number."

The excitement in her voice. That of a child who has found a forgotten and beloved toy, something valuable thought lost. But also proprietary, I hear it already. Had she always wanted this one thing that I had?

We are quiet. The buzz of static air suddenly between us. She asks, "How are things there?" and I, cowardly enough to think this is what she wants, say, "Really good. Siddharth and I are . . ."

Her voice breaking, "Akka. Stop it. Just leave him! Come here and we'll take care of you. . . ." The roar of the ocean in my ear, her voice lost somewhere in the distance between us. What remains? Only the ease with which she said the word "we."

It was predictable, of course, that they would fall in love. How did it make me feel? Did I gnash my teeth and ponder slitting my wrists because my younger and more beautiful sister had found the boy who still frequented my dreams? Not completely. I was, after all, still madly trying to win back the heart of my legitimately wedded husband. And if he was still enraptured in his blond fairy tale, it didn't matter. I would triumph in the end. Some days I was sure of it, I could hear his apologies, feel his hands on me, on that longed-for day when he finally realized that I was what he wanted all along. I believed this because he told me this was what he wanted, too. I believed it because, of course, I so desperately wanted it to be true.

In the end, it is the photographs that make me leave. I find them in his desk. My husband and her, on top of a sky-blue duvet. His hands curled around her narrow hips, the pressure of his fingers causing indentations on her white, white skin. Her golden hair falling over his lean stomach. The tension in his outspread palm as he pushes away her thigh, his head between her legs, her mouth open in agonized pleasure. She's covering her eyes with one elegant hand, with the other pressing into his hair, pushing him deeper into her. I witness: their varied acts of love, their slim bodies, the rapture on their faces.

I have not seen him in this state of abandon for years.

I wait for rage, but only a faraway ache comes. That and a raw, painful tenderness. Impossible to rage against lovers like these, whose bodies hold no secret from each other, who in the midst of their passion smile. I can see the familiar lines that radiate from his eyes, the deep groove next to his mouth when he smiles.

It is a crease I have longed to place my finger against for too long. Now I see that I am the interloper. In these years of marriage, it was always her he was faithful to. I was the other, the outsider. I pack a bag. Buy a one-way ticket to Kuala Lumpur. From there I will buy another, moving ever farther eastward. I leave the photographs scattered across the coffee table. My wedding ring, circling her profile while she sucks his cock.

ten

SARASWATHI, SRI LANKA

On that first day at the Tiger camp, there is more food than I have seen in months. I eat fragrant fish and steaming rice until my stomach is drum tight. My fingers, my mouth, my belly rejoicing; my heart aching for Amma, Appa, Luxshmi.

The soldiers have left me a blank page. They used me, spoiled me, and then threw me away like a piece of refuse. They did not expect me to survive. They should have killed me, but they didn't, and this is their mistake. Now the Tigers write upon my surfaces. I learn the ways in which Tamil blood has been spilled by the Sinhala for centuries; the myriad ways they have excluded, humiliated, and destroyed us. I learn the ways in which they hate us. I had not thought that such ferocious hatred could exist. But the memory of bullet-riddled cement walls, a perfect square of sky, reminds me that hatred is real, and that between us and them, it is the only thing.

A girl called Meena sleeps in the space next to mine. She grew up in Colombo in a family of five. She went to school with Sinhala children, played with them, trusted them. During the 1983 riots, she hid under a bed and watched as her father, mother, and brothers were found, thrown out of the house, and then burned to death in the garden. She hid inside the house and survived. Then, with their screams ringing in her ears, she came to her family in the north, looking to join the Tigers. When she talks of it, her eyes shine with hatred. When she talks of Eelam, she looks transcendent.

I learn about our Leader. About how he has devoted his life to our people. Without him, we would be slaves to the Sinhala, but he has shown us how to stand up and fight. He has given us our dignity. Without him we would be nothing.

I am given a weapon. It is heavier than I ever thought possible, bouncing against my back as I run, so that at night I am reduced to screaming sinew. But the months pass and the muscles build in my biceps, back, and legs. My lungs learn to conserve oxygen during the long, low runs across fields. My pupils dilate so that I can see at night. I learn to trust my weapon and my own ability to wield it. I learn how to track a soldier, watch him all day, close enough to touch, and how to melt into the shadows at his first suspicion. I am becoming slowly but surely a jungle cat.

Six months have passed. Months of hard training and endless lessons. My days are long, my nights sleepless. I have learned things that I had never expected to. My body, itself, has changed; it is no longer soft, but made of a certain density.

The Commandant calls in my squadron. The officers have been questioning a Sinhala soldier. He is tied to a chair, blood everywhere on his face and small, concave chest. He must have been handsome somewhere else, in some other life, with thick black hair falling over his ears and large eyes that fly from one face to another begging in silence for mercy. The Commandant cuts him loose, kicks the chair away from him so that he falls heavily on the ground. From his scream and the way they flop against the ground, I know that his wrists have been broken. The Commandant points at me, says, "You haven't killed one yet, have you?"

The soldier crawls away dragging useless back legs, trailing blood and urine like a dog run over on the rail tracks. He looks over his shoulder at me. His eyes bulging red, a stream of words in his stupid, fat-tongued language, incoherent sounds interspliced with pleas to his bastard mother, "Anaaaay ammaammammmam-mma, ammmmma."

My boot smashes hard into his right lung. He flips upside down, his arms and legs waving, helpless, red bubbles frothing at his mouth. The girls are giggling at this grown man struggling like an upturned insect. He covers his face with his arms. I push them away with my gun. I want him to see me. I straddle him, my boots on either side of his face. When his pleading eyes meet mine, I put the mouth of the rifle against his lips, push them aside so that it clicks against his clenched teeth. I hear that click and I pull the trigger.

The back of his head explodes; blood, bone, gray stuff splatters across my boots, splashes along my pants leg, even onto my hands. The girls around me are laughing. Patting me on the back. The Commandant says, "Very good," and nods.

That night, in the dark, Meena whispers, "Some girls are frightened at their first kill. They cry and even vomit sometimes. But you . . ." There is admiration in her voice. I keep my fluttering hands folded under my head; even here, even now, despite washing over and over I feel the thick slipperiness of gore on them.

I stand with the girls of my class. We are Tigers now, fully formed and as ferocious as our men, dog tags on our wrists, throats, and waist because we are not afraid to die cut up or blown to pieces. I search the small crowd until I see Amma, Appa, and Luxshmi. I have not seen them since I left home fourteen months ago. Even from this distance I can see the wet pride shining in their eyes.

The Commandant steps onto the platform where we wait. He is the bridegroom, and we the various brides. I lower my head to receive his *thali*. Instead of the ancient golden symbols of marriage, it is a hard capsule of glass he places in the hollow of my throat. Seven seconds it whispers against my beating pulse. Seven seconds to freedom. I test that frame of time, counting slowly under my breath.

One to catch the vial between the teeth. A glimmer of ice from the cold drink stand.

Two to bite down, shattering glass.

Three for the shards to slice the tongue and soft insides of the cheek.

Four to send blood gushing down the throat.

Five for the poison to slip quietly into the bloodstream.

By six darkness is falling and seven brings oblivion. The cyanide makes me smile. It will grant me victory in any battle because I am willing to die while my enemies are not. Our Leader's words ring in my ears, "Fear of death is the cause of all human fears. One who wins over the fear of death wins himself. He is the one who wins freedom from his mental prison."

I am fearless. I am free. Now, I am the predator.

We move through the jungle by moonlight, whole squadrons moving through the gray, shadowed vegetation as silently as wraiths. When we enter a village, it is almost always unalarmed. The villagers are asleep, their gentle snores echoing and mingling. When they wake, there is the inevitable cacophony, the loud begging for mercy, the calling upon long-dead mothers and prayers to various deities. I hate these terrified negotiations. The sound of Sinhala, its long syllables in these gibbering mouths, makes my rage rise. After the pleading, there is the screaming that reaches across the night sky.

We use the machete in these places because it paints the bloodiest picture. When the village is found, we want our message to be writ in red. We want to leave dead babies and bludgeoned women with streams of blood curling down the sides of their faces. To this end, I have learned to swing my machete through the flesh of babies. I have clutched the arm of a screaming toddler and swung off her head with a single blow as her mother stood with outstretched arms, voiceless in shock. I have disemboweled men and carved the breasts off their wives, sunk my knife into the hot brains of villagers. It is just like dancing under the mango tree, the weight of the machete pulling my body as I cut and weave and twirl through flesh. Flying blood splashes across my face, my mouth. I have learned to lick it from my lips. Now I am not just dancing a part. Now I *am* the Shiva Nataraja, the dancing face of death.

In this way I will never again be prey, small, trembling, and weak. We leave the villages as silently as we came. Behind us, only the lamenting of the very old remains. We let them live. Their fear extends our legend and ensures compliance and complicity.

But some nights, I fall asleep only to awaken in a bright concrete room where the sky opens to a perfect square of blue. Fear wraps its fingers around my throat, bile rises into my mouth. The uniforms materialize. That circle of men, their rough grasping fingers, the sharp ends of their rifles, my head jerked backward as the ribbon is pulled out of my hair. My braid uncoiling in rapid serpentine motions along my trembling spine. The scream of ripping cloth and my hands scrambling to cover myself. The rifle butt smashing into my mouth and then the hard cold floor, the first soldier heaving over me, the sweat gathering on his brow falling slowly, so I see each drop coming toward me, like looking up into the start of the monsoon, and I am struggling. If it falls on my skin, it will burn, but worse than that, I will forevermore smell of him so that all will know when I enter a place bringing unending corruption. But his hands are so heavy on my wrists, grinding them into the ground. And now other hands reach along my legs, rip away my underpants, and then the slap of something I can't recognize against my thigh, the hardness of it pushing, searching, digging into me. And then the soldier's camouflage uniform changes before my eyes, the formless blotches rearrange themselves into long animal stripes, khaki and green. A searing, gutting pain, a ripping of delicate flesh, a rush of hot blood. My head is jerked back and I must look into the face I know so well, as it drips its slow pollution onto my skin. The bustling mustache, the heavy middle-aged features, the reddened eyes staring into mine, claiming my body, inhabiting it. I fight then, struggle with all my strength, smashing myself from side to side, trying to throw him off, but his body is heavy, his arms muscled under the fat hold me down, his hands twist my wrists even harder into the concrete.

Moans spill out of me. They wrench me awake, return me to my mat, where I lie heaving, heart racing, teeth clenched, the sounds stuffed into my throat where they push against my gullet like undigested food. I wait for the cries to stop echoing in my head. Shame rises like a beast with shining teeth that crushes the breath from my body. Shame that the women have heard my cries and know my dreams, the extent of my sins. Know that night after night, the faces of the soldiers change into the face of the one I love the most in this world. Know that, now, nightly, it is not the soldiers who rip me apart, but our Leader himself.

I do everything I can not to go to sleep. When I sleep the dream comes and it is unbearable. The Leader is our Father. He has done everything for us. He has devoted his life to us, and yet I cannot rid myself of this grotesque nightmare. I know then that something is wrong with me. I am flawed, defective. I am corrupted. I am beyond the help of all who lie sleeping peacefully, innocent, around me.

In the mornings, the training camp is fragrant with the scent of jasmine trailing off the thick garlands that bedeck the portraits of the martyrs. Often, I go to stand under these portraits.

The martyrs are one in the set of their lips, the fixed jut of their chins, the hardness of their eyes. They look out without fear into that ultimate moment when they become the collective rage of our people. They are our Leader's most perfect weapon. They are pure, with their oneness of purpose, whereas I am corrupt and insincere in the love I profess for him.

In the Tamil villages we are served rice, lentils, some pickled vegetables on banana leaves. The villagers sit on their haunches and watch us eat. We try to make them understand that we are fighting for them, that we are making a new future for them and their families. But they are stupid people, civilians. They look terrified of our guns, our uniforms. They do not understand that we fight and kill and die for them.

Their women hover in the background, casting sidelong eyes

at us—the female cadres with our weapons, our cinch-waisted uniforms and rugged boots. They watch the way we walk. In the next months, we know, some of them will appear in the training camps ready to fight. We eat sparingly, knowing that whatever we leave will fill their children's bellies.

When we leave, we take the children of the dead. We take the children of the disappeared. But we also take a child from every family. This is the price of war. Sometimes they give us the child quickly, easily, but sometimes we have to negotiate and threaten. I hate these scenes. I hate ripping a child from his mother's arms, but it must be done. This is war and to fight we need bodies. So we take the children. We wipe the tears from their faces and take them because they are hungry, or because they have no shelter. But sometimes we take children from their families by force.

We take the children because they are easily trainable, eager to follow orders after a few weeks, small and agile enough to slip over the land unseen, and catch the enemy off guard. We take them because soldiers, no matter how battle hardened, always hesitate before children. And that moment of hesitation often grants us victory. As we leave, the villagers avert their eyes. They know that without us the children have no hope, yet still they are silently distraught.

Sometimes when I am by myself I miss the taste of our well. Water filtered through our small piece of earth, its exact mineral consistency, the taste of home. It is the only thing I allow myself to remember.

. . .

In the evenings, we watch old videos in which a younger version of our Leader performs heroic feats, running, jumping, falling to his knees, and spraying machine gun fire at an unseen enemy. I feel the women's love for him, their ardor rising in waves around me.

Sometimes we watch videos of martyrs. They are young men and women with eyes like steel. One of them, a girl younger than me, says, "This is the most supreme sacrifice I can make. The only way we can get our Eelam is through arms. That is the only way anyone will listen to us. Even if we have to die. As the Leader says, we will fight even for a hundred years for Eelam. But if we are willing to kill ourselves it will take less time."

Our Leader fills the screen. He is older now, chubby like a favorite uncle, but still with the dangerous eyes of a revolutionary, his hunger for justice unabated. He is giving a speech at a Fallen Heroes Day rally, the parents of martyrs in the front seats. He bangs his fist against the podium and says, "We have sown the seed of an ideal. We will grow it by irrigating it with the blood of our martyrs. It will grow into a luxurious tree and make our martyrs' dreams a reality."

His words make me see myself lying on the ground. I am peaceful, but fissures are appearing upon my skin, spreading, and breaking apart, so that I fall into ten thousand sharp pieces. The blood gushes out of me, soaks deep into the ground, mixes with the earth, marks it a darker red, crimson, scarlet. Something pushes at the center of the broken bits of me. A tiny sapling breaks through the ground, draws my blood into its translucent stem; it grows, feeding on me. The trunk grows thicker and thicker, becomes opaque and shoots upward dizzyingly fast, bursts into immense branches, a forest canopy, its roots reaching deep underground. It eats up my body until I am gone. But I am no longer important. This tree will bear fruit like the mango tree that I once danced under. It will provide cover for us and give us roots to anchor us in this land where we are displaced and despised. And yet, it is a tree that feeds upon blood at its roots; I wonder about the taste of its fruit.

My officers have been watching me, understanding that my courage is real, steel strong and sharp. When I ask my Commandant if I can apply, she is not surprised, but instead looks quietly jubilant. She helps me write the letter asking our Leader for permission. We work late into the night, choosing the words that will make him see my resolve. When weeks later no answer comes, I am despondent, but she says, "Wait. Wait. He does not choose you until you have written five or six times."

I am given leave to go home. I had wanted this, but on the bus ride, wearing civilian clothes, I feel unarmed, unprotected. I desperately miss my camouflage trousers, the skirt brushing against my legs feels so flimsy. I get off at the junction and walk. Villagers raise their arms in greeting, but no one comes up to me. There is a different look in their eyes now. Pride, but also fear. I am glad of this. No one will ever again speak of Appa's daughter spoiled by the soldiers. From now on, they will see me as I am, a Tiger with teeth and claws.

I walk toward the little house by the lagoon and Snowy comes out, first barking and then falling at my feet so that I can rub the soft white fur of his stomach. Amma and Luxshmi come running, they exclaim over my hair that has grown, my new skirt and shirt. Luxshmi has grown taller, Amma has grown older. They look into my face and they, too, take stock of the changes there. They take me to the house, where Appa struggles to get up from his chair. He hugs me to him, stares at me as if he cannot believe I am really here. Amma has made food, *pittu* and dried fish. Extravagant food here, but I am used to fresh curries, not these bits of fish like tiny shreds of wood. While I eat, Amma and Luxshmi talk of what has happened in the village. The various deaths, the few marriages, the buying of bicycles and availability of rice. Things that no longer interest me.

I try to talk to them of important things. What we are doing in the Movement; the new society we will build in which we will be free of Sinhala oppression. We are building a new world so that they won't have to live like this, in a mud-and-wattle, cadjan-roofed, falling-apart house. But I can tell that my words have no effect, that they are not really listening. I want them to understand that what I am doing is important, that when we finally win this war there will be food, like before, there will be prawns again in the lagoon as big as tame dogs, like the ones Appa used to tell us about. But it is useless. I inhabit a different world now and there are no bridges between that place and this.

So instead I talk to Luxshmi. I tell her about my glorious new life, the purpose I have found. I say, "You also must come. You're a big girl now. Old enough. It's time you came." She doesn't say anything. She just twists her shoulders to her ears and looks at Amma and Appa.

Appa says, "Leave your sister alone. She is too young for all this. She is planning to go to school. Study."

"Study what? Don't you realize we are in a war? She is not too young. There are girls much younger than her in my troop. She will learn discipline and strength. She will learn what it means to fight and be a warrior."

He doesn't meet my eyes when he says, "We are thinking of sending her to Colombo to study. Somehow getting her past all the blockades."

"What nonsense! Sending her to those people. The Sinhala will kill her. They hate us. Do you want her to die there? All alone among them?"

Amma breaks in, her voice half cajoling, "Why do you want to take this one also? She's the only one we have left. Anyway, she'd be a terrible soldier. She's so small she can't even carry water from the well. Let alone fight."

"She's not much younger than me when you sent me to them." I look straight at her when I say this. She looks stricken. "And look how well it has suited me." I laugh and they join me, but they are apprehensive, scared even. I don't mind. My true family is back at camp, these are strangers I knew in a different time.

When they go to sleep, I walk outside, my senses awakening with the night. I long to be patrolling with the other women, alert to every noise, my machete drawn, thirsting for the wet slide of it through flesh. When I return to the single room, I cannot sleep with Luxshmi's slitted eyes, Appa's snoring, and Amma's heavy arm thrown across me. There are too many memories in this room, waiting to sit upon my chest, waiting to steal away my breath if I sleep. I lie awake till dawn, and when I say good-bye soon after, I can tell that some heavy burden has been lifted off them.

He wants me! He has chosen *me*. Joy pulses under my skin, threatening to break out from under my bones. I am buoyant, ecstatic. The most beautiful thing has happened; I am chosen. But I cannot betray this by a single word or glance. No one can know. Not even Meena. When the time comes they will call me away. Everyone will think that I am on routine training. But I will be with the Black Tigers, learning the secrets of the Martyrs. Then I will return to my squadron and resume my old duties, skirmishes and patrols, until finally my assignment comes and I am stationed somewhere. Always with my eye on the target, following him, tracking him until the order comes and I am sent out to kill and to die.

The dreams come every night now. And it is always Him pushing and breaking into me.

I am taught Sinhala. I let its ugliness take over my tongue. A year later I am given my assignment and stationed in Colombo. I travel to the capital for the first time in my life. There I must wait for the exact time, the precise moment when my target can be destroyed. The man I have come for is a politician. He is Tamil. But he has turned traitor, fled to the south, turned his back on his people, joined forces with our enemy. I will be our Leader's weapon, his most perfect and precise revenge. I smile at the thought of our bodies, mine and the traitor's, mingled on the ground, in pieces, indistinguishable.

In the meantime, I wait, just another anonymous Tamil woman newly arrived in Colombo, making a meager living as a shop girl or garment factory worker, sending money to her family in the village, walking down the street in her shalwar kameez or denim. Lost in that teeming, steaming crowd on Galle Road.

eleven

yasoðhaRa

On the Air Lanka flight, I wake, pinned and needled in every limb, to rest my forehead against the window. Below, with the suddenness of vision, the island appears through wispy clouds, verdant green and battered by cerise ocean. I had not expected this intensity in my chest, a thudding as if malevolent gods were dancing on my heart. We stumble off the plane, bedraggled returnees, some stunned-looking tourists. The hot air hits us, sweat slides along the crevices of our skin to pool between breasts and behind knees. In the far distance, the palm trees beckon wildly like old friends come to claim us. I long to rush into their midst, to the ocean I know is waiting, but first there is the long process of arrival, lines and dull-eyed officials stamping papers. Everywhere now the sound of Sinhala and Tamil.

Pushing my luggage into the arrivals lounge, I enter a crowd of expectant faces, grandmothers and husbands, mothers and brothers, entire villages gathered to welcome home those lost beyond the dark seas. Past them, a wall of silent uniformed men hold rifles at their cocked hips.

So many familiar faces. Echoes of Amma or Mala or La in the cheekbones, the eyes, or the curve of a woman's shoulders. The stooped man who pushes a broom evokes every old uncle I have ever met. In America, it was my unconscious and secret habit to seek out island faces. When I found them, it was almost always a surprise, an occasion. Some sort of acknowledgment would always be made. Some slight and secret signal of belonging, even if hostile. We are all strangers in this land, it said, and therefore united in some way. Here, the faces are all familiar, but they look at me without recognition. I am the one who has become unrecognizable, with my foreign clothes and shoes, the sureness of my American walk. I am drowning in this sensation of dislocation when La comes. I bury my face in her shoulder and weep my jet-lagged exhaustion, my rage at what I have left behind.

Through the curtain of her hair, I see a slim man behind her. When he smiles, an ecstatic sort of smile, I am transported. The features of my childhood companion transposed over his own so that I cannot help but smile back and place my fingers behind my sister's back into his quickly grasping hand.

saraswathi

The Colombo shopkeepers speak Sinhala at me and I reply effortlessly and smile back at them. I own their tongue as if I have been brought up in this smoky, crowded city instead of in quiet northern places. Nights when I am spared that other, more ripping dream, I dream of the dawn lagoon, Amma, Appa, and Luxshmi, even my brothers.

I wake to remember. The boys are dead. Amma's face is hard, Appa is silent, Luxshmi is in the training camp. Then I know I am doing the best thing, the only possible thing.

yasoдhara

The car winds through twilit streets, a cacophony of horns, the press of bodies, crowded marketplaces, past white Buddha statues in their glass boxes, the tapered leaves of Bodhi trees spinning in the breeze. The air is smoky, wet, warm, and fragrant with green things.

At the first roundabout soldiers surround the car demanding identification papers. What is our business? Why are we on the airport road as night falls? My sister turns in her seat. Chuckles when she sees my face. Waves her American passport like a precious fetish. "Don't look so shocked, Akka. We have these magic things after all. They keep us protected from all this madness."

A soldier, he looks all of seventeen, with awkward hands and enormous eyes, takes my passport, and considers me with curiosity. When he sees me watching him, he gets shy, hands the passport back silently, gestures with his rifle for us to carry on.

I remember Alice's son, Dilshan, a boy like this one, lost somewhere in the north, his body floating in a lagoon, picked at by small fish.

They take me to the house they rent. A small, jade-hued house with red cement floors, smooth and cool as glass under our bare feet. From each room, I can hear the ocean's whispering. In the garden, mango and *murunga* trees twine about each other, dropping ripe yellow fruit and fat blue-green pods. A series of cats wind themselves around my legs and two Alsatians bound after tossed sticks and stones, bringing them back to drop at my feet.

We sit in the garden as the fireflies and mosquitoes take center stage, the frogs begin their raucous song, and the dark shadows of bats flit across the sky. I breathe in the sudden night air and feel the embrace of green, these various and infinite shades of fluorescent emerald and olive taking me over. Something coiled tightly in my chest unwinds like a spring coming undone.

Across from me, the two of them sit close to each other, touching shoulders or fingertips with the easy, unconscious intimacy of lovers. We drink Coke into which Shiva splashes potent arrack, and soon we do not mind the ferocious biting of the mosquitoes, the talk leads easily into that shared space of our childhoods, the Wellawatte house with its myriad secrets, the passageway between house and wall in which we used to hide, those long-ago Upstairs, Downstairs wars, our ferocious grandmother pitted against his formidable grandfather fighting over the mango tree. He turns to me, suddenly intent, asks, "Do you remember the blue room?" A thrill of pleasure along my spine, irritation splashing across La's face. I change the subject quickly.

We talk of the 1983 riots. Those days of knives flashing in the sunlight, disembodied screaming floating over our gate. It was terrifying enough for us, but upstairs they waited to be slaughtered.

He tells us of days spent in the dusty, sneezy space under beds, all the children packed together, half thinking it a game, only afraid when they looked at their parents' faces. The phone ringing through the house, the voices of distant relatives begging for shelter. Then the pounding on the downstairs door. A distinctly physiological understanding of fear learned then. The way the blood drains from the extremities, pools around the heart, causing cold, shivering hands and toes in that torrid sweating heat. They waited, he says, for the mob to storm up the stairs. Waited, his mother's arms around him, her heart thudding against the front of her thin cotton blouse exactly where his ear lay so that he learned the precise rhythm of his mother's fear.

Then hope, because it was not the mob that came, but our grandmother, Sylvia Sunethra. For the next few days she sent food up to them surreptitiously by the back stairs while outside the long columns of smoke rose into the air. And finally a panicked midnight run to the airport with a few suitcases holding everything they would take into their new lives.

He tells us of the years in London. All of them crowded into a flat where they slept head to toe, turning in unison like a row of grilling chickens. The early days when he spoke to no one and only watched the other adolescents, calling them names in Tamil under his breath, Moon Face, Whitey, Ugly. Days of deprivation and bad food. Later a sort of foolhardy teenagehood, fueled by what was happening in the back of his head, on the island, in the north.

The arrack makes us light-headed. A slow subsiding into silence. Companionable solitude, the hum of insects, loud in our ears. When, hours later, they go off to bed hand in hand, I drown in the sudden and sheer panic of loneliness.

In the mornings La takes me to the school. There are thirty children, each missing either one or both legs. They squeal in pleasure as we cut and color. At first it is heartbreaking, but with astounding quickness I learn their strengths, see that they are not destroyed. There is Asanga, who hops up to me on his crutches, holding up a crayoned rooster, fiery red in the comb, iridescent green-blue plumage. Shy Nirmala, who only draws stick men in boxy tanks riding mayhem over other broken-limbed stick people. Asoka, who throws his arms about my legs each time I come within reach. They sleep in two long rooms, neat cots made every morning. They ask me questions about America, is it true that everyone has a car there? And also, does everyone really have a gun to shoot everyone else on the street? One little girl sits on my lap, she says, "I wouldn't go there." But then, looking down at the curved stump of her left knee, she says, "But maybe they could send me a leg?" They know that the prosthetics come from India and America. They make my heart contract, these beautiful unbroken children. They make me forget myself. They have big brown eyes that have witnessed too much. Big brown eyes that shine with ferocious, unqualified, unrepentant hope.

Afterward La and I wander through the hot, dusty marketplace where squatting women offer us small red onions, fat green chilies, heads of garlic and ginger, twists of newspaper holding curry powder and turmeric. We walk through alleyways, heads reeling from the odor of bleeding fish twisting their death throes in the sunlight. Inexpertly, we choose seerfish and plump red shrimp. We go home jostling and laughing in a trishaw that veers madly through traffic, narrowly missing head-on collisions more times than we can count while the plastic marigold garland around the front mirror dances to the Hindi film sound track. We pass Colombo in a swirl, the crowds, the noise, and turn into the quiet lane that leads to the house. As we swing into the courtyard, the fierce sunlight switches off, dark clouds open, and we must duck our heads under newspaper, run into the house, laughing, breathing deeply, the freshly sluiced earth as seductive and potent as the scent rising off a lover's thighs.

We banish the crone who rules the kitchen and set to work, knives in a flurry through onion and chili, fingertips tugging fat shrimp out of their briny armor. I crush garlic under the flat of my knife, free the cloves from their parchment skin. La sets pots on the fire, scatters cumin and cardamom into the fragrant coconut oil. Outside, the afternoon is dark as twilight, the scent of rain and earth entering through the open windows, fluttering the flimsy white curtains like the wings of ghost insects. Rain falls inside, a small puddle forming on the red-waxed floor like a pool of molten sealing wax, melted lipstick. I go to close them, but she holds my arm. "Let it be," she says with that familiar raised eyebrow, that quizzical teasing look. I return my knife to the garlic. The scent of rain mixes with our spices, fills the kitchen.

saraswathi

There is going to be an election rally on Galle Face Green. The traitor will be there. He will be surrounded by people, heavily bodyguarded, of course. But those men cannot protect him from me. I will push through the crowd. I will carry a garland of jasmine to put around his neck. I will be so close, close enough to touch.

yasodhara

We drive through quiet Mount Lavinia lanes until we are in front of a red gate. Shiva beeps the horn once and when a small, dark girl appears to open it, I am suddenly swimming in the past. La, twisting in her seat, giggles at my expression and says, "No, it's not Poornam!" We get out and are surrounded by a pack of dancing, delightedly drunken dogs. Then I am caught in my aunt Mala's overflowing embrace, the breath squeezed out of me, like being hugged by an enthusiastic octopus, like coming home. She is laughing and pushing away tears, saying, "Let me look, girl, let me see you." She holds me at arm's length and rakes my eyes until I must drop them, her gaze too knowing, too far-reaching. She says, "Come, come inside," and sweeps us into the house on the wings of her teal-green kaftan.

Inside, it is as if time has not passed: the same photographs hang on the walls, my father, Mala, and their parents on the beach in Hikkaduwa. My father in short pants, big eyes, his hand on the shoulder of that dark scallywag sister. Beatrice Muriel looking stern and the Doctor in a sarong, his quiet eyes far away.

Mala herself and Anuradha on their wedding day, frothy veil and dark suit, luminous smiles. Photos of Poornam at various ages. "She is my daughter, you know?" says Mala. "I adopted her. Put her through school. She teaches at the university now . . . a professor of mathematics. That girl always loved numbers." There is heavy pride and possession in her voice. "People said I was mad to take in a Tamil child. They said she would murder me in my bed. But now they come with proposals for my girl. Come, let's have lunch in the garden."

She leads us outside and it is the same as in all my dreams, fragrant with jasmine, orchids spilling from trees to brush our faces, ferns uncurling tenderly, bird chatter, and the unbroken line of coconut trees. Under the avocado tree, there is a table and onto this, the servant girl places dish after steaming dish, red rice, pumpkin curry, fried cabbage, fiery coconut sambal. We swirl our fingers in bowls of cool water and lemon, and eat.

Much later, we are replete, ensconced in our chairs, entranced by the breeze in the branches, when a deep-throated chuckle breaks the surface of our shared solitude. A young woman, tall in a black-and-white batik sari, enormous eyes. A face that has grown beyond my knowing. She carries a pink box stamped with the magic words, "the Fab," and says, "So who's ready for ribbon cake?" It is Poornam. She comes and embraces me and I know the scent of her skin. She sits with us. Long, elegant fingers and dark, dark skin, as if she were really the daughter of Mala, who sits close to her, beaming. I had not realized until this moment that I had missed these two women so acutely.

. . .

Life settles into a certain cadence. In the mornings La and I take a swinging, swaying trishaw through chaotic traffic to the school. We spend our day with the children. We teach them art, but also reading and numbers. We use old, tattered books, donated paper, and cast-off clothing. As in so many places like this, there is a small ragtag team of teachers armed only with dedication. There is always the threat that the scarce money will run out, and then we spend hours on the phone, cajoling or begging. Some days a rich benefactor will make a *dana* donation to accrue merit in the afterlife, and the kids sit on the floor in long rows, cross-legged, scooping rice and curry into their mouths as fast as they can. Sometimes there is ice cream, and then we are rewarded with enormous gap-toothed smiles.

In the evenings, we three gather for dinner. We frequent the *kothu-roti* shops on Galle Road where the cook's heavy knives fall like crashing cymbals through the vegetables and roti, making the most delicious mashup imaginable. We eat at a rickety table on the pavement, the insects gathering overhead and all of Colombo swirling around us. We take walks along Mount Lavinia beach, down to where the old hotel glimmers like some remnant of a colonialist's dream and the tourists gather to watch "native" performances. At night we watch the news, there is always fighting in the north, always a steady stream of bloodshed, but here in Colombo it is possible to pretend that all of it is happening somewhere else, in some other, faraway country, while the only thing affected here is the price of shrimp coming from the northern lagoons.

Late at night there are phone calls. I pick up the receiver as quietly as I can. It is Siddharth. He sobs into the phone. He wants me back. He says he has left her. There is only me now. Just come back, he says, and we can be like we were in the beginning. I know he is lying, that she was present even in the beginning of our marriage and will always be. But I still listen, something in me calmed just to hear the sound of his voice over these broken lines. And then what shall I do when this trip is over? It's all well to live here in exile with my sister and her lover, but I can't do it forever. I must return sometime. And then what? Divorce? The word itself sounds like a death knoll, so final, stinking of failure and remorse. If I do it I shall be the very first in our whole long family line. I shall be outcast, solitary, outside the pale. And then again there is the horrified thing in me that knows I do not love him anymore, that I would only be returning out of fear. When I put down the phone, it is to see La in the backlit hallway, her arms crossed, her head shaking. But she was always the brave one, ready to sacrifice everything—reputation, family, security—for love. I'm not like her. I turn away into my bedroom. Behind me I feel the cold weight of her disappointment.

When the monsoon clears, we drive along the curving, sun-drenched, palm-lined coast southward to our father's home village, Hikkaduwa. We find a small hotel where each room connects to a cool, immaculately sand-free corridor leading down to the sea. We sit on the beach and laugh at the tourists. The Germans in their minuscule Speedos, the corned beef–faced Brits, the fat topless French women.

But we know that we, too, are only a different shade of tourist, darker skinned than these boiled lobster Europeans, and for this reason perhaps more deserving of scorn from the sarong sellers, the coconut pluckers, the mango hawkers. We live in soft-bellied, affluent places; we have forgotten our languages, our religions, our modesty. We lie on the beach in strips of cloth, turning various shades of eggplant and ebony. This obscene sun worship is a habit we have picked up in colder climes. It is unknown to our ancestors, who haunt this place.

Late at night, when even the tourists are sleeping, we slide through warm ink-black water, lie on our backs, and stare at the star-glittering sky. The sea is a bed on which we are held aloft, the stars close enough to touch. When this pleasure is exhausted, we swim to the glass-bottom boats of fishermen and tourist trips that are anchored close to shore, clamber on, and each take a post. Lanka poised on the prow, her profile, mermaid-ish in the way the wind takes her hair, throws it about, makes me remember when entering her bedroom was to swim underwater, those blue-green walls.

We drink arrack and Coke, settle into the rock and pull of the little boat. My feet rest against the cool glass, through which I feel the water run like a muscled thing. We are lulled and re-plete, sedate, when Lanka exclaims, "Look!" We follow her slim pointing arm and see silver arrows darting through water, leaping and falling, catching the moon's ghost sparkle, a school of flying fish. Under our boat the memory of a young boy immersed

headfirst in the sea, learning to swim from the fisherfolk, surrounded by schools of silver flat flying fish, surges and falls.

On our last night in Hikkaduwa, we are perched on a fishing
boat bobbing in the water when it is discovered that the last Lion
Lager has been drunk. La says, "I'll go." We hear her splash into
the water, wade toward the lighted shore. There is darkness all
around and Shiva is only a silhouette against the prow, his face
upturned toward the sliver of moon. We have rarely been alone
together in these three long resplendent months. We are silent
for minutes. Then, his voice, disembodied, "Did you ever tell her
about the room?"

My heart thudding in my mouth, "What room?"

But he, with no time for subterfuge, snaps, "The blue room.
Of course." I shake my head, will not turn toward him. It is quiet.
The waves slapping against the boat.

Then his voice says again, as if from miles away, "You left, she
came back. She was all I had left of you. Of any of you." The caring
in his voice could break me if I let it.

We hear La at the shore, entering the water. He says in a
fierce whisper, "And I love her," and I, incredulous, hiss, "Never
as much as I do!"

And then she is back, climbing onto the boat, shaking to
shower us with night-cooled seawater, laughing and bearing beer.
We are again as we were, a perfectly balanced triangle. The three
of us. My sister, her lover, and I.

In the morning, when the tide is sedate, we bob, separate

islands, weightless as cosmonauts, faces turned toward sea-reflecting sky. This very morning on waking I decide that I must return to America. Soon. Possibly in the next few days. Possibly so soon that I will carry this water's scent on my skin. By the time I reach LAX, it will be a faint memory, washed away by the dryness of the air, the loud questioning of immigration officials, and the glare of desert sun. The thought brings salt to my own eyes, it runs down my face to the greedily licking ocean. I don't know what I return to. But I have to go. I have a life I need to re-sume. Students to teach, papers to grade and write, exams to take. And yes, even a husband who cries and says he waits for me. I dare not tell La, she will be so angry, questioning everything I say. She expects me to fling it all away for the sake of freedom, but I miss the weight of that ring upon my finger; I miss the weight of his body on mine through the night. It's not love, but it's the closest thing I have to what she has found.

But there is something else also. Shiva's eyes, his voice in the dark. They bring back memories. I have to go. Soon. Before our triangle implodes.

Driving back to Colombo, sunburned and sea drenched, we are suddenly surrounded by a yellow cloud as if the car is being pummeled by handfuls of flung turmeric. We have wandered into the path of a million suicidal butterflies. Now there is a re-lentless shattering of minuscule bodies against the windscreen, until the glass is a thick sludge through which the wipers barely move. In the front seat, La holds her head in her hands. Shiva kneads her knee. She says, "Why are they doing this?" in a thick, strangled voice. And we can only shake our heads, struck dumb by the massacre.

saraswathi

I am fighting against the Leader's heavy grip, his tearing hands, throwing my body from side to side before I wake panting in the heavy, eyeless dark. I lie in my narrow bed as the first thread of silver dawn arrives and with it the man with the suit. He leads me into the back room where there are no windows. It is chilly and a single bulb throws giant crawling insect shadows onto the walls. With eyes averted he asks me to undress down to my underclothes. Then, with hands as gentle as Amma's, he pulls the contraption over my head, snuggles it against my belly, beneath my breasts. The latex runs down my body like water, all that wiring and hardware fused to my muscle and sinew seamlessly, the secret mechanisms of it hidden in my now heavily pregnant stomach.

He kneels before me and holds open the ballooning shalwar pants as if I am a child. I have to hold on to his shoulder to step into them and then he pulls them up, ties the cord precisely at my distended belly. I hold my arms up as he pulls the kameez over my head, smooths it down with his palms. He has done this many times. His fingers know where to place the latex, where to conceal the wires.

He arranges the wires so that I will be able to reach them swiftly at the prescribed moment. He makes me repeat the intricacies of our plan one more time, but I am confident, I could do this in my sleep.

A voice calls for him from the other room. When he leaves, I turn to my reflection and see what others will see, a young woman, eight months pregnant, green plastic bangles at her wrists, bright orange cloth hugging her belly. She is a ghost from a different time and place. Useless to me. Beyond her gaze, I search for my own eyes. In them I see Hope . . . and that is Everything.

twelve

yasodhara

At dusk tomorrow, I fly toward that shambles of a life I left in America. I am at home today, feigning a cold. I couldn't bear to go back to the school and face those kids knowing that I would be abandoning them so soon. It would have weakened my resolve, and that's the last thing I need. I am going back to my husband. We will work something out: some sort of compromise; isn't that what they all say marriage is about, anyway? Compromise? Yes, I can do this. He's going to pick me up from the airport and we're going to talk it out. He says he's left her. I am choosing to believe him.

I go shopping through the dusty and crowded market. I'm going to cook for La and Shiva in our shared kitchen one last time. In these three months they have become the whole of my existence, holding my memories in their carefully cupped hands like water to my parched lips. I will tell them I'm leaving at dinner and hope that the witchery in my cooking will ease their tongues.

They are both late and some American-accented voice in my head scolds, "Everyone on this island. Always late! So inconsiderate!" I put away that voice, take out my various groceries, reveling in the heft of these golden papayas that will split to reveal ruby flesh, the little fat Bombay onions and feathery greens, the heavy coconut, the fresh seerfish. I take out my knives, my pots, ladles. These instruments must perform magic tonight.

saraswathi

Chandrasekaram will come with me. He will hide in the crowd far enough away to be safe, and afterward he will take photographs so that the world will see the nature of our vengeance. We will take the bus and then walk through the crowd so that when the traitor has arrived, I will be waiting for him. I must wait until he is within a fingertip's distance, close enough to touch before I reach beneath my clothes.

Chandrasekaram and I walk together along the lane, past the loud children on their bicycles, the temple where the *pusari*'s voice rises, the scent of ghee and coconut emerging to wrap insistent fingers around my face. For a moment I remember Amma, Luxshmi, and Appa. My heart is stabbed. It is so strange. The last walk of my life and I am here with this man I barely know.

No one I love. No one who will remember me. But I shake my head and the weakness passes. I laugh at myself. They will remember me. All of them. My portrait, miles high, will hang everywhere extolling my bravery, the new cadres will come to stand in front of it, inhale the scent of my jasmine garland, be inspired by my fearlessness, my dedication. Amma and Appa will be proud. Luxshmi will be the sister of a martyr. She will be honored by all the rebels for this. I cannot give them more than this.

We wait at the bus stop with all these others, just another husband and his pregnant wife. After it has happened, they will remember me. Someone will say, "I was so close. She stood just behind me," with wonder in his voice. They will be forced to contemplate my devotion, recognize my faith, and it will make them shudder, will make the hairs on the backs of their necks rise like electricity. The thought makes me smile, my hands curved around the roundness of my belly, taut in the orange cloth.

A girl waiting in line with us catches my eye. Sinhala. My age, my height, masses of hair rising softly on the breeze, big eyes looking as if she wants to ask questions. She doesn't belong here. Something in the way she holds her head, even though her clothes are local, the cut of the long skirt and the T-shirt like everyone else's, the bangles sliding on her thin wrist, green plastic like mine. But like me, she is an imposter from somewhere else.

I can see that she's in love. It's shining in her eyes. I can see that she wants the life she thinks I live. A young husband, and a baby on the way. She wants to lay her palms against my skin and feel my baby flutter. She wants to look into my eyes and feel sisterhood. She wants me to smile at her. But she cannot see what is buried in my heart, or the strange fruit that lies just beneath it. Like the rest of her people, she sees nothing. I look away.

The bus comes. I grasp the handrails, pull myself up. The suit is heavier than I thought. It makes me waddle like a pregnant woman onto the bus. A crush of bodies, the sweat sliding over someone's arm onto my shoulder. That girl is here, too, her profile so familiar. The angles of her face, as if I have seen them over and over and over again, and she must feel this, too, because she looks my way often.

One more stop. Through the filthy windows I see the crowds gathering. I will cause such mayhem in this mass of bodies. I will cut and lacerate and detonate. I will explode in a hundred directions, send a thousand pieces of shrapnel to lodge in all this soft, pliant flesh. I can see them running, screaming, my own head lying trampled under their feet, my hair dripping pools of oily red, dusty eyes looking skyward. Where will I be then? What will these eyes be witnessing? Just one more stop . . .

Loud voices and confusion in the front of the bus. A swarm of soldiers climbing on board, pushing past bodies. The bus taking off and the smell of them hitting me as hard as fists. Please please please don't let them see me. *Tiger bitch*. But here they come, the smash of their boots crashing toward me. *Tiger bitch*. Then they are around me shouting out questions and I am trying to answer. *Tiger bitch.* And Chandrasekaram is nowhere and my mouth is opening, but no words are coming, and then there are fingers like iron around my wrist—*Tiger bitch*—and the bus lurches to a stop and I am in another place, a bullet-splattered cement room open to a perfect square of sky, and I cannot tell where the walls end and the sky begins—*Tiger bitch*—and where the voices begin and the hands end, and where I begin or end, and I am tearing into shreds and something buried deep is erupting like a land mine, like rage buried in my flesh, something settled—*Tiger bitch*—and burrowed under my heart like a fetus raising its head. *Tiger bitch Tiger bitch Tiger bitch!*

From the corner of my eye, I see the girl start toward me and I know her, but it is too late and my fingers are reaching down, feeling for the wires, and now it really is too late. . . .

Blinding light, cleansing pain, and I am dancing under the mango tree, branches spreading tenderly over my head, sunshine pouring through the leaves like emerald-flavored rain. Somewhere, there is anguish, ripping metal, and unbearable shrieking, keening, moaning, fierce shouting, chaos, and scurrying feet. But here, Amma's voice is loud and clear. She calls out the steps to the slap of her fingers on her palm and my feet move. The Shiva Nataraja is watching and I am dancing, swirling and stamping. My fingers opening like the petals of the lotus bud. My eyes long and fish tailed. My braid whipping past me in a blur. I am in motion. Unstoppable and Immaculate.

yasodhara

I chop garlic, hum along with Asha Bhosle. Delightful Asha, whose voice has reached across the planet through the throats of all those Bollywood seductresses with their supple waists and wet saris. Darling Asha, her face gathering life lines, but her voice preserved perfectly. She sings a song of longing, which, combined with imminent departures and onion fumes, proves too much for me. I push away tears before they land on sliced onion, potato, pumpkin. I would not have our last meal salted with my sadness.

Then there is an altogether different voice on the radio saying, "Central Colombo . . . bus bombing . . ." Metal fingers grasp my heart and squeeze, something biological in me smashing open, the knife flashing through my fingers, crimson blooming on the floor as I run heedless to the television, to see . . . the corpse of a bus, its iron intestines spilling in cruel cutting ribbons, shards and jagged edges of steel, a confusion of metal, wires. Dear God, what happens to soft human flesh in the midst of such metallic rage? A pushing, shoving crowd, gloved policemen laying out large lumpish things on the side of the road. It takes a moment to recognize blackened flesh, the red showing in places and seeping onto the ground.

A lady reporter saying, ". . . detonated on Galle Road at 4:43 P.M. Twelve people confirmed dead, another twenty-one seriously wounded. Unconfirmed reports attribute the attack to a female LTTE suicide bomber posing as a pregnant woman thought to be on her way to the political rally on Galle Face Green. Her target presumably the moderate Tamil politician, Krishnan Ponniah."

Blood dripping from my fingers, pooling on the shiny waxed floor next to my bare feet.

And then I am running down the street, pushing into the tumble of Galle Road. A voice in my head, "Her bus, coming this way, after work." My slippers slapping against the pavement, the choking gasping flood of my heart. A car sliding up, Shiva's voice calling my name. I crumple into the seat beside him and he says, "You're bleeding." He is staring at the front of my white trousers where deep rust stains have emerged as if I have started a period or miscarriage, some yet unnoticed female trauma. I remember the knife, the kitchen, hold up my hand. He sighs in relief, takes my hand, holds it, fingers pointing skyward. I watch as he reaches into the glove compartment with his other hand, riffles for a bandage, tears the packet open with his teeth, and binds my finger, the index of my left hand where the knife slid deep. I work to make my voice emerge. "There's been a bomb, a bus bombing . . . an hour ago . . . La . . . She should have been home ages ago."

"She isn't home yet?" Something dangerous in his voice. I shake my head, my bandaged hand gripped against my chest where my heart is flopping. "Where?" I point toward Galle Face Green and already he is swinging the car around.

We crawl through traffic toward the police barricades. Park as close as we can, run toward the wreckage. A line of policemen, terror in their eyes, rifles at their sides, skittish as blooded sharks. Shiva grabs my hand, pushes past them with the magic words, "Doctor. I'm a doctor." My nails dig into his flesh and then before us, the bus. A leviathan dragged from the depths and destroyed by the unbearable weight of air, its carapace shattered, iron entrails dragging, blood shining on the cruel jagged edges.

Shiva has let go of my hand, he is kneeling over the pavement where they have lined up bodies, the less wounded, I think. I leave him tearing cloth, staunching wounds. I am walking past, my rubber slippers sticking to the ground with every step, gore holding onto the underside of them like a beloved unwilling to let go, let go, let go. I am looking for her. Something screams that she was here, that her eyes have seen this, something feral in me smelling her here.

And then, there it is, a round object, atilt, like a child's toy carelessly dropped and forgotten. A woman's head. On the ground. Trailing tendrils of black hair and wisps of ribboned flesh. Translucent jellyfish tentacles dripping deepest scarlet, eyes gazing up into the sunlit sky, dust on her features. I see it all before gloved fingers reach down to entwine themselves into her tangled hair, lift and lower her, vanquished Medusa, death dealer, serial killer, into a plastic bag, and the policemen's bodies close off my view.

Shiva's fingers tight around my wrist, "Yasodhara, let's go. I'll drop you home before I go to the hospital. She must be home by now." The lilt of hope at the edge of his brittle, unshaven voice.

Inside the house, the phone is screaming. He runs in through the door I left swinging open lifetimes ago. I sit in the car, waiting, and when I hear him sobbing, I drop my head onto my hands and scream.

. . .

The police say, "Family members only." So Shiva drives me across town to the station. He looks straight ahead, his fingers grasping and releasing the wheel endlessly. He says, "They're not sure. It doesn't have to be her." I can't speak so I nod. "Can you do this? I can call Mala." I shake my head, ferocious. If La is there, waiting to be claimed, I know I am the one to do it.

I leave him in the car, hope and despair fighting in his eyes. I push my way through the silent crowd. All of them waiting for names. The same thoughts evident in the eyes of old men in sarongs, young women holding babies, panic-stricken mothers. "Maybe she wasn't there . . . Maybe he took a different bus . . . Maybe he's already home."

My blue passport grants me quick access. Inside all is chaos and people in uniforms shouting. I am shown a plastic chair, told to wait. I sit with my head flung backward to stare at the slowly revolving ceiling fan. A profusion of flies zigzag in the space above my head. My bowels seize and I am sure she lies here slowly turning from flesh to stone, my sister, my sister, my sister. Panic flooding my body. Like drowning. Great moaning gasps ready to erupt, but in the next moment I am adamantly as sure that she is at home, in the kitchen, mystified by the half-cut vegetables sauced with my blood, annoyed at our lateness: "Everyone on this island. Always late!" I want to wake up and describe this malevolent, unsettling dream to my beautiful sister and her lover. Sit in their garden and have sweet, milky tea, let them laugh over my paranoid imagination, my big-sister overprotectiveness. Listen to her say, "Akka, must you always imagine the very worst?" in her exasperated voice.

A young policeman comes for me. He looks harried, a scar running across the length of his left cheek, the slash of a machete in some old conflict perhaps. Something vaguely canine in his face, the large brown eyes perhaps. Above his pocket a name tag reads C. SERASINGHE. He says, "We have found a victim with the ID card of your sister. Usually we wait for confirmation . . . but . . ." Unsaid between us are the threats I used, the invocation of the American Embassy. I can feel the resentment in his gaze at the heavy privilege that grants me access, while outside a throng waits to have the same questions answered.

I don't care about his resentment or my privilege. I don't care about where and how I fit into this place anymore. I only need to confirm that my sister's body is not lying here so that I can go home to her, laugh with her about this particularly macabre episode. "Only in Sri Lanka," we will say, and shake our heads. In later years we will say, "Remember when I had to go to the morgue to identify your body?" and smile at the horror on friends' faces.

I say, "Can you show me?" C. Serasinghe shrugs his shoulders, turns, and leads me into the dark interior of the station, down loud, crowded corridors to a door.

"You have a handkerchief?" When I shake my head, he says, "Here, take. Otherwise the smell is very bad." He pulls out a soiled piece of cloth. I take it in fingers that are suddenly nerveless and fluttering like windswept leaves. He makes a noise like a disgruntled bear, pulls the cloth from me, holds it up beneath my eyes, ties it behind my head, gently gathers and frees my hair. His eyes ask if I am ready. I nod. I cannot trust my voice here behind the yellow cloth. I put my trembling hands under my armpits.

C. Serasinghe says, "Come," pushes open the door with his shoulder, ushers me into a crowded room where people walk about taking pictures. It is well lit and full of low tables that are covered in sheets under which lie lumpy shapes. The scent of burned flesh, like a barbecue by the pool at home, sweet, makes me gag. I have to swallow violently, press my fingers against my throat to ease down bile. We walk past tables, my mind struggling to reconstruct what lies under these sheets, piecing together the incongruent shapes like jigsaw pieces, the outline of a severed leg, the abrupt place where the sheet dips indicating a loss of bodily cohesion. Images that will forever populate my nightmares, a curling strand of hair, childish fingers, a man's large foot, graceful in its curve, the toes blackened and charred. This room, a circle of hell.

C. Serasinghe stops at a table, says, "Okay. You are ready?" I push fingers through my hair, imagine running from this place where the ripped-apart pieces of children lie beneath dirty sheets.

The policeman clears his throat. He picks up the cloth as if he were picking flowers with his index fingers and thumbs. Pulls it aside, a magician revealing secrets.

The mass of her hair. Her face. A bruise on the left temple like a huge crimson rose. Eyes focused on the ceiling in wonder, mouth puckered. As if she were seeing it happen. Dust on her features, sediment on the whites of her eyes, the wet shine of them dulled, immobile. Transformed into stone.

My body quaking, underground fissures rupturing in my eyes, my skin cracking open, earthquakes within me. I am free-falling through space, stars rushing like comets past me, her hair like octopus tentacles welcoming me, sucking me into her chest, which is soft and wet and broken. The edges of her ribs scraping jagged against my breasts. I sink into her like into wet red quick-sand. Pulsating screamings and shriekings burst from me, they bounce around the walls of this room, burst out into the build-ing, hurl policemen into ceiling fans, smash open the doors and crash into the street to lodge in the throats of those waiting out-side. An eruption of caterwauling, keening, mourning rising from our one throat into the smoky air of the island. The sound of pure and absolute anguish breaking out from each of us who has paid a price to the demons of war. A sound forged in the lungs of the mothers whose sons have died unnamed in the fields, the fathers whose daughters have gone to fight. A sound to make the war makers quake and flee like the ancient demons, taking with them their weapons, their land mines, their silver-tongued rheto-ric, their nationalism, their martyrs, and sacred Buddhist doc-trines, the whole pile of stinking bullshit.

C. Serasinghe tears me from her. I am unglued with a pop-ping sound, the front of me scarlet drenched. He smashes me against his hollow chest. His fingers raking through my hair, the gash of his scar against my lips as I pour out my horror.

He lets me disintegrate in his arms, until I am dissolved, pulled apart, incoherent, insubstantial. Then he drags me out of the room, his grip around my waist painful. His voice is harsh in my ear, "You are lucky. A lot of the other people have no body. Only pieces of flesh to burn or bury."

He leaves me at the station door, in the bright island sunshine. In the car, Shiva, with knowledge that will never leave his black, black eyes, waits for me.

epilogue

Before the dawn comes, Shiva shudders in my arms. His heart-beat thuds staccato under my cheek, his breathing is ragged like ripping cloth. I know he is running across the heat-dazed streets of Colombo, he is pushing past the immobile crowd, fighting his way to the bus, shrieking, keening at the impossible heaviness of his limbs. I know what greets his eyes when he reaches the center of that crowd, that bus upturned like a downed animal, spilling its metallic entrails onto the street, glinting red. In our dreams it has grown, gigantic until it dwarfs the sky, a replete beast torn open, an anaconda split after a heavy meal. It dumps flesh onto the road at our feet like macabre offerings. When he has these dreams, it is her name he whispers. I hold him close, stroke his moist and beautiful forehead, press my lips against his fluttering eyelids and whisper his name, Shiva Shiva Shiva. He shudders as he is released from the nightmare. His arms press me closer. His sleep in the shared shelter of our bed is tender once again.

Shiva and I, we fled that shattered country like tongue-tied, gaunt, and broken ghosts. After the fires, after she was burned, all we wanted was each other. There was refuge in each other that could be found nowhere else. We had shared a childhood, a house, and the murder of our most beloved. Together we formed a country, a kingdom. We ran as far west as America would allow. Not to the endless freeways and purple-hazed sunsets of Los Angeles where Amma and Thatha with their unstaunchable grief and unanswerable questions waited. Where my ghost of a husband waited, hungry. Instead, we pushed farther north to a glittering city ringed by cold ocean. When the fog lifts, San Francisco sparkles. In this most European of American cities, exile, forgetting, escape seemed possible, even common. We sought solace here, found work, bought a small house. We put down crude roots.

We have learned not to care about the state of that other place even as it burns or drowns. We cut ties, never calling across the oceans, and thus we are never woken up at 3:00 A.M. by foreign-sounding accents on the phone. We do not seek out brown faces; we do not start at the sound of Sinhala or Tamil no matter how rarely we hear them spoken. Instead we have burrowed down, picked our comrades in exile, and built a fortress about ourselves.

These days, I do not even speak of that place to myself. There is no thread of a life I want to follow there. The ocean does not call to me. I no longer long for those myriad shades of green. The island dropped away from me the moment I left it framed in the airplane porthole. This is the only way we may survive.

There is one other thing, most miraculous and unforeseen. We have a little girl, six years old and named for the ocean she has never seen, Samudhra. She calls herself Sam. She has entrancing eyes and a head of bouncing curls. When she laughs, I am pierced with a sharp joy. She sleeps with a hand curled under her cheek, the other around the fat Labrador that was once a baby with her and now wheezes and coughs climbing the stairs of our creaking old house. She likes to dress this patient dog in frills and ribbons. She calls it Dodo, which is the sound she first designated for "dog." She likes Barbie dolls, also pizza and spaghetti. She is enraptured with the color pink in all its various hues. Her weight in my arms is the most distinct of pleasures, the scent of her skin delectable. I had not known that mothering would replicate falling in love so intimately, but I have learned that it is the biology in us that reacts to both states. She has transformed us in unexpected, unimaginable ways. I still catch myself in disbelief—we are parents? Shiva and I together? After all we have seen, we have undertaken this most perilous of roles? The explaining of the world to this new creature. It seems beyond possibility.

Sam paints. The vivid lines of her childhood imaginings so certain, that I know she has inherited La's love of color, the dexterity of her brush. A year ago she brought me an advertisement ripped out of the newspaper I had picked up at an Indian restaurant, a Bharatha Natyam dancer, kohl eyed, fingers fanned into flowers. "I want to do this," she announced. So twice a week,

Samudhra dances. Her teacher pushes down her shoulders so that she must dance from an even lower squat. It will make her leg muscles develop in the proper way, the teacher tells me. She tells me that my daughter has skill in the dance. It must have lain dormant in our veins, some long forgotten memory of sinuousness.

On the hilly car ride home from class, Samudhra weaves me the stories she is learning to dance. Kunti on the riverbank, Ravana swooping down to steal Sita, Arjuna and Krishna on the battlefield. I never speak of Sri Lanka to her. I do not mention it in story or rhyme or memory. Perhaps her childish recitation is some attempt to cajole me into speaking of where we come from. These Indian stories that are not even ours, these characters we cannot claim except for the Demon King Ravana coming for Rama's Queen. I wonder sometimes if I have stolen something that is hers by birthright, if she should know the details of where we are from.

I know she is confused when adults ask her (they invariably ask), "Where are you from?" When she says, "From here, San Francisco. I was born here," they insist, "I mean your mommy and daddy. Where are they from, originally?" Their stress is on that last word, "Or-i-ginally." She says, "They're from Siri Lanka." But the words are barely audible, so that there is an almost automatic and incredulous repetition of the adult question, "Where?" Then, often, she is silent, unwilling to speak of this other and possibly mythical place that her parents sometimes, rarely, speak of.

. . .

I am in the kitchen, my blade reducing onions into long curling ribbons. Shiva and Samudhra are in the living room piecing together a giant puzzle of puppies and kittens. I hear her say, "Tell me a story. When you and Ammi were growing up. In the big house by the sea." I feel the muscles in my stomach clench, a stone drop into my belly.

"You know Ammi doesn't like when I tell you those stories."

"Please, Appa, when I grow up I'm going there anyway. Tell me about when you were fishermen. From the balcony. Pleeeeeese!" I can imagine her pursed pout, her large and wet eyes. Sam crossed is hard to resist.

"Okay. We were in the Wellawatte house. Your great-grandmother Sylvia Sunethra's house."

"Uh-hmmmm."

"We'd climb to the top story. That's where I lived with all my cousins and uncles and aunties and everyone. Your mother lived below us. We were about your age, I think."

"Tell about the fish!"

"Okay, okay. We'd take our Bata slippers off. That's a kind of shoe like a Nike, and throw them over the balcony onto the ground."

"And then you would fish for them?"

"Yes. We'd tie big safety pins to string and throw them over the balcony and try to hook the slippers. We were fishermen on a boat in the middle of the sea, and then the storms would come."

"Storms! With rain and lightning?"

"Yes. Big storms, and we would be swept all over the deck of our ship like this!"

I hear him scoop her up. Her delighted squeals as he lurches around the room with her in his arms. Playing at long-lost fishermen. In the kitchen I am trembling. My knife stilled. Has he forgotten that there was a third with us in those days? Her child-sized ghost inhabits his stories. I see her in the shadows of the Wellawatte house slipping between us, between the wall and the house into the back garden. Is it not sacrilege to talk of those days without saying her name?

But that very week, Samudhra tugs at my sleeve: "Who's this?" I turn to her and she is clutching a picture. La and I hand in hand. We are laughing. Behind us the big white house. I thought I had put away all the pictures of her. I take the photo, caress my sister's downy cheek with the ball of my thumb.

"This is your aunt. Lanka, my sister."

Samudhra stares hard at me. "You have a sister?"

"Yes, Sam, her name is Lanka. She was your Lanka Aunty. See . . . you have her eyes, her ski lift of a nose." I trace the nose in front of me, and the one in the picture.

"Where is she?"

"Sweetie. She's not here. She . . . she passed away before you were born."

"You mean she died?" Her eyes are wide. She has not experienced death yet. Not even a beloved dog or goldfish has died, and her steady concentrated stare makes me certain that she understands none of this.

"How?" The word conjures low tables, flies, that decapitated woman, her head like a ball that had rolled down the street, the octopus shreds of her blasted neck.

"She . . . she had a heart attack," I stammer.

Samudhra stares at me: "I thought only really, really, really old people have that."

"Yes, that's true but your aunt . . . she had a weak heart, you know, baby. She couldn't . . ." I grab at fairy tales to shield her from what cannot be spoken. Distract her with other tales, promises of a puppy to keep old Dodo company. She forgets easily enough. But when I put her to bed that night, her thumb already in her mouth, she clutches the wrinkled photo and I must pry it out of her sleeping grasp.

In bed Shiva asks, "Did you tell Sam that La died of"—he pauses in incredulity—"a heart attack?"

I nod vigorously. "I couldn't, you know . . . tell her. It's too much to explain. I mean, what does 'suicide bomber' mean when you're six, anyway?"

His lips press against my forehead. The tenderest of kisses. They trace their way to the corner of my left eye, along the curve of my cheek. Soft plumpness of his lip against my eyelashes. His tongue flashing out to taste my sorrow. He holds me and I know that I am forgiven, that he will not berate me for lying to our daughter, that I will not scold him for keeping Lanka alive in what little way he can. When he slides into me, it is homecoming. We ride each other like seas. Gasp and moan. We fall asleep in each other, sated.

I am reminded, a triangle is the safest of shapes. A pyramid the soundest of structures. We are three again.

. . .

Sometimes after we have put Samudhra to bed, old friends visit. We have spent these last nine years finding them and then drawing them around us. We learned early that we shared this rollicking city with other exiles from other wars and other states of disquiet. They come to talk, drink wine, and taste our curries. They might not know much about where we come from, but they know our food intimately. Around our table Americans, South Americans, Europeans, and Africans gather to lament the lack of a Sri Lankan restaurant in the Bay Area and cajole us once again to start one because, as they say, "This is incredible. So good!" They have learned that the food tastes better when the fingers are involved. And in this way we carry a sliver of the island with us, nurture and treasure it.

We had begun to feel safety. A state in which the island was a dimly remembered hallucination, some nightmare with no relevance in the waking world. But then suddenly, the news reports are full of it. Headlines burst upon us like opened monsoon skies: "Sri Lankan Conflict Escalates," "Worst Humanitarian Crisis in Decades," "Thousands of Civilians Trapped Between Army and Tigers."

My father calls from Los Angeles. He is jubilant. "It will be over within a month. Really. We have them now. Those Tiger bastards are finished. We will have peace very soon, very soon." After I hang up the phone, I stand there for a long time. What he says is an impossibility. The Tigers killed my sister. I have seen the results of their fury. I have seen what the soldiers do. I know the absolute ferocity of these enemies. They have been fighting this war for most of my life. I cannot imagine a world without it.

All around the world, the Tamil diaspora floods into the streets in protest. In San Francisco itself, they pour into the Ferry Building. There is a huge upswell of international support. The Sri Lankan government is accused of war crimes. The UN threatens sanctions. The international female pop star cries genocide. We watch in shocked silence. At what cost peace? we wonder. How many must die? And yet, how do you vanquish an enemy this brutal? What is the world becoming for us? What will it be for our child, who is both American and Sri Lankan, but beyond this, also Tamil and Sinhala?

Suddenly friends who had never mentioned Sri Lanka bring it up. "Aren't you from there? What is happening? Don't you have family there?" They can't imagine the dagger edge that slips beneath my heart at their questions.

They say, "Aren't the Tigers like freedom fighters? Aren't they fighting for a separate homeland because they are discriminated against so terribly? Like our African-Americans here?"

I try to explain. There are no martyrs here. It is a war between equally corrupt forces. I see their eyes glaze over. I realize they do not desire a complicated answer. They wanted clear distinctions between the cowboys and the Indians, the corrupt administration and the valiant freedom fighters, the democratic government and the raging terrorists. They want moral certainty, a thing I cannot give them.

. . .

And then, just like that, the impossible happens. One evening we go to dinner, return home fingers clasped and tipsy. Talking as we walk through the house, dropping our bags on the floor and turning on lights. Samudhra is sleeping at a friend's house. We have the evening to savor each other. I pour claret into two slim glasses, flirt with the idea of licking ice cream from the hollow of his throat. I stand before the open freezer trying to choose between vanilla and chocolate, tap my foot on the floor to the beat of the song we had sung together in the car, "You don't have to be rich to be my girl." Finally, I take both containers; tonight I am greedy. I'm opening the dishwasher for spoons when I hear his sharp shocked call in the other room.

I run in and he is staring at the computer screen. I take his trembling hand and together we witness. The muddy bank of a lapping lagoon. A crowd of weary-eyed soldiers in dirty green fatigues. At their feet, an overweight man flat on his back. The eyes popped open as if he is staring at the worst scenes of hell, a slack open mouth, bristled mustache, and hardened limbs, naked except for stained blue underwear, mud streaks across the belly. A startle-eyed, obese corpse. A blue handkerchief covers his head.

Shiva's arms snake around my waist. He holds me, I can feel his body shaking, my own hands curling and uncurling into fists. This fat man dead on the ground changes the course of the earth's trajectory for us. I assimilate every detail. Him. There. On the ground. Naked. Beaten. They have killed the Leader. It has happened. The war is over. . . .

. . .

The island bursts into celebration. We watch as the President returns from Jordan. Landing at Katunayake he falls to his knees and kisses the ground, behind him are two beautiful steward-esses, their palms joined in welcome. This is a man who has been accused of war crimes, whom the UN has censored for his re-lentless pursuit of the enemy at the cost of civilian lives. At this moment he is victorious. He has triumphed over the cruelest of enemies by using the cruelest of means, and all is justified in the minds of his populace. They call him King Mahinda. When asked by foreign journalists about the possibility of a truth and reconciliation commission he says, "I don't want to dig into the past. I don't want to open up this wound." He knows the wound is there, just under the surface, waiting to erupt. Over the de-cades we will witness how it heals or festers.

There is jubilation in the streets, dancing men in the hun-dreds, music all day and night, the crash of firecrackers, women banging in unison on the low round drum. In the villages they light lamps, sing songs, pass arrack bottles, cook milk rice and auspicious sweets to pass out to strangers. The temples and churches are full. Oil lamps flutter before serene-eyed Buddhas. The people give thanks. They hope.

I dream of the eighty thousand who did not live into this moment. Those who were left behind in the lagoons and paddy fields, in the cement jail cells, in the white vans, beneath the rolling waves of the ocean. Those who were broken, dismantled, disappeared; those who were shattered in bomb blasts; those who were bludgeoned, burned in tires, thrown from helicopters into the sea; those who were taken in the midst of giving speeches; those who were taken from their beds in the night; those who were lampposted; those who were pitched into the rivers; those who were taken as children; those who were pierced by shrapnel; those who lost limbs to the land mines; those who lost eyes, hearts, livers, the tender, pulsing, precious flesh; those who were called to strap bombs on and detonate themselves. I dream of the one that I can give a name to: my sister, Lanka Rajasinghe. And that other, her unnamed, unloved assassin.

Eighty thousand: it is a number beyond comprehension. I must mourn for them. I must cry and shake and tremble for them. I shall cry for a long time. And then when my weeping is spent, when I have no more sorrow to give, I shall celebrate peace. I shall wake up from these long decades of war and begin to see what we can do in peace, what sort of creatures we are when the mask of lion or tiger falls from us.

The day is coming, I think, when I will share with my child the ocean she was named after. I shall show her the island. The schoolchildren walking home. The girls in white dresses, their hair in coiled plaits, their feet shod in pristine white socks and sturdy white shoes. The boys arm in arm wearing white shirts and blue shorts, recklessly happy at release from the classroom.

I shall take her out into the country, where the buffalo stirs in the jade paddy fields, the solitary egret on his shoulder. I shall show her the creeper plants that grow giant, curling around trees and jumping into canopy, the plumeria that bursts into blossom scenting the air, the spiky insect-like orchids. We shall go high into the misty hill country where the bowed, saried women pick tea, where the flower boys race your car down twisting, turning mountain passes. I shall show her the big white house by the sea in which her mother, her father, and her aunt played games, were fed, found each other.

But it is the ocean that I long to show her most of all. I want her to learn its depths, know its many blue-green moods, and meet its finned creatures: the many-armed octopus with its all-seeing eye; the schools of silver fish that wait for the turning of the tides; the sinuous, sharp-toothed sharks. I ask that she be at peace in the bosom of an ocean-skimming boat, the sea spray sparkling across her features. I want her to know the bare-chested fishermen with their scarlet smiles and dawn-returning catamarans. They will teach her their songs and I will teach her to dive deep. To become one with the skin of the water until she feels its fluid pulse as her own. To claim this submerged world as her own.

I see her emerging from the ocean, as she will be in some distant future. She drips seawater. She has grown so tall, into a young woman with wild and snaking hair studded with drops of silver water. Her skin is shining dark, polished by sun and salt. She walks in purpose and self-knowledge, a long, rolling walk that unfolds from the hip. She is a child of the peace, the many disparate parts of her experience knit together in jumbled but peaceable unity. The waves lick away her footsteps, the sand retaining no record of what came before her.

acknowledgments

My profound gratitude to the following:

My wonderful editor, Jennifer Weis, at St. Martin's Press. From that very first phone call while I was in Sri Lanka, I knew I was in the best of hands.

The original editor of this work, Michael Meyler.

The Sri Lankan publishers, Sam and Ameena of Perera Hussein, who were the first to see that this book might have promise.

Dineli Bartholomeusz, my earliest friend from my Nigeria days who stepped back into my life after a gap of decades and led me to Sam and Ameena.

My darling writers: Phiroozeh Romer, Yosmay Del Mazo, Maria Allocco, Ayesha Mattu, Tara Dorabji, and Dilnavaz Bamboat.

The teachers: Dr. Parama Roy, Dr. Piya Chatterjee, and ZZ Packer.

Shyam Selvadurai, for being an amazing mentor and friend.

Write to Reconcile participants, you inspire me.

VONA (most especially the VONA Lucky 13).

The Squaw Valley Community of Writers.

Janet Fitch, for inspiration and hospitality.

Cathy Winkler, whose courage in writing *One Night: Realities of Rape* helped me in my attempts to understand the unspeakable.

The Tuesday St. Martin's de Porres soup-kitchen lunch crew and especially Mitchell Gilman, Julie Dyett, Naji Ali, Ben Terrall, Walter Parenteau, Merrill, Betsy, and Ellen.

Raj Ponniah and the Ponniah family. Being a part of your family is a blessing.

Family: Deva and Shiromi Aturaliye, Upali and Saras Aturaliya,

Suja and Shelly Rajapakse, Doreen Sonnadara, and Sunila and Senarath Rajawasan.

The friends who are family: Candida Martinez and Cecil Carthen, Melissa McPeters and Gustavo El Diablo Sandi, Yael Martinez and Carlos Pena Garrido and Alexsie, Nathanael F. Trimboli, Susan Ruth, Emily Guzzardi, Serena Wong and Nick Van Eyck, Melinda Weaver, Alina Moloney, Dima Dashevsky, JenKat Kwong, Jolan Bogdan and Scott Martinez and Benni, Stephen Boatright and Rebecca Lowery, Francis Vieras Blanc, and Dr. Stefanie Dunning.

Keenan Norris and Laleh Khadivi, to lifelong literary friendships indeed.

The Missildine family, great readers, writers, and editors, all!

The cousins who cheered me on: Dhumal Aturaliye and Bishan and Yosanta Rajapakse.

Dinesh Rajawasan, you're the best, even when you try to sign books in my name.

Kavya and Saakya Rajawasan and Valeena Sontidoro. Big hugs and I can't wait to see what adventures life holds for you.

The worldwide Vipassana Meditation sangha and Kaushik Ranchod, who led me to it.

Adam Griffiths, you were reading this book on the morning that the waves took you. Your spirit and your joy stay with us.

Maggie Leung and Moher Downing, loved and remembered.

The Tantulas: Namal, Shehan, and Baby Tantula—even now on her way.

Dr. Whitney Missildine, if a life is measured in love, I am blessed beyond measure.

ISLAND OF A THOUSAND MIRRORS

by Nayomi Munaweera

About the Author

- A Note to the Reader
- A Conversation with Nayomi Munaweera

Behind the Novel

A Selection of Photographs

Keep on Reading

- Recommended Reading
- Reading Group Questions

For more reading group suggestions,
visit www.readinggroupgold.com.

St. Martin's Griffin
stmartins.com

A Note to the Reader

Dear Reader,

I once heard Junot Díaz say that books have the power to transform not only their readers but also their creators. He said that one has to *become* the writer who can birth the book through the process of writing it. He said that the person who finishes writing the book is a different creature than the one who embarked upon that literary journey.

I did not live through the civil war that raged from 1983 to 2009 and took approximately one hundred thousand lives in Sri Lanka, the land of my birth. Instead I watched it from a distance, first from Nigeria (to which my family immigrated in 1976) and then from California, where we ended up in 1984 until the present.

Every year of my childhood and adolescence, however, my family spent one month in Sri Lanka. During that time, I got a taste of what people were living with, the timbre and tone of possible catastrophe, the threat of uncertainty and violence.

I remember a cousin saying that his family of four, two adults and two children, never took the same bus; they always split into pairs; in this way, if a bus was bombed, they wouldn't all be taken. I remember watching television and, like Yasodhara, seeing the devastation wrought by a suicide bus bombing. I remember being woken up in the middle of the night in Los Angeles by the phone because terrible things had happened at home.

I also remember laughter, delicious feasts, people dancing to baila and drinking arrack, my aunt's paradise of a garden, and deep familial love. People lived joyously despite all the ways their lives were prescribed by warfare in the north and east, and the fact that violence that

could erupt in Colombo and other parts of the country without forewarning.

In 2001, I was getting a PhD in English when Yasodhara's and Saraswathi's voices came to me. I had no choice but to attempt to tell their stories. The research necessary to write this book was excruciating. I often asked myself how I dared to write about a war I had only seen from the outside. Beyond this concern, I didn't think anyone would ever read this book—which gave me tremendous freedom in writing it.

When the war ended, in 2009, I finally knew how to end my novel. My agent sent it out to the American publishing houses; each one rejected it. The implication was that Americans were not interested in a war in a tiny country far away. Then, in 2012, I made contact with a small publishing house in Sri Lanka. I was extremely nervous. How would Sri Lankans take to this book? I sent the manuscript to the publishers and they loved it. They printed one thousand copies and gave *Island of a Thousand Mirrors* its start.

I realize, now, that writing this book was my way of trying to understand what had happened in Sri Lanka, and my own connection to those events. In those years of writing, this book became my obsession—as did the war itself. It was through writing this novel that I could finally lay to rest the specter of that terrible time. As Junot Díaz said, the writing of this book birthed me anew.

Publication, too, changes a writer's life. The book's reception in America has shown me that yes, Americans can care deeply about what happened in a small place very far away. In fact, people from all parts of the globe write saying they cried reading parts of this book (and I tell them I was crying when I wrote these parts). This is one way books magically connect us.

I was once at a dinner in which Daniel Handler gave the keynote; he spoke about the fact that as a child he had longed to belong to a secret society. Then, as an adult, he realized that he had always been a part of a secret society, the secret society made up of readers and writers. All of you, legions wide, who love the life of words as much as I do, who are nowhere happier than when you are deep in the midst of a bewitching book. You are my people; you are my secret society.

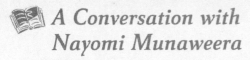

A Conversation with Nayomi Munaweera

I would love to talk about that idea of "writing home": How has living and growing up in different countries (Sri Lanka, Nigeria, and the United States) affected your life as a writer? When you returned "home" (both literally, the house of your childhood, and figuratively, your motherland), how was your writing affected?

The ancestral house I was born into and left in 1976, when we moved from Sri Lanka to Nigeria, was the one I was thinking of when I was writing *Island*. It is where a lot of the first part of the book is staged. It was lost to my family for most of the war years. So I was thinking about it nostalgically while I was in America. The house and the country were in some way equated for me. Both of them felt very far away to me.

Then after twenty-five years, we regained the house. When I went back in 2013 for the book launch, I was able to live there by myself for two months. It was also there that I got a phone call from New York saying that my book had sold in America. So there was this absolutely strange feeling of homecoming and a sense of my life arriving full circle.

And yet I was lonely in Sri Lanka, I was separated from my partner and the community I had spent years developing in the Bay and that felt isolating. I think as an immigrant and someone who has spent a childhood living in various places, home is a shifting thing; there are parts of you that are at home in different places. For a writer, this is a powerful thing because it lets you take on different voices, different perspectives more easily. Joyce Carol Oates once said something like, "I am a glass of water. I don't have a personality when I am alone." I think she meant that she takes on the tint of whatever is around her and this is an important skill as a writer—you can't be too fixed, in thought or place, you have to absorb what is around.

As for how it's changed my writing, I think the main thing is this book allowed me to come to some sort of understanding of the war. We write to work out our obsessions and my obsession with this particular topic has been exhausted. My next book, *What Lies Between Us*, is a completely different beast and I'm excited to see what readers think of it.

I have been struggling with the idea that only "uplifting" stories can heal those lost and broken. After writing this book that dispels the silence, what are your thoughts about writing these kinds of stories?

This is a common muzzle people attempt to put on the artist. If you're writing about pain, you are ignoring the good things about the community, you're painting a bad picture of "your people" to the world, etc. But trauma doesn't go away just because it's not talked about. It burrows deeper under the skin, turning necrotic, infecting the surrounding area, and psychically killing the smiling host. I think it's the writer's particular job to break these silences, to try and articulate what is most difficult to articulate.

There is a beautiful place, when the words slip under the skin and make us feel deep, profound, sometimes painful things. It took five years to write this book. It took another five years to find a publisher. It was a long journey, but I think that more than anything this is what is required of writers: endurance and some clumsy sort of faith that telling the story (if only to yourself) is valuable in itself.

Lastly, the book ends on a hopeful beat. This isn't really a question, but more of a thanks.

The writing of this book was hard enough. I couldn't bear to write a painful ending. So that ending was a gift to me as well as to the readers!

Excerpted from an interview conducted by Melissa R. Sipin from TAYO *magazine. Reprinted with permission.*

To read the full interview,
visit www.tayoliterarymag.com/nayomi-munaweera.

About
the Author

This family portrait was taken in 1976, just before my family left Sri Lanka fo
Nigeria. Our imminent departure might have been the occasion for taking a forⁿ
portrait at Acme Photo in Wellawatte, Colombo, very close to my family home. B
to front, left to right: My father, Neil Munaweera; mother Upamali Munaweerⁿ
paternal aunt Sunila Rajawasan; paternal uncle Asoka Munaweera; maternal
grandmother Sylvia Aturaliye; paternal grandfather Meemaduma Munaweerⁿ
paternal grandmother Annie Munaweera; me; cousin Dinesh Rajawasan.

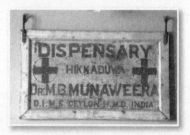

Island of a Thousand Mirrors is fiction but, as with any novel, fragments of
life find themselves onto the page. My father's childhood home in Hikkaduvⁿ
was also his father's dispensary. This sign hung in front of the house at No. ⁿ
Baddegama Road from 1952 to 1973. My grandfather's qualifications are lis
He was a DIMS—Doctor in Indigenous Medicine and Surgery. HMD indicⁿ
that he was also a doctor in homeopathy with qualifications from India,
where he studied as a young man.

Early days in Los Angeles, as a brand-new American teenager. With my pareⁿ
Upamali and Neil Munaweera, and my sister Namal Munaweera Tantula.

A weave of women. With my grandmother Sylvia Aturaliya, my aunt Nalini Sonnadara, my mother Upamali Munaweera, and my sister Namal Munaweera Tantula. 1985, Los Angeles.

At the Jaipur Literary Festival 2013.

With the American edition of *Island*.

Recommended Reading

These are a few of the books that I love. They show me what's possible when a writer is at the very height of his or her powers.

The Color Purple
Alice Walker
Alice Walker's classic text of two sisters surviving brutality in post-slavery America. The book takes the form of letters, and the characters' voices will stay with you long after you finish reading.

Lolita
Vladimir Nabokov
Nabokov's mastery over language is so powerful that the reader has no choice but to go on a ride deep into the mind of depravity. This is one of the most beautiful (and disturbing) books in the English language.

Running in the Family
Michael Ondaatje
Ondaatje's family history reveals a Sri Lanka that existed before the civil war. Studded with family pictures, he shows us a graceful and colorful world that has few remnants in our own time, sadly.

The God of Small Things
Arundhati Roy
A beautiful and affecting exploration of childhood, race, class, and love. One of the great love stories of our day, even though the lovers never speak and the story is told from the perspective of the woman's children.

We Need to Talk About Kevin
Lionel Shriver
Lionel Shriver's incredible book about a woman choosing to keep surviving after the unimaginable, her son's brutal murder of his classmates. Shriver is at the top of her prodigious powers here. A book that I return to often for its depth of language and feeling.

The Lost Daughter
Elena Ferrante
The mysterious Italian writer gives us a book that says everything that needs to be said about the mother-daughter relationship.

Wave
Sonali Deraniyagala
The author's shattering memoir about surviving the Asian tsunami in Sri Lanka while her husband, parents, and two sons did not. This is a look at grief from the inside.

Tampa
Alissa Nutting
Cutting-edge writing from an exciting new voice. I haven't heard a female voice like this in a long time, but I want more.

Jonathan Strange and Mr. Norrell
Susannah Clarke
A wonderful and hard-to-classify tome. If you get through the first fifty pages, you are in for a tremendous ride. So much fun!

Beloved
Toni Morrison
There is no greater book in the American canon than *Beloved*.

*Keep on
Reading*

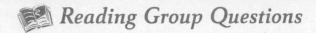

Reading Group Questions

1. In this book, Munaweera takes on the point of views of both a Sinhala woman and a Tamil woman. Why do you think she made this decision? What does it mean to try and express both points of view when the subject is a civil war? Do you think she was more successful in painting one or the other of these women? Which one and why do you think so?

2. Did your reading of the Prologue change after you finished reading the book? How?

3. This is a book that captures the immigration experience. How did Munaweera portray the pleasures and pains of immigration? Did she successfully express the divided nature of the immigrant? Did she do so in ways that reminded you of other authors or was the experience of reading this book quite different?

4. This novel has been compared to *The God of Small Things, Anil's Ghost,* and *The Kite Runner.* If you've read these books, do you think these are fair comparisons? Why or why not? Are there other authors/books Munaweera's style reminds you of?

5. Visaka and Ravan's love is thwarted but their children go on to fall in love. What does Munaweera seem to be saying about destiny, the acts/sins of one's parents, the nature of love itself?

6. The big white house on the seaside in Colombo figures prominently in this book. It is where Visaka grows up, where Yasodhara is brought after she is born, and where the Upstairs Downstairs wars take place. What does this house seem to represent in the book?

7. The riots in 1983 are described as a pivotal point in the history of Sri Lanka and in the plot of the book. Were these scenes similar to painful moments in other parts of the world?

8. Saraswathi grows up with aspirations of becoming a teacher. Do you think what happens to her subsequently is plausible? Do you think Munaweera properly describes the process by which a normal girl might become a suicide bomber?

9. The scene of Saraswathi's rape is extremely traumatic and Munaweera has admitted that it was quite difficult for her to write. Do you think the scene was necessary in the book or should literature stay away from depicting the most painful events in a character's life? Why do you think Munaweera chose to include this scene?

10. Would you describe this book as a feminist work? If so, why?

11. Munaweera has admitted that this is a book obsessed with food. Did you find this to be true? Did the book make you interested in finding out more about Sri Lankan cuisine?

12. We are taught, as young readers, that every story has a moral. What does the ending message of the book seem to be?

Read on for a sneak peek at
Nayomi Munaweera's next novel

what lies between us

Available February 2016

prologue

A child is nourished upon her mother's blood. If it is a time of starvation in the village, the crops lean, the riverbed dry, a mother takes what food there is and gives it to her child. She denies herself, mortifies her flesh, suffers in silence rather than let her child feel the smallest discomfort. All creatures abide by this law. This is the way of nature. To be otherwise is to be unnatural, to be a monster, outside the pale.

In a region stretching from the Himalayas to Japan lives an animal called the moon bear. It is named for the luminous sickle moon glowing in the midst of its midnight chest. The moon bear is the genetic originator of every bear on the planet; it is the great ursine ancestor, content to wander within its secret realms. It lives in the treetops, climbing high to huff at that celestial orb by which it is claimed. It lives on a fairy diet of acorns, honey, termites, cherries, and mushrooms; it is a peaceable citizen of these wild and lonely places.

The moon bear is not just ancient and magnificent, it is also in possession of something treasured by humans. In Chinese medicine the moon bear's bile is believed to remove heat from the body, curing tragic ailments of the liver and the eye. A kilogram of bear bile is valued at half the price of that other, shinier human obsession: gold.

Thousands of moon bears are captured and stuffed into small "crush cages." In these devices they are unable to stand upright or turn around. They may be kept in this condition for decades. Periodically each bear's stomach is slit and into the incision is inserted a tube that drains the precious health-giving liquid. Human beings ingest the bile and swear by this tonic for their various and painful afflictions.

Some years ago, at a Chinese bile farm, a mother moon bear did something thought to be outside the realm of her animal nature. Hearing her cub crying from inside a nearby crush cage, she broke through her own iron bars. The terrified men cowered, but she did not maul them. Instead, she reached for her cub, pulled it to her, and strangled it. Then she smashed her head against the wall until she died.

Why do I tell this story? Only because it tells us everything we need to know about the nature of love between a mother and a child.

one

The walls of my cell are painted an industrial white, like albumen. They must think the color is soothing. Where I come from, it connotes absence, death, and loneliness.

People write to me. Mothers, mostly; they spew venom. That's not surprising. I have done the unthinkable. I have crossed the veil into that other unseen country. They hate me because I am the worst thing possible. I am the bad mother.

But here's a secret: in America there are no good mothers. They simply don't exist. Always, there are a thousand ways to fail at this singularly important job. There are failures of the body and failures of the heart. The woman who is unable to breastfeed is a failure. The woman who screams for the epidural is a failure. The woman who picks her child up late knows from the teacher's cutting glance that she is a failure. The woman who shares her bed with her baby has failed. The woman who steels herself and puts on noise-canceling earphones to erase the screaming of her child in the next room has failed just as spectacularly. They must all hang their heads in guilt and shame because they haven't done it perfectly, and motherhood is, if anything, the assumption of perfection.

Then too, motherhood is broken because in this place, to be a good mother is to give yourself completely. It is to erase yourself. This is what I refused to do. So they shudder when they hear my name, but inwardly they smile because they have not failed in the way I have.

There are others who write. Men who find the grotesque act I have committed titillating. They send propositions and proposals of marriage that I tear up into scraps of white that match the walls of my cell. I hate their unknown, unseen faces. They remind me that in this country, celebrity is courted no matter the cause. The fact that strangers have heard your name and know the secrets of your life is supposed to be pleasing.

I never wanted this macabre interest, this unsettling notoriety. I never asked for it. I would have preferred to have been locked up and forgotten. Instead, I have become a known thing. My name, the one I had before, is gone. Instead I am named by the act I have committed. To be named thus is to be pinned down onto the corkboard with a needle piercing one's abdomen and a curl of paper underneath with one's genus and species on it in slanted writing. I have been named, and therefore you think you know my story, why I did what I did. To this I object. Perhaps this narrative is a way to undo your knowing, to say the truth is somewhere else entirely, and I will tell it in my own voice, in my own time.

And so, as all stories must open, in the beginning, when I was the child and not yet the mother . . .

Birth. My face was pressed against the bones of Amma's pelvis, stuck there, so that instead of slipping out, I was bound like a lost fish in a too-narrow stream. It wasn't until the midwife, tiring of my mother's screams, reached in with her forceps, grabbed the side of my head, and wrenched me out that I was born and Amma was born into motherhood, both of us gasping from the effort of transformation.

For three months after, there was a hornlike protrusion on the left side of my head. It subsided eventually, but for those months my parents were alarmed. "We didn't know if it would ever go away. I didn't know what sort of child I had given birth to. You were the strangest creature. A little monster," Amma admitted. "But then the swelling went down and you were our perfect little girl."

After that, the doctor looked at my mother's slimness, her girlish frame, and said, "No more. Only this one. Any more will wreck you." She had wanted scores of children filling the grand old house. She had wanted so many to love her. The love of an entire army she had created herself. She rubbed her nose against mine and said, "Only you to love me. So you must love me double, triple, quadruple hard. Do you see?" I nodded. She kissed me on the forehead, searched my eyes. I was blissful in the sun of her love, my entire being turned like a flower toward her heat.

Yes, I could love her more. I could love her enough to fill up the hole all those brothers and sisters had left by never coming.

I was born in Sri Lanka, a green island in the midst of the endless Indian Ocean. I grew up in Kandy, the hill city of the Buddhists. A city held high like a gem in the setting of the island. Mahanuwara, meaning the great city, is the name of Kandy in Sinhala. Or even Kande Ude Rata, the land on top of the mountain. It is the last capital of the Lankan kings before the British came to "domesticate and civilize," to build railroads and scallop the hills into acres of fragrant tea. In their un-sinuous tongue, Kande Ude Rata collapses, folds into itself, and emerges as Kandy. But not candy sweet in the mouth, because this place has a certain history.

In the capital Colombo's National Museum in a dusty glass case lies the sari blouse of one of the last noblewomen of the Kandyan Kingdom. Splotches of faded red stain the moldering fabric of each shoulder. The last Kandyan king was fighting the British when his trusted adviser too turned against him. Enraged, the king summoned his adviser's wife. His men ripped her golden earrings out of her flesh, so she bled down onto this blouse. They beheaded her children and placed the heads into a giant mortar. They gave her a huge pestle, the kind village women use to pound rice, and forced her to smash the heads of her children. Then they tied her to a rock and threw her into Kandy Lake as the king watched in triumph from the balcony of the temple palace. Soon after, the British conquered Kandy and took over the island for centuries.

This is the history of what we do to one another. This is the story of what it means to be both a child of a mother and a child of history.

The house I grow up in is big and old. It has belonged to my father's family for generations. It has rooms full of ebony furniture, waxed, polished red floors, white latticework that drips from the eaves like lace, and dark wooden steps that lead to my little bedroom upstairs. A wrought-iron balcony hangs outside my window under a tumble of creeping plants. If I stand on its tiny platform just over the red-tiled roof of the first floor, I can see our sweeping emerald lawns leading down to the rushing river. Along the bank a line of massive trees stretches upward toward the monsoon clouds.

In the living room is a small, slightly moldy taxidermied leopard. There are very much alive dogs in the house, but the leopard is my infant obsession. This is because the leopard lets me ride him, while the dogs do not. Amma says I should call him Bagheera, for Kipling's black leopard, but the name Kaa, for Kipling's Indian rock python, is what I choose. The sound is easier and there is something slithery in his yellow marble eyes. Exactly between these eyes is the neat bullet hole that my father's father put there. The hunting guns are locked away in a chest in my father's study, but the leopard is here as evidence of their presence.

A formal portrait of my grandparents hangs above the leopard. They are old already. My mustachioed grandfather is in a three-piece suit, my grandmother in a Kandyan osari over a Victorian blouse, ruffled and buttoned against the tropical heat. My father is a boy in short trousers, the only child of the five my grandmother gave birth to, to have survived the ravages of malaria.

The house is a kingdom divided into dominions, inside and outside, and ruled over by the keepers of my childhood, Samson and Sita. In the kitchen, Sita shuffles about in her cotton sari, her feet bare. She has been with my father's family since he was a baby. She and her sister came as young girls. Her sister was my father's ayah, while Sita set up court in this kitchen, which she has never left.

Samson is Sita's nephew. His mother has returned to the village down south they came from so long ago, but Samson stays to wrestle our garden. Once a week he cuts the lawn, balancing on his heels, sarong pulled up along his thighs. He swipes the machete back and forth as he makes his crab-legged way across the grass. His skin shines wet eggplant, and at his throat a silver amulet flashes in the sun. "Inside this. All my luck!" he says. He has pulled it open before to shown me what it holds, a tightly rolled scroll of minuscule Sinhala script, a prayer of protection bought by his mother from the village temple at a great price. She believes it will keep him safe from the malevolent influences, the karmic attachments that prey upon the good-hearted.

I am eight years old, tiny and spindly, and Samson is my very best friend. After school I race to throw off my uniform, kick away my shoes, slip into a housedress and Bata slippers, and escape into the garden. The red hibiscus flower nodding its head, yellow pistil extended like a wiry five-forked snake tongue; the curl of ferns; the overhead squawk of parrots—these are the wonders that welcome me home.

Samson speaks to me in Sinhala. He says, "Ah, Baby Madame. Home already? Come!" He swings me onto his shoulders. My thighs grip the sides of his throat, my legs hook behind his back. I reach both hands up into the guava tree to catch the orbs that are swollen and about to split, a wet pink edge in their jade skins. I grab, twist, and pull. The branches bounce and the birds rise, squawking in loud outrage. His arm reaches up to steady me. When my pockets are bulging he gently places me on the ground.

I bite into sun-warmed guava, that familiar sweet tang, small gemlike seeds crunch between my teeth. Samson is cutting away dead leaves from orchids suspended in baskets from the tree trunks.

I ask, "Why do they call these flowers Kandyan dancers?"

I already know why. These small yellow orchids are named for the dancers of this region because with petal and stamen the flowers imitate perfectly the headdresses and the sarongs, the drums and white shell necklaces that the twirling dancers wear. But I ask because I want to hear him talk and also because I want to show off what I have learned in school. I want to show how much more I know even now at eight years old because I have gone to school and he has only ever been a servant in our house.

He says, "This is the name. No? What else can we call them but their name?"

"No! I mean, did they call the flowers after the dancers or the dancers after the flowers?"

"You are the one who goes to school, Baby Madame. How could Samson know these things? Ask your teachers? Ask someone who knows these big-big things." A perfect yellow flower loosens its grip, tumbles to the grass. He stoops and picks it up between thumb and forefinger as gently as if it were a wounded insect, places it on his palm, and holds it out to me. I tug the rubber band at the end of my plait loose and settle the flower there.

He says, "Come, Baby Madame. I need your small fingers to work in the pond today." We walk over and he sits on the edge while I kick off my rubber slippers, hike up my dress around my thighs, and slip into the water. My feet in the mud, I reach into the water up to my armpits, follow the fibrous stalks of the lotus plants down to their main stem. I pull so the plants tear loose, the mud releasing the roots reluctantly. The koi come to investigate this curiosity in their midst. Their silver, orange-streaked quickness flashes all about me, their mouths coming up to nibble at whatever they can find, shins, calves, fingers. I work my way across the cool muddy water, throw the too-fast-growing lotuses onto the bank, where a mound of uprooted leaves, stems, and unfurled flowers lay open to the sky. Samson gathers the beautiful debris. He will burn it with the evening's other rubbish.

Other days I am the watcher and he the worker. I squat on the bank with a bucket as Samson wades in. He spreads his fingers wide to catch yards of gelatinous strands studded with shiny beadlike eggs, then returns to deposit these offerings in the bucket, which turn quickly into a shuddering viscous mass. Waist-high in the deepest part of the pond, he says, "Bloody buggers. Laying eggs everywhere. Pond is chockablock full already."

I say, "In France people eat them."

Astonishment on his face. "What? No, Baby Madame, don't tell lies. Who would eat these ugly buggers? What is there to eat?"

"Yes they do. Our teacher said. They eat the legs."

He stares at the water between his own legs he says, "No. Can't be. Legs are so thin. Nothing there to eat . . . Maybe the fat stomach, no?"

"No. The legs. She said."

He shakes his head. "Those people must be very poor. I might be poor like that if I wasn't with your family." A little nod acknowledges all the years he has lived with us—all my life, all his much longer life. "But even if I was on the street I wouldn't eat these buggers."

"But they are a delicacy there. In France."

"Shall we try, Baby Madame? We can catch them and give Sita to make a badum. Badum of frog."

"No!"

"That's what Baby will eat tonight. Just like the people in Fran-see. Fried frog curry with rice." He raises his arms, trailing streams of jelly in the air; he looks like a tentacled creature rising from the depths and shakes his fists so the water sparkles, lands on my bare thighs. Our laughter echoes across the pond.

In the monsoon months, the gardens are a different place, the ground sodden, the pond swollen. The sky lights up in the midst of dark stormy days as if a mighty photographer is taking pictures of our little piece of earth. It isn't unusual to come upon a flash of silver and gold, a koi flapping on the wet grass, swept out of the pond by the onslaught of rain. The river is dangerous at this time. It rushes by, carrying all manner of things—furniture, quickly rolling trees with beseeching arms held out to the sky, drowned animals. It is a boiling, heaving mass. The banks could crumble inward, the ground falling away under your feet. We all know this; in these months we keep away from the garden and the river.

Evenings in the living room, the brass cutwork lamp throws a parade of shadows on every surface. My father reads student papers; he is a professor of history at the University of Peradeniya and always has this stack of work to bury himself in. I read books in English. Stories of boarding schools and midnight feasts featuring foods I've never tasted, but yearn desperately for. I read about children who have to put on scarves and mittens and hats to go outside and wish I too had a pair of mittens. What would they look like covering my small hands? What would they feel like? How exciting to live in a snowy place and eat crunchy red apples and chocolate digestive biscuits. How exotic, how enticing. How boring my life is in comparison.

Here then are my father and I, each of us wrapped in these other worlds. My father is reading about some atrocity of the raj, shaking his head now and then, sharing out bits and pieces with us. This is how, of course, I first heard of the Lankan lady mashing up her children's heads. My father is denouncing colonialization and the history of imperialism while I, thoroughly colonialized by the very books he had approved for me, secretly dreamed of some other more desirable and colder childhood. But a third person is with us, and it is her presence that brings us all together.

My mother sits and stares at a page in a Mills & Boon novel. Sometimes she sighs loudly, declaratively. Sometimes she leaps up, puts on music, grabs my hands, sends my book flying, says, "Come, child! Dance." Anxiety and joy flood through me in equal measure. Joy at her closeness, anxiety at the thought of what my ungraceful feet are doing under me.

She holds me, her hands on my haunches, pushing them one way and then the other. "Like this, like this, sway your body, move, child. Don't be so stiff. Move around." My elegant, beautiful mother. I can read the messages in the arch of her supple, fluid body: "How is this my child? So different from me, so stiff and so serious?" I can't tell her that I am not serious. That it is only this unexpected closeness to her that is making me awkward and gawky. In the garden with Samson, in the kitchen with Sita, I can dance mad baila like an undulating dervish. I can lose myself and be just a whirl of motion. I can be silly and unfettered and ridiculous. But here with her, I am tongue-tied and thick-footed.

Her hands push me away. Quick footsteps. The bedroom door slams, reverberating through the house. My father looks up from his papers and says, "Your mother is delicate. We need to treat her carefully. You understand this, don't you? The need for care."

Of course I do. She is my mother. I know better than anyone that she must be handled with diligence, like all things precious and dangerous.

Sometimes on the weekends when I wander down to the kitchen, she is already there. She says, "We don't need Sita today. I sent her to the market. I'll make you breakfast myself." I sit at the table and watch. She talks fast, her housecoat wrapped over her nightdress, her hair pulled into a gushing ponytail on the very top of her head, cascading down in an inky waterfall to her elbows. She says, "I'll make pancakes. The way you like. Thin. Crispy like an appa." Her fingers crack eggs on the rim of the bowl, slide them in with one quick motion. "Just the way you like."

I watch this mother, the one that appears sometimes. She is demonstrative, coming over to hug me, so I open my nostrils wide to inhale her scent—like nothing else, the smell of this woman. She pushes a bowl at me. "Here, you whip the eggs." She heats oil, tilts the pan to coat it. Pours the batter onto the hot oil and swirls it so that the thinnest of crepes emerge. She flips these onto a plate, sprinkles sugar granules on the hot surface, squeezes a lemon over it, rolls up the little package, and passes the plate to me. I love the sweetness and the bite of the lemon, the hot delicious crepe. She watches me with hungry eyes. She never eats while I do. Watching me is enough for her, she says.

This too happens. I'm playing outside her locked door, waiting and wishing for her. I'm being careful, but somehow the big doll slips from my fingers, falls banging on the wooden floors. Her bedroom door whacks open and she comes for me. The clutch of her fingers around my upper arm is like a tourniquet. Her face close to mine, she hisses, "I told you to be quiet. I need to rest. I *need* to sleep. Migraine is splitting my head apart. You *need* to be silent. Do. You. Understand." Important information is being transmitted. Yes, I understand. I must not make noise. I must be quiet; I must let her rest. By the age of nine I have learned the lesson of silence perfectly.

In every house on this island, in a frame as extravagant or as meager as the family's fortunes can afford, is the talisman of the wedding portrait. Without this photograph the house cannot stand.

The wedding photograph of my parents is in a heavy gold frame poised in the center of the living room wall. It shows my mother enwrapped in a Kandyan osari, her eyes huge, the gleam of lipstick on those virgin lips. Her neck is weighed down by the seven concentric gold necklaces that go from encircling her throat to dangling at her waist. Her hair is bisected by a ruler-straight

part, on one side of it an ornament in the shape of a dazzling sun-
burst and on the other a curved crescent moon.

Next to her, my young father-to-be wears the costume of the
Kandyan kings. In later decades it will become fashionable for all
young grooms to don these garments, but during this period, the
early 1970s, they are still reserved exclusively for the old Kandyan
families. So he wears it not as fashion but as a marker of a certain
heritage, a certain history. Here on his feet are the curved slippers, and above that, the various complicated sarongs. One's eyes
move upward to the maroon matador jacket studded at the shoulders with sequined lions. On his head is a tricornered crown, itself topped with a small golden bodhi tree. The only costume in
the world perhaps where the male's outshines the female's.

They don't look at each other, these two. They face the camera and barely touch. They are not smiling; smiles were not requisite in those days. This is one of the only photographs that has
survived, so it remains here large on the wall. If my mother had
had another, she would have replaced this one, but she doesn't,
so it is the one that endures.

When Amma is in a bright mood she tells me how matches are
made. We are Sinhalese Buddhists, and this is how it has always
worked. When a son comes of age, a mother makes inquiries. The
matchmaker comes to the house wearing his cleanest white sarong and swinging his black umbrella, sheaves of astrological
charts and photographs of girls in his battered briefcase. He sits
in the best chair and makes his pronouncements. "The Kalutara

Ratnasomas have four daughters of marriageable age. No sons. The mother must have very bad karma. The eldest girl is ready and they are eager to find a boy for her so that they can also start looking for the younger three."

When he leaves, the women of the family gather to compare the girls he has suggested. Beauty, lineage, docility, and culinary skills—these are the subjects of comparison. And then a girl is chosen. For a doctor son, an engineer son, a mother can expect a pretty, fair-skinned daughter-in-law from a good family. For a son who drinks or who is lame, who shouts so the neighbors can hear, a dark girl or one who has done badly at her O levels will do. A dowry of course changes everything. A father will collect money for years to marry off a daughter. A father of many daughters is an unlucky man: he will work tirelessly, and after his girls are married off, will have nothing to show for it.

Everybody knows that happiness in marriage is not expected. It is a possibility, of course, but it is not the reason one gets married. If it happens, one is lucky, but marriages are arranged for many reasons—financial, social, as a calming agent on the hot tempers of young men and the possible waywardness of young girls. Happiness is hoped for but is never an expected consequence.

Amma says, "We didn't do it like that. We broke the rules." I can tell she is both proud of and ashamed about this. They had been on an up-country bus. My father, a young man on his way to the university; Amma, a girl of unknown pedigree, certainly not someone his parents if they had been alive would have approved of. He had seen her, her bare arm snaking up out of her sari blouse sleeve to hold on to the swaying strap of that bus, which moved like a boat. She was willowy in her printed sari, her feet in leather sandals, the toenails painted the lightest blush of pink. He had looked at these toes and then dared to look at her face, and she had not looked away, as almost any other young woman would have done. Instead she had held his gaze for the briefest moment, and he had been snagged on that glance.

She says, "He had a nice shirt. I knew he was a Peradeniya boy, and that was all the difference." She continues, "He passed me notes after that. On the bus. He was so nervous. He didn't even need to take the bus. He had the car. But that one day it had broken down and he had taken the bus, and from then on, every day he took the bus and I was there."

He'd had his friends make inquiries. They learned that she was poor. Her sister and she were living with relatives after the parents had been lost in some typhoid complication. Her dowry was meager. What she did have was beauty, and for my father, who owned this house by the river, whose own parents had died, and even more important, who was rich enough to do as he pleased— including studying something as useless as history, getting a doctorate in it, and then teaching it at the university—this was enough.

They saw each other on the bus for months. He passed her notes that declared his undying passion, slipping them into the open mouth of the shopping bag at her feet or into the cheap unclasped bag under her armpit. She never responded either in word or through letters of her own. She never even looked at him again. That initial meeting of his gaze, that was all she could declare. After that everything was up to him. "A girl can't be cheap," she says. "You have to maintain yourself. Do you understand? You have to keep your pride. Without that, a girl is nothing."

They met formally thrice before they were married. He went to her relatives' small, battered house and was fussed over and served weak tea and plain cake on two occasions. Once he had escorted her to the cinema, where a thin, sweating aunt had sat between them and they had watched the earnest Professor Higgins labor over the guttersnipe Eliza Doolittle's vowels before falling in love with her. The young professor sat in the dark and wondered if he could enact a similar metamorphosis with the girl who sat on the other side of the thin aunt. Meanwhile, the girl was rigid with terror and excitement at the spectacle of the moving giants above her. It was her very first movie. She was seventeen years old, and her suitor was twenty-nine.

After the movie they went for falooda and Chinese rolls. The thin aunt had gone off to the bathroom and the young man had realized that what he had seen in her eyes when she first met his gaze on the bus had not been passion or rebellion but desperation. It was frightening to realize this, but it did nothing to assuage his desire. He was hooked.

They were engaged and her relations were jubilant. Most incredible, this bridegroom had not asked about dowry, had not mentioned the requisite plots of land, refrigerators, or houses that were usually expected. His own family was livid. An extensive collection of aunts and uncles and cousins and assorted jetsam of the far-flung family refused to come to the wedding. There were only the groom's colleagues and their wives. On the bride's side, only her older sister, some of her badly dressed family, and a few of her young school friends, shy around the older people. It was a truncated and odd assortment in a country where extravagant weddings are a national pastime. And then even in this small gathering, all around the couple, a hum of gossip,

One professor's wife bows her head close to another's, says, "Do you know? They met on a *bus*?"

The other takes a shocked suck of air. "What? Can't be."

"It's true. I heard from Sujatha's son."

"These modern girls. They'll do anything to catch a good one."

"Yes men. Can you imagine if his parents were alive to see?"

"They must be turning in their graves. Such a good old Kandyan family."

"Yes. What to do? The world is not what it was. All the old rules are broken."

They, the newlyweds, heard the whispers and ignored them. They ran out to his car in a hail of rice. No more buses for them. Then they were alone. They were not used to each other's scents or tastes. The bride had only ever shared a bed with her older sister. They had never kissed or held hands. But this was normal and natural. For it to be otherwise would have been unthinkable. In this place and time, one did not dip a toe into marriage; one plunged into it, fully dressed.

There is only one other wedding picture in the house. It sits on my mother's dressing table, and when she sees me looking at it, she says, "I was just a child. Only seventeen. And I had you the next year. You were with us from the very beginning. It was always the three of us." She considers the picture and tells me the story yet again. "Only those two photographs. The photographer went out and got drunk after the wedding. Got in a fight and destroyed his camera. All the rolls were ruined. I cried for a week when they told me. Thank god, at least Aruna Uncle had a camera. Otherwise even these two we wouldn't have."

Beneath the glass of its frame, the photograph still shows off its cobwebbed crinkles. I had been small, maybe four or five. I had awoken in the middle of the night to loud voices. I had slipped out of my narrow bed and gone to stand in the hallway that led to their bedroom. I saw his arm raised and this photograph in its previous frame hurled across the room. Heard the crash of it against the wall. He saw me then. He came to the door, put his finger to his lips. *Shh,* he was saying, I must be quiet. I must be good and go back to bed. He closed the door.

Later either he or she had taken the picture, unfurled it, and put it in a new frame. It was something I learned then. That you could take the crumpled remains of something destroyed and smooth them into newness. You could pretend certain things weren't happening even when you had seen or felt them. Everything done can be denied.

Sometimes at twilight she goes out to stand at the line of trees by the river's edge. She watches the dark water flow by her bare feet.

I watch from a window. I know my father is watching her from a different window in his study. His hand is curled around a glass of arrack. He will drink for hours and then he will fall asleep in his chair. I have found him there, his head lolling on the student papers, the empty glass dropped from his nerveless fingers onto the floor, making a pungent puddle by his bare feet. I don't wake him. I have done this before and he had looked at me with some terrible warning in his eyes, so now I always let him be.

Now from our separate windows, we watch her. She does not belong to us, but to some other state, some other mood, and even if we called to her, she would ignore us or stare back at the house, past us in the windows as if we did not exist. When the sun drops as suddenly as a shot bird, all we can see are her earrings, jagged lines of silver that dart from the tips of her earlobes to the silhouette of her rounded shoulders. We watch these lightning flashes until they too disappear.